MW01520317

Killing Bobby Fatt

and other nasty bastards.

A Roger Storm novel

Jonathan Harries

RHINO BOOKS

Rhino Books
An imprint of Jonathan Harries Ink
PO Box 183
New York, NY 10013

www.jonathanharriesink.com

ISBN: 978-1-950628-00-1 (print)
ISBN: 978-1-950628-01-8 (ebook)

Library of Congress Control Number: 2019903619

First edition

Contents

Foreword

You've probably seen the disturbingly common Facebook and Instagram posts that show stashes of rhino horns and tusks confiscated from poachers. Or trophy hunters proudly posing with the dead leopards and giraffes they've just shot. The pictures are normally followed by hundreds of comments from angry people that range from, "Disgusting ... I hope they rot in hell ... I wish them a horrific death," to increasingly exasperated expressions of horror and outrage.

If you're one of these people, then *Killing Bobby Fatt and Other Nasty Bastards* (and its predecessor *Killing Harry Bones*) should be just up your ally.

It's easy to understand why we're all outraged by these barbaric acts of senseless violence and cruelty. We've seen pictures and films of amazing animals in the wild on TV or perhaps been lucky enough to go on a safari. What I—and I imagine you—can't quite comprehend is why some people feel the need to kill and stuff animals. It must involve a level of narcissism that is totally incomprehensible to most of us.

I've spent a great deal of time wondering if sometimes the difference between right and wrong in the killing of big game animals is not the act itself but rather the motivation for the act. The thing that recently sparked one of my sleep-depleting ruminations on the subject was an article I read about a trophy hunter in Chicago who'd donated his taxidermy collection to an obscure university. In the article he spoke about how none of the animals was endangered and all had been hunted legally. He claimed that hunters are "very good conservationists," and that trophy hunting not only provides skins and meat to locals but creates jobs in impoverished areas. He talked about how he'd shot an elephant in Mozambique during the civil war (forgetting to mention that 90 percent of Mozambique's animals were wiped out during that war and are only now making a comeback thanks to the efforts of entrepreneur and philanthropist Gregory Carr, an amazing human being). He said he'd been on a jaguar hunt in Belize and provided money to build a school, which I assume made him feel that killing a highly endangered animal was all worth it.

I'm not singling this person out specifically. There are hundreds of stories like his on the Internet where men and women surrounded by dead and glassy-eyed lions and leopards, polar bears and oryx pose proudly, defying anyone to raise an objection. They all love adventure, and talk about the thrill and the hardship of the hunt. They all donate the meat of the elephants or baboons they've slaughtered to the locals and they are all "conservationists."

The issue I have is that all of these are simply justifications for what they've done. None explains their motivation. Not one of these trophy hunters can say they set out to kill a rhinoceros because the meat could feed a village. If feeding a village was their intention, then the $67,000 they paid to the hunting company could buy about 140 cows—and my gut feel is that eating beef is preferable to chewing on a rhino. They can say they promote conservation, but if you've ever compared the terrified behavior of animals in a hunting preserve to those in an area reserved for photographic safaris, that argument becomes spurious and delusional. Even if you ignore the traumatic behavior of the game, you have to question what continuously taking out the alpha male or female of the species does to the gene pool.

There is no question in my mind that herds have to be culled and people have to eat and keep warm and some of the poachers—particularly the ones who tend to get caught—are doing it to feed their families. But the animal traffickers in Vietnam and Laos, the big game hunters in America and Europe, the South African farmers who breed lions for hunting, the people who wear furs from animals tortured in traps or have handbags made from exotic reptiles because they look beautiful—those are the people whose motives I question and actions I despise.

The sad truth is there is no real answer.

But happily, there is revenge. And that's what the Roger Storm books are all about.

My books are dedicated to all the people who find the senseless destruction of wildlife abhorrent. The real conservationists and anti-poaching squads who put their lives on the line for what they believe. The incredible animal organizations dedicated to reducing misery and saving animals in every environment. My friends on Facebook and Instagram who expose the killers every chance they get. And finally, the people who go into the few remaining places where one can still see the magnificent herds and prides and be in awe simply because animals look a lot better alive on the plains than they do on some rich asshole's wall.

Just as a matter of interest, in *Killing Bobby Fatt and Other Nasty Bastards,* I've used the actual names of the most notorious animal traffickers in the world. Look them up on the Internet or read about them in the paper. You can see what they do and how they evade authorities or bribe their way out of trouble. The good news about fiction is that I get to do anything I like to these bastards.

And believe me, I do so with a great deal of relish.

Just about everything I make from these books goes to charities and organizations dedicated to helping all animals. So thank you for buying it.

My thanks go to Melissa Mazzeo, who has been an incredible editor and done so much to bring my books to reality. To my sons, Simon and Steven, who are both devoted to animal causes. Lastly to my wife, Jennifer, who encourages me every day and thinks I type too loudly.

Kindest regards,
Jonathan Harries

Prologue

It was early.

That time of morning when young people run, and old people walk their dogs.

Bobby Fatt, founder and president of one of Canada's largest outerwear manufacturers—a man neither old nor young, whose activity was neither running nor walking—was out with his wife's golden retriever, Bessie. Their forward motion—more of a shuffle than anything else—took them along a secluded area on the Belt Line Trail, a few kilometers from Bobby's home in the Bridal Path area of Toronto. Bobby was panting heavily, and the pain from the bunion at the base of his big toe was excruciating. The bright orange running shoes that had been custom-made by one of the company's chief shoe designers hadn't helped one bit, and he made a mental note to get his assistant to fire the asshole.

Physical activity was not something Bobby enjoyed. His knees throbbed, his lungs felt like deflated footballs, and the outdoors, in contrast to the controversial company mission statement he'd drafted—"Without Chilly Canuck the

Great Outdoors Would be Shit"—depressed the hell out of him. In fact, the only reason he'd taken up "jogging" was to avoid an early morning encounter with his wife, whom he'd begun to despise as much as she despised him. Bobby looked at his watch and decided that if he turned around now she'd be on her way to yoga.

He stopped for a minute to catch his breath and let Bessie relieve herself next to the path. He too needed to pee rather badly and looked around to see if there was anyone nearby. Satisfied there wasn't, he stepped towards a thicket, pulled down the front of his running shorts, and squeezed out an enlarged-prostate-style trickle. His sigh of relief was interrupted by an awful groan coming from a thick clump of trees about four meters from the path. Bessie gave a shrill bark and darted into the undergrowth.

"Hey, hey! Stop, you stupid dog," Bobby yelled. "Come back here."

Bessie, however, was a free spirit with an untrained retriever's sense of adventure and disregard for instruction. The groaning intensified, and Bobby, who under normal circumstances would not have responded to a call for help from another living creature, cursed loudly.

"Bessie! You goddamned mutt. Get back here at once." Had Bessie appeared, Bobby would have continued without the slightest twinge of conscience. She didn't, and so, not wishing for further rebuke from his wife for letting Bessie off the leash, he walked gingerly toward where the groans appeared to be coming from.

"Hello? Hello? Who's there? Do you need an ambulance?"

Whoever was groaning groaned even more vociferously. Bobby gave one last curse and stumbled through the thicket into an open space where a very large man sat against a tree. He was holding onto Bessie's collar with one giant hand and scratching her belly with the other.

"What's wrong with you?" asked Bobby. "And I'd appreciate it if you'd let my dog go."

"Of course," said the big man, scrambling to his feet with an agility Bobby would not have associated with someone whose moans had so recently indicated severe trauma. "And there's nothing wrong with me, but thanks for asking anyway. I'd heard you were a coldhearted, uncaring bastard. Clearly people were wrong about that."

For a moment Bobby was speechless. Of all the slings and arrows that could have been tossed his way, "coldhearted" was, in his admittedly inflated opinion of himself, totally unjustified. "How dare you imply that? Do you know how much money I give to different groups and charities?"

"If you mean the National Firearms Association or global-warming deniers or conservative think tanks, then yes, I do. To be fair, I'm talking about people who feel your attitude to the humane and ethical treatment of animals leaves a lot to be desired."

Bobby didn't need to hear any more. He knew exactly where this was coming from. Over the past few years, his company had been inundated with letters and protests from thousands of environmental warriors and other crazies who objected to their use of coyote fur on their products.

"Oh, Christ. Don't tell me you're one of those animal rights activists? I suppose you sent me the *warning* letter too?" He said *warning* as if he were mimicking someone with a speech impediment.

"I did. Well, to be totally honest, the people who employ me did. They believe in a soft first approach. Personally, I wouldn't waste my time with warnings. They never work. I find my own methods of persuasion far more effective."

Bobby began to back away. "Are you threatening me?"

"No, I'm more of an action person than a threat person."

"Look, I don't talk to you people. If you've got any questions, speak to our corporate lawyers. Now, if you don't mind, I'm going to put my dog on her leash and continue my jog."

"Oh, but I do mind. I mind very much. So, don't go anywhere just yet. It's you I want to talk to, not your lawyers. I really want to give you an opportunity to reconsider before taking this to the next step."

Bobby's palms began to sweat. "I'm not interested in you or your arguments or my 'opportunities.' If you've got any issues with what we do, read our policies. Everything we do to those vermin is legal."

"Oh, it's definitely legal. But you have to ask yourself: Is it ethical? I mean, I spend a good deal of time in very remote places, and my Patagonia jacket keeps me very warm. They're a very ethical company as you no doubt know, and as I understand, very profitable. Now stop backing away. You're not going anywhere until we're finished with this conversation."

Bobby shook his head. He was getting tired of talking to the stranger and had no desire to compare brand attributes with a dangerous lunatic. In his experience people who were concerned with the welfare of animals were rarely violent, but this one seemed different. He took out his phone. "I'm done with this conversation. I don't know who you are, but leave me alone or I'm going to call the police. Come on, Bessie."

But Bessie didn't move. Bobby snorted and turned his back on the stranger, confident Bessie would follow him to the path. He hadn't taken two steps when a massive fist slammed him between his shoulder blades. He gave a gasp and began to topple forward just as the stranger grabbed the back of his running shorts and yanked them down. The thought that he might be sexually assaulted lasted less than one second as the ground rushed up to meet him. There was an awful clang, and Bobby screamed in horror as the jaws of the coyote trap, perfectly positioned just thirty minutes before, fastened themselves on his now-exposed scrotal area, imprisoning his balls and penis. As the initial shock dissipated, the pain hit, and he vomited up the protein shake he'd bolted down before he left his house. Then he gave a low moan that would have been a precursor to another full-on shriek had the big man, unfazed by the green regurgitation, not clamped Bobby's jaw shut and stuck a syringe into his neck.

"In case you're wondering what I'm injecting you with, it's amiodarone HCL. It's an antiarrhythmic drug that will keep your heart beating normally—for a while at least. That's the good part. The bad part, just in case you were thinking of yelling for help, is that I mixed it with a really strong dose of cocaine, which should paralyze your vocal cords in seconds. There's also a little good news with the cocaine: it should ease the pain a little and give you a boost of adrenaline. Here, I'll remove my hand and you can try to scream."

Bobby, who was wavering between semi-consciousness and full-on lights out, opened his mouth. All he could manage was a whisper.

The big man leaned forward. "What's that?"

"Why . . . are . . . you . . . ?"

"I did give you an opportunity to talk about this earlier, so don't blame me. Think of it as the universe paying you back for the thousands of coyotes your company tortures to death every year so that a bunch of rich, unfeeling, or perhaps unaware people—I'll give them the benefit of the doubt—can look good, and you can make even more money."

Bobby opened his mouth once again. This time the scream was silent. He desperately tried to turn over, but the trap, which was anchored to the ground, didn't give. The pain, eased somewhat by the cocaine, still felt as if an alligator was giving him a blowjob.

"No, don't try to turn over; you'll rip your entire scrotum off. You don't want to do that just yet. Now, I'm sure you rationalize your actions all the time. People who put their own pleasure before the suffering of animals usually do. They always have a self-rationalized reason for slaughtering animals. It 'promotes conservation' or 'the local tribes reap the benefits.' One trophy hunter in Zimbabwe told me that the Bible states clearly that God gave man dominion over the animals. I gave him the opportunity to discuss that directly with his God. I know, you just want this to stop.

Sorry, I get carried away with this sort of stuff, and I can see you really don't feel like listening."

Bobby's head began to spin from the cocaine, and he felt himself going in and out of consciousness. In his now undecipherable whisper, he pleaded with his assailant to help him. But his face was in the dirt, and not even the God that Bobby pretended to worship every Sunday could hear him.

"I'm sorry Bobby. I don't like to see suffering in any living being, but I'm afraid I have to be a little hard-hearted in your case. I know how many anti-cruelty organizations have tried to reason with you. The problem is you've ignored them, just as you did me a few minutes ago. This was the only way I could think of to get you to listen. Now, you'll notice the jaws of this trap don't have those sharp teeth. Just like the ones your company claims to use. Although, of course, I have my doubts, knowing some of the people you hire to do your trapping. Even without teeth, it's the force that snaps the bone and cuts through the skin of the animal. I'm sorry I had to use it on your dick and balls, but it's too small a trap for a human leg. There is, however, one chance for you get out of this, I'm pretty sure, painful predicament."

Bobby lifted his head slightly and threw up again. Then he began to laugh hysterically.

"Ah, too much cocaine . . . I'll have to work on the formula a little more. Anyway, as I was saying, coyotes can escape one of these traps, and mothers with cubs usually do, by chewing through their legs. It's not easy, I warn you, and, of course, very few survive for long with three legs. Unless you've practiced auto-fellatio, you'll never be able to get your mouth close enough, but if you pull really hard and you can withstand the pain, you may be able to rip your scrotum off. And this would be the time to do it. Move really quickly before you lose too much blood. Then get to the path, and if someone finds you and gets you to the hospital, you may be able to survive. Though, I really doubt that's going to happen. But give it a go. You have nothing to lose."

Bobby didn't even try to whisper. His eyes rolled back, and he slumped into a fetal position. Just before he passed out, he managed to turn his head just enough to look at the big man. He saw his face with its sharp cheekbones and strong jaw. He peered briefly into the dark eyes and saw they were devoid of sympathy. The man's thick black hair had been drawn up into a pony tail, and he looked to the now-delirious Bobby like a character out of *The Last of the Mohicans*. He laughed again. And then there was nothing but a swirling cloud of pain and darkness that slowly pulled him down into oblivion.

"You may come around again in a few minutes. The pain will be awful, I'm sorry to tell you, and I'll be gone by then. One last thing: I'm going to take Bessie with me. She's a really lovely dog, by the way. So long, Bobby. Don't forget to think about all those coyotes you tortured in your traps. Their suffering should take your mind off your own."

With that final piece of advice (and it was pretty much final, because Bobby's heart exploded a minute or so later, killing him instantly), Ishea Payamps—half Puerto Rican, half Lakota, ex-marine, ex-special forces, currently employed as a mercenary and animal-rights activist—pulled the dead Bobby out the thicket so that his bright-orange, running-shoe-clad foot, still in the trap, was visible to anyone passing by.

"Damn. Too much cocaine, too little amiodarone. I have to work on that formula."

Then Ishea took off down the trail with a jubilant Bessie in tow. He left her tied to a pole outside the Fatt house with a note to Bobby's widow telling her where to look for her husband. Then he walked to a busy street, took a taxi to Toronto International Airport, and caught a late flight to London and a connection to the island of Zanzibar.

A month later, Lilly Fatt, widow of the late Bobby, who'd taken over the business after her husband's rather unfortunate but not entirely inappropriate death, announced that the company would no longer be using coyote fur to enhance the appeal of its coats. Some shareholders were extremely upset that she'd given in to "those goddamned weirdo PETA people," as one of them put it. But when sales shot through the roof as the rebranding opened up a whole new market, most agreed it was a very good move.

Chapter 1

In which Roger Storm has an unexpected encounter

Hunter's Folly Private Game Reserve,
Limpopo, South Africa

Two hippos had made their way from the muddy waters of the Limpopo River to graze on the neatly manicured lawn in front of Roger Storm's personal tent on his 23,000-hectare private game reserve. His was the simplest of the six permanent tents—though in truth they were more like luxury hotel suites than the image that is normally conjured by the word "tent"—but it had, he thought, the best view of the water and the vast expanse of the Northern Tuli Game Reserve across the Limpopo River in Botswana.

"If I was back in the real world," said Roger as he handed a fresh Amstel Light to his friend, Brian Morris, who'd flown in from Australia the day before and arrived at the camp that morning, "I'd start a lawnmower company to compete with John Deere called Jack Hippo. Those guys can restore order to an overgrown area the size of a football field in under an hour. And as an added bonus take out unwanted guests."

Brian laughed. "Yes, I think I read somewhere that they kill more people than any other animal."

"That's what I used to think too. But in reality, they're way down on the scale compared to mosquitos, dogs, tapeworms, and, of course, the most dangerous species of all: humans."

"The way you said 'humans' sounds to me like you've lost any liking for your own species."

"And that's true. I have. I don't like people for the most part—with, of course, a few exceptions. But as I think back on my life, especially to what happened a year ago and all the people I worked with and everything I read about what we're doing to the planet, it's pretty obvious—and of course this is just my personal observation—that we're all so driven by greed and a godlike sense of superiority to any other living organisms that we're headed for total annihilation, and we're determined to take everything else down with us."

Brian sympathized with his friend. He'd known Roger since elementary school, and in his opinion, Roger had always been an overly goofy, inordinately sensitive individual who took everything far too seriously. He could only imagine what the horrors of Roger's Ethiopian nightmare in the company of the notorious Freddy Blank had done to his psyche. "You sound awfully bitter, Roger, my friend. Justifiably so perhaps, but maybe you've been out here too long."

"It's only been a year, so that's hardly an issue. Look, I know I sound that way, but I'm not really bitter. I just feel more aware than I've ever felt, more conscious of what's going on around me. And I'm determined to do what I can to save what I can of the good things, no matter how small and no matter what it takes. In a million years I never thought I'd ever get an opportunity to be a part of something so incredible. So as horrible as my time in Freddy's company was, I got this place out of it, and perhaps that's made me more appreciative of the few things we humans haven't destroyed."

"Well, so long as you don't go too maudlin on me. It's not that I get to see you a lot. Hey, that one hippo looks like he's making a beeline for us. He's not going to come up on the deck?"

"No, he won't. He'll walk right by the tent. They only attack things in their path, and we're not in it. They come out the river just about every evening at this time, keep the lawn trimmed, and hang around my tent for God knows what reason. But I guarantee you not to eat us. Cheers, mate. I can't tell you how great it is to have you here."

"Cheers, Rog." Brian clinked bottles with his old friend, and the two of them settled into the two chaises that constituted the furnishings on the small hardwood deck. "This really is unbelievably beautiful." Brian paused for a moment to look around. "You know, in a million years I could never have imagined you being in a place like this. You were pretty much wiped out last time I saw you. In fact, if I'd had to put money on it, I would have bet you'd be dead."

"Well, as awful a thought as that may be, you're right." Roger took a sip of his beer and stared out over the lawn and across the river towards the vast wilderness beyond.

3

The sun had dipped below the horizon, turning the bush from gold to a deep purple. The hippos, despite their bulk, had mysteriously disappeared into the shadows. In the distance a lion roared. It was killing-time in the bush.

Roger continued, "The last time I saw you was at my mother's funeral in Melbourne. About a month before I met our newly resurrected and subsequently 'unsurrected'—if such a word exists—friend, Freddy. God, I was depressed. I'm being over dramatic, I know, but it felt like I was in a bottomless pit of pure funk. Worse than I've ever been. And hardly any of it to do with my mother's death. Though the funeral probably wasn't the most appropriate time to tell my brother that I intended to commit suicide. Really pissed him off."

"You were also pretty drunk, as I recall."

"I suppose I was. It's hard for me to even imagine what shit shape I was in back then. Pounding back vodka from early in the morning, every single day. I was utterly hopeless. No control over my emotions whatsoever. Divorced. Fired from my job by that perfidious fucker Harry Bones, the most miserable bastard imaginable, and with absolutely no prospects. You can hardly blame me."

"Nope, I don't suppose I can. Well, I'm glad you're better, old friend. I'd really hate for both you and Freddy to be dead."

"If he really is. Who knows with Freddy? I'm convinced he died trying to rescue me in Ethiopia, but then again, he has a habit of coming back to life. As you know, it certainly wouldn't be the first time."

Brian took a long sip of his beer and thought back to the headline on page four of the London Daily Mail from ten years ago that proclaimed in bold type, "Cat-loving Conman Dies in Mysterious Suicide." Freddy, who'd been as close to Roger and Brian as they'd been to each other growing up, and whose exploits and antics were legendary in school and infamous in early adulthood, had supposedly died in an apparent drug-related suicide in London after being accused of fraud and money laundering. He'd resurfaced in Paris a year ago as head of an international arms company and involved Roger in a crackpot scheme to save Africa's wildlife and displaced people, the details of which Brian had just heard that afternoon. "Well, I have to say, other than your desire for the destruction of mankind, you do seem really content, Rog. I'd say 'happy,' but I'm not sure that's right. Something's clearly missing."

Roger laughed. "Yes, something is missing. I had a real chance at love. Or at least I thought I had...." He paused for a second. "Anyway, despite my angst, which as you know—because you've known me a long time—is a passing aberration, I'm content for the first time in a long time because I'm doing something I honestly love, with a person I like, and in a place that defies description. Can you think of anywhere more beautiful?"

"No, it's magical. That's for sure."

The lion roared again. This time the roar was answered by another that seemed as if it was only a few hundred yards away. Brian looked startled.

"Don't worry," said Roger. "They're across the river. Our prides are north and south of here. Too far away to hear, but I imagine they're about to kill something for their dinner as well. Talking of which, we should head up to the dining room."

"So...." Brian, ignoring the suggestion, drew the "so" out slowly. "You've told me the whole weird adventure, but the one thing you've avoided is the death of Harry Bones. Are you going to tell me about it?"

"I'd rather not go into it...." The one person Roger did not ever want to have to think about again was Harry Bones, whom he blamed for the desperate state he'd been in when he'd "mysteriously" bumped into the supposedly dead Freddy in Paris. Harry Bones had met his end by digesting tetrodotoxin from improperly filleted pufferfish, making hundreds of people whose lives he'd ruined ecstatic.

"You know, of course, I'd never say anything."

"I know you wouldn't. But it's not quite as simple a discussion as you think. And the fact that there's even a speck of suspicion in your mind, is why."

"That's not why I'm asking," Brian lied. "It's just that the story doesn't seem complete without knowing what really happened to him."

"And it may never be, I'm afraid. Look, you know the circumstances of his death—poisoned sushi—but you don't know just how many people wanted to kill him. Harry Bones fired people left and right and ruined so many lives that the list of suspects was endless. I think the cops closed the file when they realized the sheer number of people who had motive."

"Yes, but not everyone had opportunity."

"Of course not. Including me if it makes you feel better. Look Brian, you're my oldest friend—my best friend—and even though we only see each other every couple of years, it always feels like I saw you yesterday. So, put the lawyer side of you away and think of me the way you always have. I'm no different. I haven't suddenly become capable of murder."

"Please, mate. I'm not judging you or even questioning you. But with everything you've been through, I honestly wouldn't blame you. Being shot at by crazed mercenaries, beaten up by Albanian torturers, meeting ghosts from the past, and having a love affair with a beautiful assassin would change most people. I'm just curious, that's all."

"I've known you too long to lie to you, so I'm not going to start now. But you have to understand that whatever answer I give you will change our relationship."

"No, it won't. Come on, we've been friends for over forty years."

"Yes, believe me, it will. If I say, 'Yes, I did have a part in killing him,' you'll always think of me as a murderer, and your conscience won't allow you to get over that. And if I say, 'No, I did not kill him,' you'll always wonder if I was lying. So, you have to let it go. I've thought about it a lot and it's the only way. It's the same thing I told both my sons. In any case, if it makes you feel better, the cops never even put me down as a person of interest in the death of Harry Bones."

Brian nodded and stared up at the at the sliver of moon that hung over the horizon.

Roger smiled at his friend. "Look, Brian. I want to see you for as long as I can, and I want you to think of this place as yours too, because while Freddy gave me the money to buy it, he would have wanted you to feel at home here. I'd really like you to come whenever you like and stay for as long as you like. But it's never going to work unless you can move on from what you're thinking."

"I understand what you're saying, Roger. First, it's extremely generous of you to ask me here, and I do want to see you more often. Or at least more often than we've seen each other in the past twenty years. But...."

"But what?"

"No, you're right. I don't really want a *yes* or *no* answer. Our friendship's more important than a dead asshole. So, okay. I promise I won't ask you again." Brian had known Roger since they were in the fifth grade. Their friendship had been both profound and complex at times. Yet despite the years and vast distance between them, Brian would have said that it was unshakable. He'd always believed that he had a deep understanding of Roger, but uncertainty had begun to creep in. He took another slug of his beer and looked over at his mate. He knew Roger was right about how he'd feel, but he also knew it was too late to go back to how things were. It was true, despite the fact that Roger hadn't actually answered either way, that he would never see him again through the same eyes. Roger was different. There was a hardness to him. It was subtle but unmistakable. Whether that meant he was able to kill someone, Brian didn't know. A sudden sadness came over him, and he made the decision to return to Australia in a few days.

He'd have to come up with an excuse, which Roger would no doubt see through but understand.

Brian gave a deep sigh. "I'm kind of jealous that you got to see Freddy again."

"Well, don't be. Those few weeks were horrific. It took me months to recover from that awful beating I took in the monastery in Ethiopia from that psychopath Demetri Guria—who was Bulgarian, not Albanian by the way—and his awful boss, Geoffrey van der Borrekens. And to get over Conchita Palomino...." Roger took a deep breath. "Although I'll probably never get over her."

"You really loved her?"

"I did. Or at least I thought I did. Either way, she was the most amazing woman I've ever met." He felt a sudden pain in his chest, and he knew it was the aching hole that opened up every time he thought of her and wondered if their relationship had just been as crazy and big a farce as the whole harebrained scheme Conchita and Freddy had dragged him into.

"Anyway, it's probably best you remember the Freddy from our childhood. The fun days before he went totally off his trolley. Burning down the school, stealing diamonds...."

Brian laughed. Freddy and his antics were not things you could easily forget.

"If it's any consolation, Freddy did talk about you a lot, and I have a feeling there's nothing more he would have wanted than to be here with us. Now, come on. We really do need to go and eat, and then you can get to bed. I bet you're exhausted and starving."

"I am rather tired, and the beer's going straight to my head."

"So, let's walk up before you keel over, and I'll introduce you to my partner Gosego Modise. I'm sure he's got something terrific planned for us for the next few days. No one you'll ever meet knows the bush better, and there's a ton of stuff to see." Roger gathered up the empty beer bottles and grabbed a flashlight.

"Don't you have a gun?" asked Brian as they headed out towards the main lodge.

"No, I'd never carry one. We're perfectly safe, and I'd never kill an animal out here. This is their home. I'm just a caretaker."

But, thought Brian as he walked alongside his friend, *you'd have no compunction about killing a human.* He stopped himself and felt awful for still thinking that. Roger was the same Roger. No different to the timid, non-confrontational boy he'd grown up with. *And yet* . . . He pushed the thought aside. *No, Roger couldn't actually be a murderer.* But the thought wouldn't go away. It was well and truly lodged in his brain. He was more convinced than ever that Roger had played some part in the murder of Harry Bones.

The main lodge area was a well-lit and beautifully furnished open-thatch and concrete structure. Huge leather couches surrounded a magnificent coffee table made from the wood of a jacaranda tree, and various other loungers and tables gave visitors the impression that they'd somehow wandered back in time to the camp of some aristocratic British explorer. The property was large, but the camp in relation to some of the others in the area was small. Roger had planned it that way. He wanted visitors to enjoy the bush as much as he did, just not a lot of them. The prices were ridiculously high, but it had been rated the top private game reserve in the area for both the experience and the cuisine.

Gosego Modise was sitting at a table with two of the guests discussing everything they'd seen that day. He waved to Roger and Brian as they walked into the dining area, and both of them went over to the table to greet the guests.

"This," said Roger, "is Brian Morris, my oldest and best friend from Perth in Australia. "And these," he said to Brian, relieved that he could actually remember their names, "are Maggie Marden and Mark Piggot from London."

The three guests shook hands, and Roger thumped Gosego on his shoulder. "And most important, Brian, and no offence Maggie and Mark, this is the famous Gosego Modise. My partner, the most feared poacher hunter in the area."

Gosego stood up, his six-foot-five frame making Brian and Roger seem like dwarves. Brian stuck out his hand, but Gosego ignored it and grabbed him in a bear hug, nearly crushing his ribs in the process.

"Aha," he said, "Brian Morris . . . I have heard a lot about you. The good and bad. Well, if you are still a friend of Roger Storm after forty years, you must be as special as your friend has told me. You must also be a very patient person. I have only known Roger for a year, and already I can't stand the bastard. Seriously, how could you be friends with such a lazy and useless person?"

Brian looked for the grin, but there wasn't one. Maggie, who'd been smiling the whole time, looked down in embarrassment. Mark snorted dismissively and shoveled his salad into his mouth, smacking his lips in an annoying way. Then Gosego burst into a smile and let out a chortle that sounded like a rampaging elephant. "Hau, what's wrong with you people? I'm joking. Let the world outside go. There is no stress here. This is paradise, where everything is beautiful." He grabbed Roger in an even bigger bear hug. "This man, even though I'm not joking about him being lazy and useless, is my best friend. So, Brian, you are going to have to share him with me. Here, the two of you sit down. I have stuff to do, but I will see you before you go to bed, and we can talk about what I have planned for tomorrow."

"Do you mind if we join you?" asked Roger after Gosego had gone.

"Oh," Maggie almost tittered. "That would be lovely. Your partner told us a little about you, but you can fill in the gaps. You know, the secret stuff that the other guests don't get to hear."

Roger grinned and gave Brian a disconcertingly direct look before answering. He knew exactly what was going through his friend's mind. "There aren't too many secrets around here, Maggie. What you see is what you get, I'm afraid."

"I very much doubt that. There's a sense of mystery about you...."

Roger laughed politely as he and Brian sat down at the table just as a waiter came over with Mark and Maggie's main course.

"Oh, my God," said Brian, peering at the food. "Is that Chicken Peri Peri?"

"Yes, that's what we ordered," Maggie replied, taking a bite. She chewed for a few seconds and sat back. "You know, this is even better than Nando's."

"I wouldn't go that far." Mark hadn't said a word up till then, clearly annoyed at Maggie's blatant attempt at flirting. "But you probably don't know Nando's."

"Hell, yes," replied Brian. "They're all over Australia."

"As good as Nando's is," Roger responded, "I'd have to agree with you, Maggie. Our chef is from Mozambique, where they basically invented peri peri dishes, and his are bloody brilliant. He crushes his own chilies. Mixes them with some mysterious oil that he refuses to divulge the source of and marinates the chicken for days. If you like the chicken, wait till you try the peri peri prawns. Hopefully they'll arrive tomorrow. Served with his special fries...."

"Well, that one thing hasn't changed." Brian elbowed Roger. "You're still working on the next meal before you've eaten the one in front of you."

"You see," Roger responded with a grin, "same old me."

Roger asked the waiter to bring them a bottle of the 2013 Herdade do Esporão Verdelho. "It's the perfect wine with peri peri," he said to Maggie and Mark, who were drinking a reasonable chardonnay. "Very dry and citrusy. Goes great with the spiciness of the chicken. You must try it." He was trying neither to impress Maggie nor annoy Mark, but he succeeded on both counts.

"Really, hmm...." Maggie said, picking up a drumstick and sticking it in her mouth in what Brian thought was an extremely provocative gesture. "Well, maybe I'll have a glass with you." There was a slight emphasis on the *you*.

"I'll take your word for it. This stuff is just fine, thank you," Mark said, not liking the way Maggie was gawking at Roger at all. He swallowed half a glass of the chardonnay in what would have been clear to anyone observing him closely, anxious jealousy. He knew his wife's predilection for outdoorsy men. Though how Roger qualified as such with all the young guides around was beyond his comprehension. He sniffed loudly and drained what was left in his glass.

"So, tell me, Roger, how did you acquire this establishment?" Before Roger could respond, Mark grabbed the wine bottle from the waiter, who was hovering in the background, and filled his glass until it was on the verge of overflowing. He took another huge sip and, with barely concealed disdain and a rather obvious curl of his upper lip, interrupted Roger as he was about to answer. "You sound sort of South African but with an American twist and, no offence meant, you don't really look like a bush person. More like someone who's spent his life prancing around an office."

"Well...." Roger replied, totally ignoring the slight. He paused for a second and rolled the wine around his mouth in a way, judging by her giggle, Maggie thought was particularly charming. "No offence taken because I'm really not a 'bush person' as you put it. Like Brian, I grew up in South Africa, and then in the late '80s, while apartheid was still in full swing, both of us left. I went to the US and Brian went to Australia."

"So, why did you come back? I mean, and again no offence, you seem more of a dabbler than someone who likes hard work. What we would call a 'floater' in my business."

"Don't know the term, but it sounds mildly disagreeable," Brian said, jumping to his naïve friend's defense. "What business are you in?"

"I'm in toilets. Biggest company in the north of England. We manufacture the Thomas Flushless Toilet. It uses sonic waves to break up the fecal matter."

"Jesus, Mark. Must you talk shit while we're eating?" Maggie rolled her eyes.

"Well, shit it may be, but shit is what paid for your trip, my dear. The toilet's named for a personal hero of mine, Thomas Crapper. Perhaps you've heard of him?"

"Who hasn't," said Roger, giving Maggie a wink. "I think of him at around 7:30 every morning."

Mark began to grind his teeth in an alarming manner. "You're definitely a bloody floater." He looked over at Maggie, who seemed to be drooling, and cleared his throat loudly to distract her. It sounded as if he were about to cough up a small pigeon, and Roger wondered if he should thump him on the back. Mark's growing indignation at what was going on between Roger and Maggie went totally over Roger's head. He was enjoying himself.

"I'm not really sure why you keep calling me a 'floater,' but to answer your original question, I grew up going to game reserves and loving wildlife, and I guess, though it wasn't something I really thought about till a year or so ago, I've always wanted to live on a private game reserve."

"How very interesting," said Maggie, fluttering her eyes. "You must have been very successful in business to be able to buy something like this. I'm sure it cost a fortune."

15

"Well, it wasn't cheap, that's for sure. But as to my success, let's just say I was lucky. Anyway, I managed to get this place, and with Gosego, we've turned it into something quite special."

"Yes, you have," said Maggie, whose flirtatious glances had gone from subtle to something akin to a python eyeing a bush pig. "You're a mysterious man, Roger. I'd really like to know more about you."

"Well that's not going to happen tonight," said her husband, throwing his napkin down on the table in an indelicate display of defiance. "We've an early morning game drive, so let's go to bed." He added a conciliatory "my dear."

"Good advice," said Roger. "Someone will knock on your door at five. Get some rest. You'll have a wonderful drive tomorrow. I believe you're going to look for our southern lion pride. Sleep well."

As Maggie was almost dragged from the dining area, she looked back at Roger and once again fluttered her eyelashes.

"Good God," Brian laughed. "If he weren't around, I think you'd have some company tonight. You'd better be careful. Mark looks like a dangerous bastard who'd punch your lights out with little provocation. Of which I might add, you're giving him plenty."

"Oh, come on. I wasn't doing anything. I'd never do anything to make Mark mad. Maggie's the wild one. Did you see the way she kept fluttering those artificial eyelashes at me?"

"Perhaps, but be careful. He thinks you're a 'floater,' though he never answered my question about what it means."

"No doubt something nasty to do with fecal matter, but who cares?" Roger replied with a grin. In truth he felt quite pleased with himself. He hadn't had any female company since his last night with Conchita in the wilds of Ethiopia, the day before she had tumbled off the walls of the monastery to her death on the rocks below. Maggie was a good-looking woman. A little ragged around the edges, to be sure. But then again, so was he. Mark seemed like an honest guy, and Roger, despite having enjoyed the flirting, had no intention of doing anything that would come between Maggie and her husband.

Just as he and Brian were finishing the last of their wine, Gosego came back. He had a huge grin on his face. "Good news, my friends. The black rhino female has given birth."

"Oh, Jesus. That's fantastic news Gos!" Roger jumped up and pumped Gosego's hand in sheer joy.

"I guess congratulations are in order," said Brian. "I'm assuming it's a rare occasion?"

"Yes, it is," replied Gosego. "We have the only breeding pair of black rhinos in the area. This is enormous news because black rhinos are almost extinct. So, you gentlemen had better get some sleep. We're going to track them really early tomorrow morning."

After Roger saw Brian to his tent, he made his way to his own. He was tired and slightly inebriated and worried about Brian. He could sense the void that had opened between them, and he knew there was nothing he could do to close it. He supposed he could have told him the truth about the death of Harry Bones, but he'd decided never to tell it to anyone ever again.

Roger found the door to his room slightly ajar and cursed loudly. The baboons must have been in again as they

17

had been two days ago. He only hoped they hadn't wrecked the place. He flicked on the lights and let out a loud shriek. Lying on the bed was a very naked Maggie Marden.

"What the hell?"

"Is that any way to greet a lady?"

"Oh, my God, Maggie. What are you doing?"

"What does it look like? I'm lying here waiting to give you the best blowjob you've ever had in your life."

"No, please. Maggie, you have to put your clothes on and go back to your tent. This isn't right."

"What? You don't find me attractive? Well take a look at these." She jiggled her large breasts at Roger who, despite his initial reluctance, felt himself getting aroused.

"No, you're very attractive and those . . . Well, they're spectacular." The sheer impact of Maggie's mammaries moving side to side a few feet from his face had thrown Roger into a tailspin. He put out his hands and then stopped. He took a deep breath. "No, Maggie, we can't...."

"What? Don't tell me you are a 'floater'?"

"Look, I'm not being a piece of shit. Why do you keep calling me that? I just don't think—"

"Mark means you're flamboyant, gay. Not a piece of shit, you idiot. Now, are you going to come over here or not?"

"Oh, really? Well, if that's what you think, allow me to show you." Roger launched himself onto the bed and landed headfirst in the vicinity of Maggie's ample buttocks.

Thirty minutes later, as he snuck Maggie back to her tent, he had to admit she hadn't exaggerated about it being the best blowjob of his life. He felt exhausted, drained both of energy and seminal fluid.

Two hours later a frantic banging on his door pulled him out of a deep, satisfied sleep. For a minute he panicked, thinking it had to be Mark wanting to pound him into small pieces. Then he recognized the voice. It was Gosego.

"Roger, wake up! Something terrible has happened. The rhino and her baby ... They're dead."

Chapter 2

IN WHICH TWO SIDELINED COPPERS FIND THEMSELVES BACK ON THE FIELD

Bundeskriminalamt, Wiesbaden, Germany
A few days later

Chief Inspector Constantin Darmstaedter was bored. Things had been slow in Division ZI into which he'd been unceremoniously dumped after he and Inspector Matthew Bunter of Interpol had failed, in the eyes of their respective superiors, to bring to justice the organization responsible for killing off a number of wealthy trophy hunters in Africa. Division ZI dealt with information management, and Darmstaedter's job for the past few months had been to update the agency's DNA analytics database. For the tenth time that day, he wished he hadn't promised both his wife and current mistress that he'd give up smoking once again.

"Gott verdammt!" he yelled, smacking his computer in frustration as yet another error in his entry popped up. He was about to deliver another blow to the quivering laptop when his phone rang. Much to his surprise it was his old pal, Matthew Bunter.

"Matthew! What a great pleasure to hear from you."

"Ah, Constantin, old chap. And it's equally lovely to speak to you again. It's been over a year."

"Yes, indeed. A year in hell, I must tell you. They punished me by putting me behind this damned computer instead of out in the field. I'm about to pull my hair out."

Bunter knew Darmstaedter was totally bald but declined to point that out. "So sorry to hear that. Well, hopefully, then, I've got some good news. Are you free for lunch?"

"Ja, I'm free for anything. Lunch, coffee, or a hundred-meter hike with stones in my socks. Anything to get me out of the office. When are you thinking, Matthew?"

"I'm thinking right now. Today. I'm downstairs in your lobby."

"You're joking."

"I most definitely am not. I was just talking to your new boss—is it Floppi Nussbaum?"

"It's Floppi Haselnuss, actually."

"Right, I knew there were nuts involved. Anyway, nice chap."

Darmstaedter grabbed his leather jacket off the coat rack and closed his computer. As boring as he found his English counterpart, with his erroneous interpretation of German names and his constant Sherlock Holmes impressions, his invitation was exactly what he needed. He couldn't imagine that anything Bunter would have to say would constitute good news, but even indifferent news was preferable to anything he'd been doing.

"Matthew!" Darmstaedter rushed up to his old friend with his arms out, forgetting that Matthew was not someone who embraced willingly. At the last minute he pulled back his left arm, and Bunter shook his right hand with as much energy as the pickled herring Darmstaedter had eaten for breakfast.

"My God, look at you, Matthew. Very cool for an English policeman. What has happened?"

Much to Darmstaedter's surprise, Bunter had shed his navy blazer and grey slacks for jeans and a paisley shirt. His ginger hair, which had been cut in a regular "short back and sides" style the last time they'd worked together, now hung over his collar. Even the one thing that annoyed Darmstaedter the most about Bunter, his ginger moustache, was gone.

"Well, Clare thought I was a little too formal to be seen out with her, and you know how opinionated she can be."

"Ah yes, the mysterious Clare...." Darmstaedter pictured the brilliant computer hacker who'd helped them the year before to identify Der Felsen, the company supplying the mercenaries who'd been responsible for driving tribes off their traditional land for the neo-colonial powers who were buying up huge parts of North and East Africa. "So, you are still together?"

"We are, though it's hard to keep up with her if you know what I mean."

Darmstaedter nodded as if he knew exactly what Bunter meant. In fact he didn't because Bunter meant from a social perspective and Darmstaedter assumed a purely sexual one. "Well, my friend, you can tell me about how you are *bumsen* Clare and why you are here without any warning over lunch. And I have just the place in mind if Interpol is picking up the bill."

"I've never heard of *bumsen*, but knowing how your mind works, Constantin, I can only imagine. So, no. You will not be hearing about any of our private affairs. But yes, Interpol will be picking up the bill."

Twenty minutes later, Darmstaedter and Bunter were sitting at a corner table at Webers Wikinger in Wisebaden's old town ordering the city's best schnitzel with the big white asparagus that had just come into season and a bottle of 2013 Mittelheimer St. Nikolas.

"Excellent choice," said Bunter, taking a sip of the dry Riesling. "Different to some of the other Rieslings we've drunk together. A good finish."

"Ja, ja. It's much more intense than the Mosel Rieslings," Darmstaedter said with a hint of frustration. He knew Bunter had very little knowledge of wine. Not that Darmstaedter did either, but he wanted to get to the real reason the Interpol policeman had visited in person rather than called. "But I'm sure you didn't invite me to lunch to talk about wine or girlfriends. Though I really do want to hear about Clare's and your love life. Does she still have that big rubber ball? Have you fucked her on it again?"

"I can't believe you remember that ball, you randy bastard. But you're right—that's not why I came to Wiesbaden so suddenly. This is...." Bunter took out his iPad and opened up a story in the *Toronto Star* from two weeks before. He passed it to Darmstaedter, who began to read out loud.

24

"*Toronto billionaire fails to free himself from animal trap. Dies horribly.* Hmmm. *Bobby Fatt found dead in a pool of his own blood after trying to free himself from a coyote trap by unsuccessfully ripping off his penis. Police suspect environmental groups* . . . Mein Gott, what are you getting at, Matthew?"

"I suspect you know exactly where this is going. Take a look at the next story."

"*Los Angeles socialite strangled with her own Shahtoosh scarf.*" Darmstaedter read through the story about a wealthy woman who, despite an anonymous plea, continued to illegally purchase the scarves, which were made from the endangered Tibetan chiru and banned in most countries. Her husband, a private banker, had come home to find her lying on their bed with one of her many Shahtoosh scarves wound tightly round her neck.

"I don't know, Matthew. I'm still struggling to see the connection...."

"Come on, Constantin, use that big noggin of yours. It has everything to do with the case we worked on a year ago."

"You're not suggesting . . . No, you don't think?"

"Oh, yes I am, and I do."

"Ishea Payamps?"

"The very same. Think about it. Both of them get anonymous letters—those are in the police reports not the news articles, by the way—asking them to stop in the name of humanity. Both ignored them. Soon after, both died in what some would say is a manner similar to how the animals used in their fashion items died."

25

Darmstaedter tapped his front teeth with his knife and shook his head. "Ja, but it's very floppy."

"You mean flimsy. Yes, I can see you're skeptical." Bunter took a bite of his schnitzel and chewed thoughtfully. "So, I'm going to tell you something not mentioned in the press. A jogger out on the same trail at around the same time that Bobby Fatt was murdered saw a very big man with long black hair going into the woods. He took particular notice because, and I quote, 'he looked like a First Nation's chief returning to his ancestral land.' To top that off, a security camera at the house where the socialite lived shows a picture —a very blurred one, mind you—of a man fitting the same description."

"It is as you English say, a 'long shot,' but I suppose it could be Payamps. I mean, that's very close to how Roger Storm described him to us in London. But these seem very different types of killing for him, no?"

"They do, compared to the killings of trophy hunters and poachers in Africa. But take a look at the next story."

Darmstaedter swiped through to the next story about George Parker, an American big game hunter from Texas who'd gone to Uganda to shoot an endangered lowland bongo antelope in a section of the rainforest. He claimed it was one of the only animals he hadn't killed.

"And it will also be the last animal he ever kills, I presume?"

"Yes, it most certainly will, unless of course he can aim with his arsehole rather than his eyes. As we've seen before, his wife was sent his head, neatly mounted on a piece of plywood for easy display." Bunter took back his iPad and

26

put it in sleep mode. "And then, there is what happened a few days ago in South Africa."

"I'm all ears."

"Very nearly," said Bunter, marveling at how large Darmstaedter's ears were. "It happened on a private game reserve at about five o'clock. There may be a few names you don't yet know, but here is one you will."

"And who may that be?"

"Roger Storm."

"You're joking. Roger Storm?"

"Oh yes, the very same. He owns the game reserve."

As they finished their schnitzels and drank the wine, Bunter filled Darmstaedter in on the remarkable email he'd received the previous afternoon from a Colonel Patel in Johannesburg, and when he was done, Darmstaedter sat back and smiled.

"So, Matthew." Darmstaedter regarded his friend thoughtfully. "This could be very good news. Good news for the animals, and for me . . . for us."

"Yes, old chap, you and I have been reassigned to the case. My boss called Herr Haselnuss yesterday and he's agreed. You're officially off desk duty. Cheers!" Bunter clinked his wineglass against Darmstaedter's. The clinking was a little too forceful and he spilled his wine onto his half-eaten schnitzel.

"I wonder why Director Haselnuss agreed? He seems to hate me," Darmstaedter mused.

"Knowing you, most probably because you slept with his wife."

"Well, I did, but long before he was moved up to his current position. I don't trust people who hold a grudge for that long."

"Anyway, my boss sent his assistant to tell me, and I've never even seen his wife."

"Ja, well, I suppose we both embarrassed our organizations a little. We definitely should have been able to apprehend Payamps. Anyway, thank you Matthew. I shall enjoy working with you once more."

"Yes, my dear friend, and I too. As Sherlock Holmes liked to say, 'The game—'"

"Shut the fuck up with Holmes, Matthew. Now, where the hell do we start?"

Chapter 3

IN WHICH SOME OF WHAT MATTHEW BUNTER TOLD CONSTANTIN DARMSTAEDTER IS EXPLAINED

Hunter's Folly Private Game Reserve, Limpopo, South Africa
Very early the previous morning

It took Roger less than five minutes to wash the residue of Maggie's saliva off both his face and his genitals. He threw on a pair of long khakis and a t-shirt. Then, grabbing his thick jacket, he walked over to the front of the lodge where Gosego was waiting at their Land Rover.

"Christ, Gos, this is the worst possible news. How the hell could this have happened? I know we had guards on them 24/7!"

"We did, Roger. But these bastards must have been waiting for the half an hour it takes to rotate the guards. I guarantee the rhinos were by themselves for no more than thirty minutes. The poachers must have been monitoring them the whole time . . . just waiting. And if I find differently, then heads will definitely roll." Gosego sounded like an impending thunderstorm.

"Look, Gos, let's not blame anyone just yet. Your guys have done an amazing job this year, and we haven't lost a single animal so far."

"Till now."

"Yes, till now. You're right, and I can't even begin to tell you how I feel. I'm honestly trying to remain as calm as I possibly can. And I'm upset, not with the guards, but with those sons-of-bitches who still buy rhino horns. Those are the guys whose heads I'd like to see roll."

Roger thumped the side of the Land Rover with his fist. "I hate to say it, but I suppose it was inevitable. We know these goddamned poachers have gotten so sophisticated with their tracking equipment."

"It's still our fault. We got lazy. And I'm blaming myself. I should have had a back-up team. I'm really sorry, my friend. To lose a black rhino and her calf—nothing could be worse."

"No, I don't suppose it could. But," he said, putting his hand on the big man's shoulder in as reassuring a gesture as he could manage, "if anyone can track those bastards— and perhaps it's not too late—it's you."

"I'm going to try, believe me. Hopefully the trail is still warm."

Roger thought back to when he'd first offered Gosego a full partnership in the private game reserve he'd bought with the money left to him by Freddy and Conchita. The thing he'd liked most about the huge man—other than the fact that he knew and understood the area, its animals, and its people better than anyone Roger had spoken to—was that he'd immediately loved Roger's idea of calling the place "Hunter's Folly". Many of the other farms and reserves in the area allowed trophy hunting, and Roger had made it abundantly clear with signs and notices that both poachers and hunters would be shot. He wasn't sure if it was actually legal to take a potshot at a human, but so far no one had challenged him. Gosego was not only a totally committed conservationist, but he'd been responsible for tracking down and arresting countless poachers in the area. Most of them were locals trying to make money to feed their families. Once they'd had the errors of their ways patiently explained to them by Gosego, they were offered salaries to work for Hunter's Folly as trackers. Two hunters who had "inadvertently" wandered onto the property had not been as lucky. One had been seriously injured when the Land Rover that was taking him to the police station hit a nasty bump and he was thrown out into a camel thorn bush where a number of the inch-long thorns embedded themselves in his crotch. The other had suffered massive trauma to his right hand when Gosego had tried to confiscate his rifle and it accidently went off. He would never fire a rifle again.

"I should wake Brian," Roger said as Gosego began to back the Land Rover away from the lodge.

"I wouldn't do that. What we're going to see isn't something he will easily forget. I arranged for him to go with Johnny Sithole when he takes Mark and Maggie to look for the southern pride. It will be better for him and perhaps prevent Maggie saying something to Mark about where she was last night."

Roger cleared his throat and smiled sheepishly. He knew there wasn't a thing that went on in the camp that his partner didn't know about. Gosego grinned and punched his friend's leg. "Roger, Roger, Roger. Always something new to learn about you, my friend. Just don't fuck too many of our guests; it'll ruin our reputation. Not as a game lodge but rather a place owned by a virile man."

"Not to worry. I have no plans to become anything other than a lover of wildlife. Now, I'd rather not talk about it if you don't mind."

Dawn had broken over the bushveld, and the early morning cold that had seeped into Roger's bones despite his heavy jacket began to ease.

"There they are," said Gosego, pointing to another Hunter's Folly Land Rover on the side of the dirt track they'd been travelling on. Two of the trackers were waiting in the vehicle to walk them to the carcasses. The way they avoided eye contact with Gosego made it clear to Roger that they'd already been suitably rebuked. He nodded a reassuring greeting and followed them into the bush. It wasn't the first time he'd seen a poached animal, and he hoped he wouldn't throw up again.

He nearly did, though. The scene was horrific. The mother was lying on her side with the baby nestled close to her belly as if it had been trying to drink. It was clear she'd been shot with a high-powered rifle and her horn carefully removed with a hacksaw. The baby was no bigger than a Labrador, and its umbilical cord was still attached. It had no horn as yet, and the fact that they'd killed it for absolutely no reason made Roger even sicker. He looked back and felt himself tearing up at the senseless destruction of two such beautiful creatures, and he wished more than ever he could find whoever had been behind it and kill them. He turned his face up to the still-pale sky and opened his mouth in a silent scream of rage.

He was preempted by one of the young rangers. "It moved! The baby moved!"

Roger looked down as Gosego ran over and felt the little rhino. "Yes, yes, it's still breathing. We have to move quickly." He picked up the baby, who was struggling to lift her head. "She is in stress and she needs to feed. Here, Sammy, you take her. You and Roger drive to Dr. Stobbs. I will call her now."

"But—"

"There's no time, Roger. You go with Sammy. Melusi and I will try to track the poachers. It's better you're not with us. Call me when you're at the doctor." Gosego handed the barely moving rhino baby to Sammy, who, despite his size, struggled with the hundred-pound calf. He eventually got a decent grip and scrambled through the bushes back to the Land Rover. Roger followed obediently.

"Let me drive," said Sammy, plonking the baby in Roger's lap and nearly crushing him in the process. "I'm going to go fast, so hold on tight. This poor animal's been through enough."

Roger held on as tightly as he could as the Land Rover crashed and bumped through the bush and onto the main road. The one thing that almost broke his heart was how the baby rhino stared at him. Its large eye, though slightly dull as its life ebbed away, seemed to have tears in it. He shook his head sadly. "Hurry, Sammy. We have to save her."

The Limpopo Wildlife Rescue Mission was on a 2,000-hectare farm about six kilometers from Hunter's Folly. It was run by Dr. Susan Stobbs and her husband, Stuart, a tech entrepreneur who'd sold his business and put the millions he'd made into his wife's project to rescue the area's orphaned and wounded animals. Both were waiting on the porch of the hospital as Roger and Sammy pulled up.

Susan ran up and took one look. "Oh, my God. Quick, bring her inside and let's see what we can do. She's really weak . . . Hurry, man. What's wrong with you?"

Roger was grunting and sweating and realized he'd lost all feeling in the legs from the weight of the rhino. "Nothing, but how about someone helping me . . . Sammy?"

In the end, Stuart, who was twenty years younger than Roger, lifted the little rhino and together with his wife carried it into the hospital. A few minutes later when he'd recovered some feeling in his legs, Roger joined them in Susan's surgery.

The little rhino was lying on its side on the floor on a plastic sheet. Susan had given it a sedative and was listening to its heart with her stethoscope. "I think we're going to be lucky. You may have got her here just in time. Her heart's nice and strong, which is good. The problem's going to be to get her to feed." She covered the calf with a thick blanket. "We'll monitor her round the clock and start her on milk as soon as she wakes up."

"What sort of milk will she drink?" asked Roger, who was feeling quite useless.

"We use baby formula mixed with full cream milk. It's my own formula, but it's worked on a lot of the baby rhinos that come in."

"Is there anything I can do right now? Anything you need me to—"

"Nope, there's nothing you can do at this stage. But you interrupted our breakfast, and you look like you could use a cup of tea yourself. Come on, the staff will call me if anything changes."

Susan and Stuart led Roger out the surgery towards their house, a few meters away. It was a relatively large house that looked like most of the lodges in the area, with concrete walls painted a dark cream color and a thick thatch roof. There was a big, open porch with well-used but comfortable chairs set round an old wooden table on which rested a large teapot and a plate of scones.

"Those look good," Roger said, eyeing the scones and accompanying dish of cream and pots of jam. "I'm starving."

When Stuart had poured them each a cup of tea and Roger was on his second scone, he sighed deeply and looked up at his hosts. "Thank you both so much. I'm Roger Storm, by the way. I own Hunter's Folly together with Gosego Modise."

"Oh, we know Gosego well. He's a great chap. And we know all about you," said Stuart. "You're not the most popular owner in the area with all your warnings to hunters. Plus, of course, the 'accidents' that happened to those two who were on your property a few months ago. You know, they had to remove the one's private parts because of the thorn damage?"

"Yes, I heard that. Son-of-a-bitch tried to sue me. Well, too damn bad. I feel really strongly about trophy hunting, and I'm not going to make any apologies."

"Oh, no need to apologize at all; we're totally with you. As much as I dislike the poachers—because we treat so many animals suffering from gunshot wounds or horrible cuts from snares and what have you—at least they're just trying . . . well, for the most part, to feed their families. But trophy hunters—I'd personally shoot the bastards." Susan popped a scone into her mouth with a loud smack of her lips.

"Well, I'm glad you feel the same way. I was beginning to think I was the only one around here with strong feelings about it."

"Well, you're not, but a lot of the land owners around here—not all of them, mind you; our numbers are growing—justify hunting as a form of conservation. And of course, it is in a way, but a rather perverted way." Stuart refilled his cup and lit a cigarette.

"I'm not sure I totally understand."

"Well, look at it this way. The reason hunters want to conserve animals is to shoot them. So, it has nothing to do with preserving the species per se. And the reason I say that is because no one is shooting the old or the sick. They want the alpha lions or the biggest tuskers or the kudu with the longest horns. So, they're weakening the DNA. Creating fragile species. And, of course, the guys who own the farms are breeding animals the same way they breed dogs in puppy mills. It's really very sad."

36

"It's sad and sick," said Susan, "because ultimately, it's about greed and arrogance, not about doing anything good for conservation or local tribes. The only benefit goes right into the bank accounts of the hunting companies. So, keep up what you're doing, Roger. It's the right thing. Now, I'd better go and check on our baby."

"Before you go, I want to make sure I pay for everything. You have to let me know—"

"We don't charge for our services," said Stuart, standing up with his wife. "What you can do, though, if you'd like is make a donation to our fund."

"Of course," replied Roger. "If you can email me the info, I'll send you a check as soon as I get back."

As he stood up to say goodbye, his phone rang. It was Gosego. "How is the baby rhino?"

"Good, I hope. He's still alive."

"Well that's excellent. And more than I can say for one of the poachers that killed her mother. He is most certainly dead."

Chapter 4

IN WHICH ROGER GETS SMITTEN BY A BLACK MAMBA

Hunter's Folly, Limpopo, South Africa

The big veranda at the main lodge was more crowded than Roger had ever seen it. The six guests, back from their early morning drives, were sitting at tables eating huge breakfasts, chatting excitedly and staring at a group of eight women dressed in camouflage who were drinking tea and eating biscuits from the large glass container at the serving table. Brian was sitting with Mark and Maggie, who looked up and much to his horror blew Roger a kiss.

"Roger," Gosego yelled, "come over here. We need to talk to you."

Roger waved at Brian and walked up to Gosego, who was talking to a clearly-in-charge woman with long dreadlocks who was almost as tall as Gosego. They'd been talking in Setswana but stopped and immediately switched to English when Roger appeared.

"Roger, this is Sergeant Bontle Warona of the Black Mambas."

"Very nice to meet you," said Roger, shaking her hand. "But I didn't realize the Black Mambas were operating in this area. I thought you were over in Balule Game Reserve and Kruger?"

"We have only been in this area for a month," she replied in an accent that echoed the high and low tones of her native Setswana. "We trained with the teams up in Balule for six months. But we can talk on the way; there is something urgent you have to see."

"What?" Roger asked. He was exhausted and still hungry, and all he wanted was to have a proper breakfast and take a nap.

"The Mambas came across the poachers just before I called you. You need to see for yourself."

"Okay, but I have to talk to Brian first. Just give me five minutes."

Bontle nodded, somewhat impatiently Roger thought. "Five minutes max, and then meet us in the front."

Roger had no desire to engage with Maggie or Mark, and so he asked one of the waiters to tell Brian to meet him in his office just off the main gathering area.

"What's going on, Roger? Who are those women?"

"Look, I'm sorry about this morning. Poachers shot the mother rhino at about four, and I went with Gosego to the scene. We thought the baby was dead too, but she's okay, and I had to take her to this vet who runs a rescue organization nearby. That's why I couldn't be with you."

40

"No worries," said Brian. "That's horrible and I totally understand."

"And as to the women, they're an anti-poaching unit called the Black Mambas. It's an all-female team that was started a few years ago near the Kruger National Park, and from what I understand, they're incredibly effective. I had no idea they were even in the area, but apparently they are, and they've found the poachers. They want me to go with them to see . . . God knows what. Bodies? I don't really want to see them, but they're on my property."

"I'd like to come with you."

"I don't think that's a good idea, Brian. You're here to have fun."

"Look, Rog," Brian said, putting his hand on Roger's shoulder. "We've been friends for ever, and after all the ups and downs you've been through over the last year with a bunch of lunatics, I think you could do with a sane person at your side. So, I'm coming whether you like it or not. If nothing more than to keep you out of trouble."

Gosego raised his eyebrows when he saw Brian, but Sergeant Warona greeted him politely and didn't seem to object when he and Roger got into the lead Land Rover. The two-vehicle convoy set out with the sergeant directing Gosego along one of the tracks that lead to the north of the main lodge. The track went away from the river past rocky outcrops and tall nyala trees, and then after half-an-hour turned west back towards the Limpopo. As they got close to the river, the bush gave way to riparian forest with greenish-yellow fever trees. No one said a word, and the only sound was the low whine of the engines as they plowed through the thick sand. Even the birds seemed to be taking a rest in whatever shade they could find. The temperature had climbed to 85 degrees, but Brian and Roger were the only ones sweating.

"From here we walk. It's only about fifteen minutes. The rest of my squad will meet us where they have the poachers."

They climbed out of the Land Rovers, and the Mambas fell into line behind their sergeant, who set off at a fast trot. Gosego kept up with her, but Roger and Brian, who were the oldest and least fit by a long way, soon fell behind.

"Can you see them?" asked Brian, who was leaning forward trying to catch his breath.

"No, but they can't be that far ahead. We should try to catch up. This isn't a good place to be on our own."

"What do you mean?" Brian asked as he shuffled after Roger in the general direction of where they'd last seen the backs of the Mambas.

"I know there's a group of old male elephants in this area, and I'd rather not come across them without Gosego around."

"Jesus. Well, I bloody hope they're somewhere else. I have no desire to be trampled to death by an elephant."

"We'll be fine. Just keep your eyes open and listen for breaking branches."

"I can't hear anything. They've probably moved off. Are you sure you know where you're going, Rog?"

But Roger hadn't the faintest idea, which is why the big bull saw them before they saw him. He'd wandered off from his friends to eat from a particularly luscious-looking mopane tree when he sensed the intruders. He turned his head and examined them carefully. He was not a big fan of two legged creatures. His memory, fading as he aged, was still capable of recalling when one of them had killed his brother. He fanned out his ears and began to make a noise like an out-of-tune oboe. Then his trunk began to swing back and forth in a slow, almost hypnotic rhythm. Roger and Brian froze.

"What do we do?" Brian asked, slowly taking up a strategic position behind his friend.

"I'm not sure...."

"What the hell do you mean? You have to know. You live here." Though he was whispering, Brian's voice went up two octaves.

"Well, I can never remember whether you should hold your ground or back away. Depends if it's a mock charge or a real charge, and I always get confused whether their ears should be flat or flapping . . . I think we should just stand still. Or maybe we should back up. Oh, look. His ears are back down and his trunk's curling in. That's a good sign—I think. Let's just move off to the side."

But it wasn't a good sign at all. The elephant did not share their confusion as to what the appropriate action was when confronted by a member of the opposite species. The off-key oboe swelled to a full orchestra, and with one decisive stamp of his front foot, he began to charge. Roger wanted to run, but his feet wouldn't move. His bowels felt like they were about to explode, and he realized he and Brian were dead men.

"Wave your hands! Wave your hands!" The voice came from a clump of trees to Roger and Brian's right. "Wave, you idiots! Like you mean it!"

Roger, in what felt like slow motion, raised his hands and began to wave. It felt slow, but when he thought back to the moment later, he realized it had been a frantic gesture. Brian stepped out and was doing the same thing. A huge cloud of dust erupted from the dry sand as the elephant stopped. He gave one more flap of his big ears, took a last look at Roger and Brian, turned around, and ambled back to the mopani tree.

"Holy fuck!" Roger said as his heart rate returned to just slightly above normal. "This is already a little too much for one day. Are you okay?"

"Yes, I'm fine," said Brian, "but I nearly peed in my pants. Man, that was close. But who shouted to wave our hands? It didn't sound like Gosego."

"You're right, it didn't." Roger walked over to where he thought the voice had come from. He looked around but couldn't see anything in the shadows. Whoever it was that had provided such sound advice hadn't left a trace. "It wasn't Gosego, that's for sure." He peered into the undergrowth again, but there really was no trace. Not a footprint in the dust nor a broken twig nor even a bent blade of grass. The deep voice that had given them the warning must have belonged to someone who was an expert in bushcraft.

At that moment, Gosego and one of the Mambas appeared. "Roger . . . Brian, what the hell are you doing? Can't you see? There's a big bull elephant over there!"

44

"No kidding," Brian replied, his breathing still dangerously fast. "He charged us . . . nearly killed us."

While the whole incident had terrified Roger, there was something about the strange voice that made him even more uneasy. "Gos, I don't know exactly what happened, but someone yelled at us to wave our hands when he charged us. And it didn't sound like you."

"No, it wasn't me. I would probably just have wished you a safe passage to the next life. It was probably Satan, who has a more appropriate death planned for a non-believer like you. But let's not wait right here for that big bastard to charge again. Come this way, but I warn you: what you're going to see isn't going to be very pleasant."

Even *extremely unpleasant* wouldn't have been an apt description of the scene up ahead. Six of the Mambas surrounded three totally disheveled and morose, visibly injured, and blood-spattered poachers who were shackled together and sitting uncomfortably on the ground. The fourth person was in slightly worse shape than his counterparts. He was propped up against a fever tree, and from the fly-covered stumps that hung out the sleeves of his expensive safari shirt, it was clear he wouldn't be scratching his nose any time soon. Not that it mattered really, because where his nose had once been, there was now a huge and very impressive rhino horn pushed through the back of his neck and up into the roof of his mouth, dislodging soft tissue, bone, and cartilage, till it emerged from what looked like a massively enlarged nostril. For the second time that day, bile rose up into Roger's gaping mouth.

When he'd recovered somewhat and seen to Brian, who was muttering softly as he lay in the shade of a large tree with a wet cloth on his forehead, he went over to Gosego and Sergeant Warona, who were interrogating the poachers in their own language.

"What do they say, Gos? Who did this?"

It was Sergeant Warona who answered. "They're telling us that they can't say...."

"Can't say or won't say?"

"Well, they insist that the man who did this—a very big man, and not a white man or a black man, they're sure of that—made them swear not to say anything. I'm not certain what he threatened them with, but they're scared out of their minds. I'm sure my girls could persuade them to talk, but we'll leave that to the police. They should be here soon. What's wrong with you? You look like you're going to be sick."

"No," said Roger, "I'm not going to be sick. Why does everyone think I'm some sort of weak imbecile?" He wanted to tell her that he had a horrible feeling he knew exactly who'd killed the poacher but decided to keep quiet for the moment. He wandered over and took a quick look at the rhino-horn-nosed man. The damage to his face was so great that it was almost impossible to tell whom he might have been. He was definitely not European or African but could, Roger thought, be Asian. The man was wearing nylon safari pants to match his blood- and snot-covered shirt and expensive hiking boots. He seemed to have a piece of paper folded in his top pocket, and Roger began to reach in to remove it. The sergeant, who'd seen what he was about to do, slapped his hand away.

"Are you crazy? You don't touch a thing till the police get here. One of my troops is waiting for them on the road now. So why don't you go and sit with your friend over there in the shade and drink some water." She handed him her canteen and turned away, giving Roger time to admire her slender body.

Roger took a large gulp of water and walked over to where Brian was slowly recovering. The feeling that he knew exactly who was behind the horrific killing and warning shouted to him and Brian was overwhelming. He put his head in his hands and rubbed his eyes. He could picture Ishea Payamps squatting next to him in the hill temple in Ethiopia, the still-wriggling hand of the treacherous Zecheriah Corn on the floor by his feet, and the insane cackle of Geoffrey van der Borrekens echoing through the ancient building. Ishea had saved his life, but he wasn't someone Roger had any desire to meet again.

"My God," said Brian, who'd recovered somewhat and managed to sit up. "She's quite beautiful."

"Who are you talking about?" Roger asked, trying to bring his mind back to the present.

"Who do you think? The sergeant. Don't think I didn't see you staring at her ass."

"Was I? Sorry, my mind was somewhere else entirely." He took another careful look at Sergeant Warona, who was in deep conversation with the other Mambas. Brian was right, but "beautiful," Roger decided, didn't do her justice. He'd noticed how tall she was back at the lodge, but he hadn't quite realized just how imposing, almost intimidating, she was. Her body, even covered in loose camouflage fatigues, looked long and sinewy. Her head, at the end of what Roger thought of as the most perfect neck he'd ever seen, was held high. Not proudly, but with a regal superiority that did its bit to diminish everyone around her. She must have felt him staring, and she turned towards him and smiled. It was a *fuck-you* smile rather than a *fuck-me* smile, and Roger, as he had the first time he saw Conchita Palomino, tumbled head-over-heels in love.

His brief reverie was interrupted by a piercing voice that demanded, "What in the name of bloody hell is going on here?"

Two policemen dressed (rather inappropriately for a bush investigation) in drab blue uniforms and showing signs of minor encounters with thorn trees walked up to the group. *Walked* was perhaps not an apt description of the ambulatory technique of the two fattest cops Roger had ever seen. Their movement made him think of snails with bowling balls on their backs instead of shells. But for the fact that one was black and the other white, they could have been twins.

"It's not very pretty, Lieutenants," said Gosego, shaking the hand of each policeman in turn.

"'Pretty' would not be the word I would first think of," said the white policeman. "Would 'pretty' be the word you would first think of, Lieutenant Mothibi?"

"It would not, Lieutenant Steenkamp," replied his black counterpart, peering at the rhino-nosed corpse. "Heinous would be more appropriate."

"Yes! Heinous would be a much more appropriate word. I am quite surprised that you'd think this even somewhat 'pretty,' Mr. Modise. And in the future, I must ask you to please refrain from inappropriate, unnecessary, and misleading adjectives before Lieutenant Mothibi and I examine the scene."

"Um, yes, of course, Lieutenants," said Gosego, who was unfazed by the Keystone Cops routine. "I'd like you to meet Sergeant Warona of the Black Mambas. She and her squad tracked the poachers." The two cops looked her up and down.

"Ah, yes. We heard you were in the area," said Lieutenant Mothibi. "Well, this is a very good start for the Mambas. Very good. To capture so many poachers without even the use of firearms. Hau! I'm impressed. Is this not impressive, Lieutenant Steenkamp?"

"Very much so, Lieutenant Mothibi. But 'impressive' is not quite the word I'd use. How about *awesome*, as the Yanks like to say?"

"Talking of *Yanks*," interjected Gosego before the two fat policemen could high five each other again, "this is Roger Storm, my partner."

"Oh, Christ," spluttered Lieutenant Steenkamp. "The bloody American who wants to kill every hunter in the area. You, man, have no idea the bloody trouble you've caused us. Throwing people into thorn bushes, blowing their hands off. Unacceptable behavior."

"Well, in all honesty what happened to those two trophy hunters was entirely their own doing. The warning signs are really clear: *Trophy Hunters will be Dispatched.*" In any case, while I do despise trophy hunters with a great deal of passion, I wouldn't actually condone killing them. Poachers like this guy here, on the other hand, I'd have no problem killing. It would give me immense satisfaction to rid the planet of his type."

"Are you bloody crazy?" asked Lieutenant Mothibi. "This is going to be too easy. You just admit you want to kill poachers, and what do we find?" He pointed at rhino face.

"Bloody brilliant, man." interjected his partner. "Case closed as far as I'm concerned. Roger Storm, we're arresting you for the murder of this man—whoever he may be. And don't think the law will be lenient just because you've confessed."

"Are you two insane?" Roger spluttered. "I certainly did not confess, and I honestly don't think this is a good time for jokes."

"Jokes? Jokes?" Lieutenant Steenkamp grabbed Roger's right arm and spun him around. "Lieutenant Mothibi, would you call this whole situation a joke?"

"I would not, Lieutenant Steenkamp. As you have always said, there's nothing funny about murder."

"Whoa, hold on Lieutenants." Sergeant Warona stepped up to the pair, who were trying to fasten handcuffs to the struggling Roger. "Seriously? You just assume this man killed the poacher? Just like that? No examination of the scene? No questions? Have you even understood how the poacher died?"

"No need to tell us how to do our job," replied Steenkamp indignantly. "And for your information, it's pretty obvious how this poacher died. Someone pushed a rhino horn through the back of his bloody head."

"Well done, Lieutenant. And that would have taken great strength, no?"

"Yes, it would. Incredible strength is a better way of putting it."

"Okay, and do you honestly think this man, Roger Storm, is capable of such strength? I mean, just look at him."

"Well," said Mothibi, "not really. He seems quite weak, in fact. Like a bit of a sissy."

"Exactly," said his partner. "I would go a lot further. He's not a 'bit of a sissy;' he's the genuine article."

"What the hell is wrong with everyone?" Roger pulled his arm from Steenkamp and stood up. "First, Mark calls me a 'floater,' and now these clowns call me a sissy. You know I've been through more shit in my life over the last year and a half than most of you over your entire lives combined. So why don't you just fuck off."

Brian, who up to that point had been observing the absurdity with amused interest, walked up and faced the two Lieutenants, who were clearly having second thoughts about arresting Roger. "Lieutenants, my name is Brian Morris. I'm an attorney. Not that Roger will need my services, but if he does, you can be sure that the first thing that will happen will be to sue you for wrongful arrest and unnecessary force while making said arrest." Brian turned to look at his friend. "How's your arm, Roger? It looks like Lieutenant Steenkamp was particularly brutal." He winked at Roger, who got the message.

"It hurts like crazy. I think he may have dislocated my shoulder." He groaned and rubbed his right shoulder in a rather unconvincing way.

"Ag, please," said Steenkamp. "I didn't hurt him one bit. You see, he *is* a sissy. But fine, then let's just get down to business." He took out a small notebook and a pen. "Where were you last night, Mr. Storm?"

"As it happens, I was with Brian and Gosego and some guests till about 9.30. Then I went to bed, and then Gos woke me at four to say someone had killed one of our rhinos. After that I was with everyone you see here. Honestly, this is ridiculous."

"Ridiculous to you, maybe. But extremely interesting to us. Because most criminals are caught by the details, Mr. Storm. So, you were alone between the hours of 9.30 and 4 this morning. That's–"

"Five-and-a-half hours," his partner jumped in. "Plenty of time to commit murder."

"Lieutenants, think about it—if you're capable of doing so. Mr. Storm didn't even know that the rhino had been killed before Gosego woke him, and in any case, Mr. Storm was not alone during the hours of 9:30 and 4:30."

"Jesus H. Christ," yelled Roger. "And why does everyone know my whereabouts? First Gos, now you. I suppose Mark knows too. He's probably waiting to punch me in the guts."

Brian just laughed and slapped him on the shoulder. "No worries, mate. I think they have a pretty open marriage."

The two policemen, whether realizing the ridiculousness of their initial assessment or losing interest totally in their chief suspect, had moved on to the body. The walked around the tree a few times looking for any signs that the killer may have left, but the ground had been badly compromised by the Mambas and Roger.

"There's a piece of paper shoved into his pocket," Roger said.

"Like we didn't see it," replied Steenkamp, pulling out the note and taking a look.

"I guess they're not concerned about forensics," Brian whispered to Gosego, who was standing next to Brian and Roger observing the two policemen at work.

"No, they're not, mainly because the nearest real forensic team are hundreds of kilometers away, and the body would be rotten from the heat or chewed up by hyenas by the time they got here. In any case, he was a poacher, and despite what Steenkamp said, no one's overly concerned about killing them."

Steenkamp looked up from reading the note. "Who the hell is Vixay Keosavang?"

"I have no idea," replied Roger, assuming the Lieutenant was asking him.

"Well, I do."

Sergeant Warona had joined Gosego, Roger, and Brian from where she'd been consulting with her troop. "Anyone in the anti-poaching business knows that name. Vixay"— she pronounced it wee-sai—"is the most notorious animal trafficker in the world. He's a Laotian who probably controls 60 percent of the illegal trade in animal parts. He's been written about in newspapers, online reports, you name it. He and The Bach Brothers are responsible for some of the worst poaching crimes in Africa. But up to now, no one has been able to touch them."

"Well," said Steenkamp, taking another squint at the note, "something will touch him pretty soon—that's for sure."

"Who?" asked his partner, taking the note and fiddling in his pocket for his reading glasses.

"It's not so much *who* will be touching him as *what* will be touching him. Because whoever shoved a rhino horn through his son's head and cut off his hands is sending those hands to Mr. Vixay in the hope he gets the message about his criminal undertakings. And, yes, also his nose."

"Well, I guess that's poetic justice," Brian said.

"Poetic justice and touching it may well be," replied Steenkamp, taking out his radio. "But the fact remains: Whoever killed him is probably still in the country, and it's our job to apprehend him. So, if anyone has any thoughts on who it could be, now would be a good time to speak up. No? No one?"

Gosego nudged Roger and whispered, "Tell him about 'Satan.'"

Roger hesitated and looked at Brian, who nodded his head in encouragement. "Well, Lieutenants, there is something I should probably tell you. When Brian and I were trying to catch up to Gosego and the Mambas, we were charged by an old bull elephant—"

"Really, Mr. Storm, do you think we're idiots?" Lieutenant Mothibi interrupted. "You're going to tell Lieutenant Steenkamp and me that the crime involved the participation of animals?"

"No, of course not. What I was about to say before you jumped to another ridiculous conclusion is that someone yelled at Brian and me to wave our arms to stop the charge. Someone we couldn't see and who'd disappeared by the time I got to the spot where we heard the voice."

"And," said Mothibi, sounding suddenly quite perceptive, "you recognized the voice?"

"I don't know. Maybe . . . but probably not."

"Don't mess with us, man. You're in enough trouble for withholding information about your whereabouts. *Maybe* and *probably not* is not a clear answer. Either you recognized the voice or you didn't. Now, which is it, and don't waste our time or we will arrest you for obstruction."

"Well, it's not that easy. It sounded like someone I was with over a year ago. But he disappeared...."

"And who was this mysterious person?"

"I'd rather not say."

"Well, I'd rather not have to eat a lot of Raisin Bran for my constipation, but I have no choice. And neither do you. Now tell us who the hell it was, or is, or could be, or may be!" Steenkamp had gone from a bright pink to a vivid red.

"Okay, calm down," Roger said. "It sounded like Ishea Payamps, a man who saved me from a bunch of mercenary killers in Ethiopia."

Both policemen put their notebooks back into their pockets and shook their heads in unison.

"You know what, Mr. Storm?" Lieutenant Mothibi said. "Mercenary killers, Ethiopia, mysterious voices . . . I think it's best you accompany us to the police station where you can tell us the entire story. And your lawyer friend here, he can come with for the ride. There is more going on here than simple murder. My feeling is that this will become a much more complicated situation."

"Yes," agreed Steenkamp. "Complicated is a good word, an excellent word. But 'complicated' isn't going to be the half of it. No, no, no, no. You two, follow us."

"I'm really sorry about all of this, Brian," Roger said as they sat in the back of the police van as it bounced over the corrugations of the dirt road that led from Hunter's Folly to police headquarters in the small town of Alldays.

"No worries, Rog," Brian replied, giving his friend a pat on his shoulder. "First, I'm going to have some great stories when I get back home, and second, you have nothing to worry about. As incompetent as these guys seem, there's got to be someone in charge with a bit of sense. Just tell them what you know."

As it turned out, Brian was right about one thing and totally wrong about the other. The chief of police in Alldays was a recently graduated, highly intelligent young man who listened to Roger's story calmly and with a great deal of interest. He made detailed notes, and after asking Roger to stay put on his game reserve until they'd finished their enquiries, he had the lieutenants drive him and Brian back to Hunter's Folly. Where Brian was totally wrong was in believing Roger had nothing to worry about.

Three days later, shortly after Brian had flown back to Australia, in a sprawling mansion in Paksan, a small town on the banks of the Mekong River in Central Laos, a distraught father sat in an armchair draped with a tiger skin and vowed to slowly separate every limb from the man he believed was responsible for killing his son.

"You will find this man, Roger Storm," Vixay Keosavang said to his lieutenant, Punpitak Chunchom, "and you will bring him here. Then we will see how long it takes for him to die."

Chapter 5

IN WHICH TWO SLIGHTLY JET-LAGGED
INSPECTORS EAT SAUSAGE, MAKE A FRIEND,
AND FORM A PLAN

Joburg, South Africa

"I must say, I absolutely love this," said Matthew Bunter, spearing another piece of the spicy sausage that preceded every meal at the Butcher Shop restaurant in Mandela Square in Joburg's northern suburb of Sandton. He and Constantin Darmstaedter had flown into South Africa that morning from Frankfurt to meet with Lieutenant Colonel Nagesh Patel, who headed up the anti-poaching forces in the South African police's elite *Hawks* division.

"We call it *boerewors,* which translates as 'farmer's sausage,'" replied Patel, a short, rotund man with an impressive handlebar moustache and a spark of unmistakable passion in his dark, hooded eyes. He regarded his European counterparts with a great deal of skepticism. As far as he was concerned, they were enjoying themselves a little too much to be taken seriously, staying at an expensive hotel and eating at a restaurant that no South African policeman, except for those taking bribes, could ever afford. He shook his head and thought about what his father would have said if he could have seen his son sitting at such an excessive place eating what he would consider overly large quantities of food. His father had been a political prisoner on Robben Island towards the final death rattle of apartheid where, on top of all the other degradations, he had been almost starved and had emerged, when all prisoners were released, with an inability to eat more than small mouthfuls of food. It had taken the older Patel a long time to get over the fact that his son wanted to join an organization that had once been responsible for his apprehension and torture.

But Nagesh Patel had been obsessed with animals since a high school trip to the Kruger National Park, and while he was one of only a few Indians who'd joined the police, he was a strong voice in the dramatic transformation of the force from an instrument of authoritarian rule to democratic, non-racial rule. Patel's only problem was that he was scrupulously honest. He'd never taken a bribe in his life and had been a whistleblower in several cases that had resulted in the conviction of a number of his colleagues. The problem was the Laotian, Chinese, and Vietnamese syndicates behind most of the poaching of rhino and elephants in Africa paid enormous sums to politicians and government stooges who saw the declining herds of animals as a way to enrich themselves rather than the country as a whole. Patel had been threatened more times than he cared to think about, but he was resolute and refused to be intimidated.

The zeal he applied to his job and the success rate of his teams had gotten him international attention and numerous awards from wildlife organizations around the world. He'd accepted none of them, purely on principle. The fact was Lieutenant Colonel Nagesh Patel was principled from his well-manicured toenails to the end of his immaculately trimmed moustache. He had more endurance than a squad of Kenyan marathon runners, and he was loyal beyond reproach—more than anyone or anything, to the animals he had sworn to protect. In truth, like Roger, he had very little time for people.

By the time the main courses arrived—the beef kebab for Darmstaedter, pork spare ribs for Bunter, and the vegetarian option for Patel—both the European policemen were convinced that Patel had no life outside his job whatsoever. In fact, he seemed somewhat impatient with their stories and culinary observations, which were copiously fueled by two bottles of the 2011 Hartenberg Shiraz, that he, who hardly ever touched alcohol, wasn't drinking.

"Gentlemen, I'd really like to get down to brass tacks. I'm busy and you, no doubt, are tired, and if we are to work together in a productive and efficient manner, then we need to stay focused. So please, enlighten me on this Ishea Payamps."

"Of course, Nagesh," said Bunter, who'd attacked his ribs like a warthog eating grubs, leaving his face covered in barbecue sauce. "But perhaps you'd tell us why his name came up in your investigations? We've had him on our radar for the past year, especially over the last two weeks, and we were flagged the minute you entered his name in the Interpol database. It would help to have some context."

"Very well," replied Patel, pushing aside his half-eaten meal and taking out his notebook. "His name came up after the murder of the son of Vixay Keosavang on a private game reserve in the Limpopo province. I assume from your response to my email, that you both know who Vixay Keosavang is and what he does?"

"We do." Darmstaedter took a long sip of his wine. He hadn't slept much on the plane, and he was beginning to get a headache. He pulled out an article he'd printed from The South China Morning Post on Vixay Keosavang's tiger farms. "We have been tasked with both disrupting and destroying his organization and that of the other notorious animal traffickers, The Bach Brothers. But we don't know how Vixay relates to Ishea Payamps?"

"Ishea Payamps is the chief suspect in the murder of Vixay's son, whose body was discovered by an anti-poaching squad looking for the killers of a female black rhino. The owner of the reserve, an American named—" Patel consulted his notebook, "Yes, Roger Storm, informed our officers that—"

"We know this Roger Storm. He was mentioned in the report too."

"How would you know him? He doesn't seem like an international criminal."

"Maybe not. But Constantin and I are well aware of *a* Roger Storm. A South African-American who featured rather prominently in a case we were involved in a year ago. And seeing as the case also involved Ishea Payamps, I'm going to assume it's the same person. However," Bunter raised his hand as if to twiddle his absent moustache and smearing even more barbecue sauce on his face, "when we last saw him, he barely had two pennies to rub together and was on his way back to Chicago from London after a rather bizarre adventure."

"Well, *this* Roger Storm paid nearly twenty million dollars in cash for a 23,000-hectare game reserve, and he appears to have a lot more money."

"Everything makes sense," Darmstaedter said, "and yet nothing makes sense. All is in place, yet nothing is in place."

"I'm not sure I understand," Patel said, eyeing the tall German curiously.

"Don't mind him," Bunter replied. "When his brain starts revolving in that giant noggin, it's best to simply let things play out. The results are normally excellent."

Patel nodded politely. "It seems we both have information to share. So why don't you start by filling me in on your case, and then I'll tell you about mine. And perhaps while you talk, I'll have a glass of wine. Just a half-glass as I don't really drink."

By the time both parties had downloaded all of their information, they'd gotten through another two bottles of wine, and Bunter and Patel were discussing cricket. Darmstaedter, who didn't understand the game at all, had sat quietly thinking about everything he'd heard. His headache was getting worse, but he had a strong sense he knew precisely what the next steps should be.

"Attention!" he said, slapping the table to disrupt his colleagues. "Here is precisely what is going on. None of this is coincidence. Whoever is paying Ishea Payamps is planning something big in the global fight against Vixay and The

Bach Brothers. And Roger Storm, just as he was last time, is being set up to play a role. We need to visit him as soon as possible. I have a feeling he is the key in this whole shadow plot. It is also my belief that his life will be in danger."

"Why do you say that, old boy?"

"I say that, Matthew, because in the culture from which Vixay Keosavang has emerged, the slicing-off of a nose is the greatest insult imaginable. No father can allow that to go unpunished."

"Well, as it turns out," said Patel, who was beginning to slur his words, "I had planned on visiting him tomorrow. Why don't you join me?"

The next morning at 11:00, a Cessna 185 belonging to The Hawk's Anti-Poaching Division landed on the rough airstrip a kilometer from the main lodge of Hunter's Folly Private Game Reserve. Lieutenant Colonel Patel had never been airsick before. Then again, he'd never consumed so much red wine at one sitting.

"If any of you throw up on my plane on the way back," said the pilot as he disposed of three bags of vomit in an old oil drum, "I'm going to push you out over that crocodile-infested river."

Chapter 6

IN WHICH ROGER STORM LEARNS ABOUT HIS IMPENDING DEATH

Hunter's Folly Private Game Reserve,
Limpopo, South Africa

Unlike Patel, who spent any free time in the bush, neither Darmstaedter nor Bunter had been on a safari before, and though the ride to the lodge was pretty uneventful in terms of large animal sightings, the small herds of impala and zebra lounging about drowsily in the mid-day heat helped ease the remnants of their hangovers. By the time they were sitting in the shade on the veranda sipping lemonade and waiting to meet with Roger and Gosego, all three policemen felt slightly less nauseous.

"Herr Storm," Darmstaedter said, uncoiling himself from the low leather chair, "I'm not sure you will remember me or Inspector Bunter of Interpol, ja?"

"Yes, I do, Inspector Darmstaedter," Roger replied, shaking hands with both policemen. "Though to be honest, I didn't think I'd ever see you again."

Patel stuck his hand out. "I'm—"

Roger didn't wait for him to finish. "Of course I recognize you, Colonel Patel, from all the papers you've written on poaching. This is a real honor to have you here." He was genuinely excited and pumped Patel's hand till he was interrupted by Gosego clearing this throat. "I'm so sorry. This is my partner, Gosego Modise."

Now it was Patel's turn to be impressed. "Ah, Mr. Modise. Your name is well known in my department. If you ever want a job with us, I hope you'll let me know." Roger looked for the smile but there was none, and he realized that Patel was deadly serious.

"Thank you, Colonel Patel, but I prefer it out here with this guy. Though after all the trouble he causes, God knows why." He laughed and slapped Roger on the back. "Can we assume this visit has to do with the man who was killed a week ago?"

"Ja," said Darmstaedter, who, as tall as he was, was dwarfed by Gosego. "However, there are many questions that need to be answered, and so we should assume nothing."

"So, it isn't about the dead poacher?"

"I'm saying you shouldn't assume it is about the dead poacher."

"Well, what should we assume it's about?" asked Roger, getting confused.

"I'm saying don't assume anything."

"Well, we have to assume something, or why are you here?"

Patel was getting as confused by the German police inspector as Roger. He was also getting annoyed. "Of course it is about the poacher, for God's sake. But it's also about Ishea Payamps. What's wrong, Mr. Storm? Does that name ring a bell?"

Roger's hands began to feel clammy and he broke into a sweat.

Darmstaedter ignored him and glared at Patel. "I can see your methods are more direct, Colonel Patel."

"No, they're just clearer. I don't have time for subtleties and confusion."

"I'll tell you what," said Gosego, sensing the need to lessen the tension. "It's almost lunchtime. Or brunch, actually. Why don't you join us, and you can ask as many questions as you like."

Roger felt an old familiar panic begin to percolate in his stomach, and once again, as he'd been a year ago in a restaurant in Paris when he first saw his previously dead friend, Freddy Blank, he was overwhelmed by the feeling that awful things were about to happen. He was glad to have Gosego for moral support, but he wondered if Brian should have stayed. He knew there'd be legal questions that he wouldn't know how to answer.

"Are you okay, Mr. Storm?" asked Bunter. "You look like you're about to faint."

"No, no, I'm fine, thanks. Just a little tired. Good food and a martini will fix that."

Gosego looked at his friend with a concerned expression on his face. He'd hardly ever seen Roger drink during the day. But Roger had been withdrawn since Brian left, and Gosego knew there was something worrying him. Roger had talked to him briefly about what had happened in Ethiopia and how he'd been left the money for Hunter's Folly, but, Gosego sensed, he'd always stopped short of the real story. It wasn't in Gosego's nature to ask too many questions, and so he'd never pushed his friend. All he knew was that Roger was a caring and generous man who'd gifted him 50 percent of one of the most valuable properties in the Limpopo region. Roger trusted him entirely, and he was determined to do the same.

Colonel Patel dismissed the small talk that accompanied the eggs, bacon, sausage, and fruit and the large martini that Roger knocked back as if it were an orange juice. "Mr. Storm, we have a number of issues that we need to have a very serious discussion about. I'm sure Inspectors Bunter and Darmstaedter have questions relating to your previous encounters, but I'm most interested in one name: Ishea Payamps."

"Look, Colonel," Roger responded, signaling the waiter for another martini. "As I told the police chief in Alldays, I only *thought* the voice of the person who yelled at us to wave our arms when the elephant charged sounded like Ishea Payamps. It's almost ridiculous to think it was. I mean, what the hell would he be doing out here? In any case, I never saw any trace of him or anyone else. That's the truth. Now, would anyone like a drink? I recommend the martinis. They're excellent. We use Monkey 47 Gin from the Black Forest region in Germany. It's 94 proof, so you'll probably need to take a little nap afterwards."

"Mr. Storm," said Patel, his dark eyes boring into Roger's skull with an intensity that made Roger decidedly uncomfortable, "we didn't come all this way to talk to a drunk man. You need to answer all of our questions before you take another sip. I'm deadly serious, as you will be very soon. Only without the serious qualification."

Gosego gave the waiter the universal finger-across-the-throat signal to cancel the second martini and put his arm on Roger's. "It's been a rough week for him—"

"We appreciate that, Mr. Modise, but this is not some casual discussion."

"Mr. Storm." Bunter swallowed a large piece of bacon and reached into his briefcase. "I wasn't going to get to this until a little later, but, as Colonel Patel has already indicated, there's something rather startling you need to hear. So, I will tell you this something now, and it isn't great news as far as you're concerned." He held up a piece of paper that looked like a printout of an email and waved it in front of Roger's face. "It's a report that Inspector Darmstaedter and I picked up this morning, and though I agree with Colonel Patel that you should stop your tippling for the moment, when you hear what it is, I have no doubt you'll want to bolt down another few martinis. Which you are free to do after we're done."

"Fine," said Roger, who was feeling a little lightheaded after slamming the martini down so quickly. "I won't have another one now if you're going to be so damned snotty about it. What's this report?"

"Yesterday, a small plane coming from Brazzaville in the Congo landed on a private airstrip on the Botswana side of the Limpopo River. There were two passengers, a man and a woman, who disappeared into the bush before the local authorities could find out exactly who they were. We, however, believe them to be Punpitak Chunchom and Loy Chanthamvonga, the two trusted lieutenants of Vixay Keosavang. Our agent in Brazzaville identified them and was able to get their flight plan. We have no doubt that they're on their way here."

"What for?" asked Gosego, who suspected he knew the answer already.

"To kill you, Mr. Storm, or more likely to capture you and take you to Laos."

"Either way," Darmstaedter said, "it's not going to be something you will enjoy. Whatever Ishea Payamps or some other 'mystery' person did to Vixay's son will seem like a peaceful death compared to what they'll do to you. I have no doubt Vixay has some fiendish torture in mind."

"Jesus!" Gosego said. "Why Roger? He had nothing to do with the death of Vixay's son. I mean, why not me or the Black Mambas? We were all there!"

"They may well be after you too; our agent didn't say. Perhaps he got Roger's name from the Hunter's Folly ownership records. Or maybe some local farmer that his son may have been in contact with gave him the name. There could be another reason entirely. Whatever it is, it's Roger's name they have. That's why if we're going to help you, Roger, you have to tell us everything."

"I will tell you everything," Roger said, almost squeezing the empty martini glass to get the last drop out. "But seriously, I don't know any more than I've already told you."

"Fine," said Bunter, "go over everything again in as much detail as you can. Leave nothing out as you describe the events that led up to this moment. Nothing is trivial, nothing unimportant. As Sherlock Holmes once said, 'To a great mind, nothing is minute.' And Mr. Storm, you are in the presence of a great mind: that of Inspector Constantin Darmstaedter. Inside that giant head of his is a brain beyond any you have encountered."

Darmstaedter, who'd been about to scowl at Bunter when he brought up Sherlock Holmes, smiled at the compliment and closed his eyes as if he were about to solve the Riemann Conjecture.

Roger looked at the three policemen. Bunter was sloppily mopping up what was left of his fried egg off his plate with a piece of toast. Darmstaedter, with his eyes closed and his nostrils flaring with each intake of breath, bore the expression of a Tibetan monk contemplating his or someone else's navel. Patel, who'd said very little and eaten even less, rested his elbows on the table and stared at Roger. He looked like a Schnauzer with his bushy eyebrows and mustache, and yet for some reason Roger felt he could trust him.

"Where would you like me to start?"

"Why don't you begin with exactly how you got the money to buy this place? You clearly didn't have it before we met you in London. We obviously have an idea, but we'd like to hear it from you. In your words," said Bunter. He was speaking slowly and more deliberately than he had a few minutes before.

"No, that's true. I was pretty much on the bones of my ass when we last met in London. But all of that changed pretty rapidly as soon as I got back to my apartment in Chicago. There was an invitation and airline ticket to the Cayman Islands waiting for me with the doorman. The letter—or invitation—was from an Archibald Rossiter of the Grand Cayman Bank. You can check him out—"

"Ah, rest assured: someone has already spoken to Mr. Rossiter."

"Okay, well then you do know everything."

"Yes, though Mr. Rossiter refused to reveal anything. So, as I said, we need to hear it from you."

"Fine, I can understand why you don't trust me entirely."

"Actually," said Darmstaedter, opening his eyes, "we don't trust you even a little bit. Everything we've ever heard from you is beyond the norms of probability and reason."

"You know, I never asked for any of this. So there's no need to be so damn rude."

Darmstaedter nodded as if he agreed with Roger, closed his eyes again, and waved his hand for Roger to continue.

"Anyway, when I met Archibald the next evening, he informed me that I'd been left—or maybe given; I don't know what the legal term is—the sum of $55 million for services rendered."

Constantin whistled. "And you were not surprised? That is a great deal of money."

"That's what I told Archibald. He didn't seem to believe it was excessive in his dealings with Freddy and Conchita.

Anyway, he assured me that it wasn't from their international arms company, PaloMar, because as you told me, their assets had been frozen. But it was most definitely from Conchita and Freddy."

"Hmm," said Bunter, "and why would you say that?" His hand had begun to tremble, causing him to spill coffee on his white shirt. "Shit!" He tried to dab at the stain with a wet napkin, but the shaking had intensified, and the rubbing made the stain bigger.

"Isn't it obvious? I mean, who else would pay me for 'services rendered'? In any case, there was a message that said, 'Freddy and Conchita want you to be happy.'"

"Herr Storm," Darmstaedter said, not even bothering to open his eyes, "nothing is obvious, and the obvious is nothing. What may seem obvious to you is nothing to me. So, as my colleague said, give us every fact, no matter how trivial it may seem to you." His breathing took on the semblance of low snoring, and Roger was sure he'd gone to sleep.

"Well, other than Archibald taking me to dinner, and I could tell you what we ate, I'm not sure what else there is. I declared all the money back in the US for tax purposes. I'm sure you can check that out. Even then I still had more than enough to buy this place."

There was a moment of silence followed by the unmistakable sound of snoring coming from Darmstaedter. Roger paused and looked over at Patel, who still hadn't moved. His eyes were open, but he was breathing deeply. He turned to Bunter, whose head was resting on his chest.

"Christ, Gos. I think these buggers have all fallen asleep."

"You know, they stink of booze. They're probably totally hungover."

"Do you think we should wake them?"

"Probably not. Let's just finish eating and see what happens."

They didn't have to wait long. A vervet monkey who'd been observing the meal from the branch of a huge sausage tree around which the dining area was built finally decided it was safe to drop onto the table to grab what was left on Patel's plate. Roger and Gosego, who were used to the sudden appearance of the hairy thief and considered his actions routine, didn't flinch. Darmstaedter chose the moment to open his eyes, and he screamed.

"Verflucht nogmal! Ein haariger Kobold!"

His scream woke Patel and Bunter, who both shot off their chairs at the sight of the intruder. The monkey stuffed his mouth with as much toast and fruit as he could from Patel's plate, and then, grabbing Bunter's coffee cup, shimmied back up the sausage tree.

"You were saying, Inspector Darmstaedter? Right before you were very rudely interrupted...." Gosego said with a broad grin.

Roger wanted to laugh, but his annoyance at what he thought of as totally hypocritical behavior on the part of these people who'd had an issue with him having another martini prevented him from emitting anything more than an unmistakable snort of pure derision.

Colonel Patel was the first to recover. He cleared his throat and splashed water on his face. "Look, Mr. Storm, we aren't here—well, I'm certainly not—to check up on the legality of your sudden wealth. To be honest, we have checked as best we can, and while it is unusual, and some would say suspicious, it appears to be quite legal under South African law. No, what we're here to find out is whether Ishea Payamps—and let's not beat about the bush in that respect, because the probability is that he is the killer—is here or not. From what my two colleagues tell me, he's been killing poachers and hunters in a number of different countries, which makes him suspect number one in the murder of Vixay's son as far as I'm concerned. We are also here to try to help you not become the victim of Vixay Keosavang's vicious assassins."

"Yes, it's rather unfortunate," Bunter stifled a yawn, "but Ishea's actions have made you the potential chump of a blood-chilling revenge. That's the trouble when you mingle with psychopaths."

"Why would you call him that? You don't know him."

"Don't need to." Bunter yawned. "His actions fit the mold."

"I have to say something, and if it annoys you or pisses you off, then too fucking bad. What Ishea Payamps is doing is trying to save what little is left of the creatures that make this world a beautiful place. The people you assume he takes out are hell bent on destroying animals for their own disgustingly selfish desires. What makes those people better in your eyes? Because they don't break your laws? Well, they break the laws of the universe. So when you talk about him out here where those sort of things count, you'll show him some respect or you can get the hell out of here."

There was a deathly silence, and everyone looked down at their shoes. Then Gosego spoke. "What are you planning to do, and what would you suggest we do here? Because I'm telling you now that I'm not allowing those two people you mentioned to harm Roger. We don't carry guns here on Hunter's Folly, but we do have a few rifles in the safe, and I will make sure that every qualified ranger and tracker we have carries one or some other weapon."

"That's probably a good idea," Patel said, "but you must understand that these two are highly trained killers, and I'm pretty sure that your people won't be able to stop them without someone getting hurt or killed. But yes, we do have a plan."

"Or at least a proposal," Bunter interjected, looking at his notebook to make sure he got the names correct. "Punpitak Chunchom and Loy Chanthamvonga, and of course their boss, Vixay Keosavang, are three of the most-wanted, non-terrorist-classified criminals in the world. They've been untouchable in Laos because of the corruption, but out of the country they are fair game, if you'll forgive the pun."

"A good one, Matthew," said Darmstaedter, who'd recovered from the monkey attack. "I like it. One of your better ones, for sure."

Bunter smiled at him. "Thank you, my friend."

"Excuse me," said Gosego, "can we get back to your plan, or proposal, or whatever it is? Hau, hau, hau."

"How? How, you ask? All in good time, sir."

Patel, who was getting tired of his colleagues going off on tangents, once again took control of the situation. "*Hau* in this case is an expression of impatience, Inspector Bunter, not a question. I'm going to be totally frank with you, Mr. Storm and Mr. Modise—"

"That would be refreshing," Roger muttered.

Patel ignored the sarcasm. "There are two issues. The first is Ishea Payamps. Now, while he clearly is important, there probably isn't much we can do about him at this moment, because in my opinion a man of his talent and resources is most likely already out the country."

"We don't know for certain, but we'll assume Col. Patel is right," Bunter said, looking directly at Roger. "Ishea Payamps is only partially the reason we're here. In order to satisfy our bosses back home and not land ourselves in hot water again, Inspector Darmstaedter and I will have to be quite certain. But under the current circumstances, his apprehension will have to wait."

"Yes, yes," Patel said, puffing his cheeks and expelling the air out his nose like a Bulldog. He was getting a little tired of his British colleague's constant need to interrupt. "I do understand you, Mr. Storm, and personally, I'd rather give Ishea a medal than apprehend him. But you also have to appreciate that we are policemen whose job it is to uphold the law. Anyway, at this precise moment, the threat to your life, Mr. Storm, by Vixay's lieutenants is the more pressing issue than Ishea."

"You won't get any arguments from me on that."

"No, I don't suppose I will. However, and this is where we may well get an argument from you, is that we want you to be the bait."

"What do mean? Use me as bait?"

"Just that. We need to make you as visible as possible in order to attract the killers."

"Are you crazy? Use me as bait? Absolutely not. That's ludicrous. Why the hell should I put myself in more danger? First you say Ishea is using me, and now you want to do the same thing. So let me repeat myself: no-fucking-way!"

"Don't worry, Herr Storm," Darmstaedter said, leaning forward and patting Roger's head as if he were reassuring a child about to jump off a diving board. "You will be protected."

Roger felt the anger swell up inside him. He clenched his teeth and banged the table. Then he began to rub his forehead and breathe deeply.

"Are you okay, Roger?" Gosego had never seen Roger quite as agitated.

"No, I'm not. I'm really not. I'm suddenly back in the middle of a nightmare that I can't seem to wake up from." He stood up and began to pace, talking more to himself than anyone else. "You know, just over a year ago I was a middle-aged advertising executive. Out of a job, I suppose, and I'm pretty sure, on the verge of becoming an alcoholic. The most dangerous thing that could have happened to me would have been to fall off the couch in my apartment in Chicago or choke on an olive. Suddenly, all hell broke loose. I was drugged, God knows how many times, I was kidnapped, shot at, tortured, had the woman I loved tumble off a cliff in front of me, and after all of that, my oldest friend thinks I'm a murderer. That's not the sort of thing you get over easily. I didn't, and I doubt I ever will. But then peace returned, the kind of peace that was unimaginable to me, and over the past eleven months I've lived what I believed was going to be the most remarkable life anyone could have. Running this incredible game reserve with a man who's become my great friend. Out here, in the middle of the bush, where it's hard to be anything but happy. And now the whole damn thing's starting up again."

"Roger," Bunter said. "You don't mind me calling you 'Roger'?"

"No, I don't. In fact, I'd rather you did. I hate the formality."

"Good. Well, we can all sympathize with what you went through before. But what you're going through now, old chap, is really of your own choosing."

"What the hell do you mean?"

"You took the money. No one forced it on you. And while you put it towards something good and worthwhile, deep down you must have known it was dirty. And so, I'm afraid along with dirty money comes risk and danger. So, as the Yanks say, 'man up' and stop wingeing. What we're suggesting could actually help destroy a major part of the poaching industry, which will benefit everyone. You have a chance to do something really worthwhile. Now, why don't you have that second martini and listen to our plan."

"You know, he's right, Herr . . . uh, Roger," said Darmstaedter. "This is your opportunity to do something good for the world."

"Who else wants a martini?" asked Gosego, signaling to the waiter. "I'm going to join Roger."

Bunter and Darmstaedter nodded, and Patel, against his better judgement, put up his hand, hoping it would make him feel better.

The awkwardness of the moment was shattered by a loud bellow as a herd of elephants made its way out the bush towards the waterhole in front of the lodge. It was a female herd with a number of babies, who immediately began to play with each other in the mud. Roger had witnessed the scene a hundred times before, but the sight of the huge pachyderms, almost ochre-skinned from the red Limpopo dust, slowly began to calm him. He looked at the others who were equally caught up in the magic, and at that moment he knew Bunter was right. He waited until the martinis arrived and everyone had sat back around the table.

"You know what? Everything you said about it being my choice—well, I can't argue with that at all. And if I sounded petulant and 'wingey' as you put it, Matthew, then I apologize. At the time I was in such pain and feeling so bloody desperate that I did believe the money that was given to me was payment for everything I'd been through. But I hope I've done something good with it, as you say. And I really want to continue doing it. I'd really like to spend the rest of my life helping to preserve Africa's wildlife. At the same time, I don't want to die or be tortured again."

"Of course not, uh, Roger." Patel had a hard time accepting informality, but here he was drinking a martini with a bunch of what in his opinion were all, with the possible exception of Gosego, certifiable lunatics. "We don't want you to die either, and that's why we are here to catch those two bastards and protect you."

"You mean the three of you?" asked Gosego.

"Ja." Darmstaedter regarded him curiously. "The three of us. We are all experienced policemen, and while Inspector Bunter—Matthew and I have not worked with Nagesh before, we are more than confident of his abilities. Is this an issue?"

"Not an issue. But how will you guarantee Roger's safety against those two assassins? I'm not certain we shouldn't get more people."

"My friend," replied Darmstaedter, sounding rather arrogant to anyone who didn't know him and perfectly normal to anyone who did, "have you heard of Sun Tzu?"

"Enlighten me, please." Gosego had studied Sun Tzu when he'd been at officer's training school during his five years in the military, but he was getting tired of what he perceived as pure arrogance on Darmstaedter's part. "And just before you do, let me ask you if you've heard of Sun City? It's a big resort not far from here where we could put Roger up until the danger is past."

Darmstaedter flicked his wrist in a gesture of dismissal. "Sun Tzu said, 'If you know your enemy and you know yourself, you need not fear the result of a hundred battles.' These are things I learned from my father, who was an army officer."

"Interesting. However, if you know yourself but not the enemy, you will also suffer defeat. I may have read that part somewhere. Now, from what you've said, you don't know

81

the enemy that well. So I think Sun City sounds like the safest thing to do."

"Absolutely not," said a now-flustered Darmstaedter. "He stays here. They will come for him, and we will be waiting."

"What happens if they decide to shoot him from a distance?"

"No, that won't happen. They want him in person. They will come for him; I am certain. They may employ stealth tactics. They may make a frontal attack. But they won't be able to outthink me—I mean, us. And then, like mice that have walked into a trap filled with Cambozola cheese—my favorite by the way—we'll have them."

Roger, who was feeling decidedly tipsy from the second martini which he'd slammed down in sheer desperation, leaned back a little too far in his chair. "Excuse me, I think—"

He never finished the sentence. As his chair toppled backwards, a .338 Lapua Magnum bullet fired from a twenty-six-inch Stealth Recon Scout sniper rifle travelling at approximately 960 meters per second came within two centimeters of Colonel Nagesh Patel's upper lip, shearing one entire half of the handlebar mustache he'd so carefully cultivated for twenty-two years.

It was fortunate for the rest of the party that Loy Chanthamvonga had failed to fit a sound suppressor to her rifle. The shot that had come from directly behind the water hole spooked the herd of elephants which, with loud trumpeting and clouds of red dust, turned and retreated hastily into the bush, narrowly missing the two Laotian assassins who were hidden behind an acacia tree.

Five minutes later, when it was clear that no more shots were imminent, Roger staggered to his feet and turned to Darmstaedter, who'd emerged from behind the couch. "I thought you said they wouldn't try to shoot me."

"I don't believe they did. I think they wanted to shoot Nagesh, or me and Matthew and probably Gosego, before they came for you."

Chapter 7

In which Roger Storm realizes that the present is simply the past in a different pair of shoes

Hunter's Folly Private Game Reserve,
Limpopo, South Africa

It was dusk when Gosego and Sergeant Bontle Warona reported back to the group after leading a party of rangers and Black Mambas to scour the bush around the camp.

"Anything?" asked Colonel Patel who, despite Roger's offer of a razor, hadn't shaved off the undamaged side of his mustache.

"No." Sergeant Warona poured a cup of tea and plonked herself down in an armchair in the inside dining room that now served as group headquarters. "We found a casing...." She pulled a spent shell out her pants pocket and handed it to Patel. "But the elephants destroyed any tracks. The only thing I can tell you is that they won't get close tonight. I've posted my Mambas with Gosego's rangers strategically

85

around the camp. No one is going to get through. At least, without us knowing about it."

"I hope they'll be safe without any guns," Bunter said.

"They'll be fine, don't worry," said Gosego. "They're trained to survive in the bush; the two Laotians are not. Well, not African bush for sure. But, now, will you listen to me about getting Roger out of here?" Gosego was calm, but there was a hint of tension in his voice. "No one, not you or any of us, will be safe until he is away from here. Luckily, we don't have guests tonight, but four are arriving tomorrow, and we have to make sure they are going to be okay, because it's too late to cancel them."

"He's right, Constantin," Patel said. "There are too many lives at stake now."

"Fantastic," said Roger. "Now that your lives are in danger, you're fine to call the whole thing off. But it was fine to offer me up as a sacrificial goat."

Patel ignored him. "I'm going to call the pilot to be here at first light, and we'll get Roger to Sun City or somewhere else until this is over. I'm also going to request a helicopter and more men to come to help us search for those two bastards."

Bunter shrugged and Darmstaedter nodded in agreement. "I agree. Reluctantly, I must point out. But I think, as dangerous as it may be, we should perhaps stay here until they have been caught."

"Not caught—killed," Patel said, rubbing his lip. "I'm ordering my men to shoot on sight."

"I can't endorse that, Nagesh. Interpol would have my balls for bagpipes if they found out we hadn't set out to capture rather than kill. And I'm sure Constantin will agree."

Constantin shook his head, not so much at the thought of shooting poachers but at the absurd suggestion that testicles could be converted into an obscene-sounding musical instrument. Patel looked carefully at Bunter, then pulled himself up to his full five-foot-four, and in a voice that sounded to both Bunter and Darmstaedter like a televangelist expressing his righteous indignation, said, "That, gentlemen, is too damn bad. This is my territory and my decision. You are guests, nothing more. These people . . . these poachers . . . these murderous employees of that swine Vixay are two of the most disgusting creatures imaginable. I'd say we're dealing with animals, but animals don't behave this way. No, they are too dangerous to try to capture alive. I refuse to allow them to spill one more drop of blood—animal or human—on the continent of Africa." Then he sat down as if his proclamation had sapped him of all energy. "No, it's kill on contact as far as I'm concerned."

"Tell me, Nagesh," Constantin asked, "would you be so keen to kill them if they hadn't shot your very fine mustache off, hmm?"

Patel bristled, or would have, had his upper lip been in full possession of its recently damaged follicular masterpiece. "Quite irrelevant. These two are on the most wanted list of just about every country involved in wildlife smuggling. I assure you: No country wants to go through the expense of a trial."

"I am totally with Colonel Patel," Roger chimed in. "I say we kill these two fuckers and leave their bodies out for the hyenas." He was on his fifth martini of the day and beyond caring.

"Listen, Roger," said Bunter. "I think you should probably go to bed. Your tent may be the safest place for you tonight. We can stay here and marshal our thoughts."

Gosego walked over to where Roger was sprawled on the couch. "He's right, Roger. Here, I'll take you back, and we can put some of the rangers outside your room." He took Roger's elbow as his friend staggered up from the couch.

"Fine, as long as you can get one of the waiters to bring me some food and one more martini. Goodnight, everyone. Let's kill those bastards tomorrow." He held onto Gosego as they made their way through the darkness towards his tent. There was an eerie silence about the bush, and it made Gosego uncomfortable.

"You know what, Gos? I really meant it."

"You really meant what?"

"What I said earlier. That you are my greatest friend."

Gosego squeezed Roger's arm affectionately. "Well, I appreciate that, but you have many good friends. Don't forget Brian."

"Yeah, well he's convinced that I killed Harry Bones. I could tell from the minute he asked me that we couldn't have the same relationship ever again. It made me sad, Gos."

"You'll have to tell me about it one of these days. In the meantime, why don't you go in and take a shower—you stink by the way—and I will have some food brought up. I'm going to get a rifle and take first watch."

"I don't suppose you could talk Sergeant Warona into taking watch? Not that I don't feel safe with you, but you know...."

"My friend—my horny friend—let me tell you this: The sergeant is so far out your league you have no idea. She's also half your age. Are you not ashamed of yourself?"

"Not really. Well, that's not true. I am ashamed of myself for so many things, but she's so damn beautiful. You know, Gos, she reminds me of Conchita. I miss her terribly. You would have liked her."

"I'm sure I would. Now, go inside. You're drunk. I will see you later."

Roger stumbled onto the porch and opened the door. The room was dark, and he fiddled for the light switch, which, in his inebriated state, proved to be elusive. When he finally found it, he flicked it on, but much to his annoyance, nothing lit up.

"For fuck's sake," he said to no one in particular. "Why the hell didn't anyone check the bloody lights?" He stumbled around the room feeling for his flashlight, but that too seemed to have vanished. He turned around and began to walk to the door to go back to the main lodge when something wound itself round his neck. At first he thought it was a snake that had fallen from the ceiling. He shrieked in panic as whatever it was tightened around his windpipe, cutting off his air.

"If you utter another sound," said a voice in a distinctly non-African/-British/-German accent, "I will strangle you."

"Oh, shit," thought Roger as he felt himself sinking into unconsciousness. "I'm going to be tortured again."

Chapter 8

IN WHICH ROGER IS PLUCKED FROM THE FRYING PAN AND PLOPPED INTO THE FIRE

Hunter's Folly and beyond

It took Roger several minutes to realize what had happened, and even then, he was totally discombobulated. There were several things he knew for sure:

1) His head hurt like crazy from the martinis
2) His mouth felt like he'd swallowed a hedgehog
3) It was very dark
4) He was somewhere in the bush
5) He was slung from a pole that he could tell, despite his disadvantaged position, was being carried by two sturdy people

The rest was a positive blur. He remembered Gosego taking him to his room and the lights not working, and the mysterious "snake" around his neck, but that was it. His painful musing was interrupted by a voice.

"We have to put him down. He's too heavy." The voice had a distinct Tswana accent.

"Yes, he is a fat man, like a bush pig," agreed a second man with a similar accent.

"Do not dare to put him down," said a third man with a totally different accent. "We are paying you to transport him to the airfield." Roger had no need to think about the third man; he knew exactly who it was, though he couldn't remember the name.

"If you put him down," said a female voice, "you will not be paid. This I promise."

But the strain on the shoulders of the two bearers from Roger's not-insubstantial bulk outweighed the threat of a severe reduction in their wages. With a thud that knocked the breath from his body, he was dropped to the ground. The only relief, and it was at best negative pain, was the lessening of the pressure from the ropes that bound his wrists and ankles to the pole. He groaned loudly and received a hard kick to his exposed thigh.

"Fuck, ow, Jesus!" he yelled. "What are you doing?"

Someone knelt down next to him and grabbed his hair, pulling his head back so that he could see, despite the darkness of the bush, the face of a young woman. He tried to think of her name but once again couldn't remember.

"Shut up, shut up," she hissed, reinforcing her admonition with a stinging slap to Roger's face.

Roger felt the bile rise up as whatever was left from lunch competed with the martini-induced fermentation process taking place in his stomach. Fear replaced shock and he began to moan softly.

"Pick him up immediately and let us be on our way." Punpitak Chunchom was angry.

"No," said the one pole-carrier. "My shoulder is killing me. We are halfway to the airfield and he is awake. Make him walk from here...."

If he had further helpful suggestions, his abilities to provide them were severely hampered by a subsonic bullet fired from a Glock 14 fitted with a sophisticated sound suppressor in the hand of Loy Chanthamvonga. The man gave a surprised gasp and collapsed on the ground next to Roger.

"Oh, that's brilliant," said Punpitak. "What a genius move, Loy—you idiot! What are we supposed to do now?"

"Precisely what this dead fool suggested. We make this swine walk the rest of the way and—" She turned around to the other pole-carrier, who'd frozen when she'd shot his comrade. But he, being no one's fool, had vanished into the dark bush. "Oh well, at least we saved Vixay some money."

"You know, we are supposed to be a team," said Punpitak. "Next time you decide to do something so dramatic—and stupid—please discuss with me. Now, help me cut these ropes. We've already wasted too much time."

Roger smelt the garlic on Punpitak's breath before he got a full glimpse of the pock-marked face of Vixay's most loyal lieutenant. Roger closed his eyes hoping he'd wake up from the nightmare before someone hit him or kicked him again. "Open your eyes, pig-dog. Take advantage of everything you can see. Before long, you won't have eyes to look with when we pull them out your miserable head with red-hot fish hooks." Punpitak cut the ropes securing Roger's hands, and Loy did the same for his feet. Then, grabbing him by the hair, Punpitak pulled him up into a semi-standing position and put the tip of his knife just under Roger's left eye.

"Make one sound, you babbling oaf, and I will pluck out your eye like a ripe lychee. I'm sure my boss won't mind one less eye to work on. Now, you will walk between me and Loy, and if you make any wrong move, I will cut you." He pricked Roger's buttock with the knife to make sure he got the message.

Roger squeaked in pain. He tried to say something, but the sheer horror and insanity of the situation had robbed him of the ability to speak. He started to amble forward, but while the adrenaline had masked the effects of the alcohol-fueled headache, his movement was severely hampered by the reduced blood flow to his limbs.

"Move, you worm," said Punpitak, giving Roger a brutal shove that sent him tumbling forward into Loy, who stumbled and dropped her gun.

"Idiot!" yelled Loy as she bent down to try to retrieve her Glock. Roger had landed face down on the hard ground, and try as he might, he couldn't move. Exhaustion had finally overcome fear.

"Use your phone to give me light," said Loy as she scrambled around on all fours searching for her gun.

"You crazy bitch. You are useless. I can't turn on the light. Those black women are around her somewhere."

"You call me that again, you cancerous pig bladder, and I will kill you where you stand," Loy said, the Glock once more in her hand.

"Really? You, who have jeopardized this mission at every step of the way. First, you miss the Indian policeman with what should have been a simple shot for you. Then, you shoot the bearer and lose your gun. I can't wait to tell Vixay about this. Why he chose you to accompany me on this mission is beyond me." Punpitak took out a crumpled pack of cigarettes and a cheap Bic lighter. It was the act of a complete and desperate idiot. Not because minutes before he'd warned Loy about using the flashlight on her phone but because the flare from the lighter illuminated his face for no more than three seconds, giving Loy ample time to aim her Glock.

Roger hadn't understood a word of the conversation between the two poachers, which was conducted in a combination of Laotian and Thai. He was too busy trying to curl into a fetal position and hoping the two clearly angry people would forget about him.

As it happened, Fate was on his side.

At that moment, a large leopard leapt from the tree nanoseconds before Loy could squeeze the trigger to kill Punpitak. Its front paws hit Loy's shoulders, breaking her left clavicle. Then, as she staggered backwards, it buried its incisors in her throat, piercing her jugular as if she were a baby impala. She fell with a gurgled shriek on top of Roger, whose ability to process any new aspect of his predicament was severely hampered. He gave a soft whimper and lay perfectly still. Punpitak, unaware of the protocol required during an attack by a large predator, gave a shrill yell and began to run in the opposite direction.

Had Roger been able to follow Punpitak for no more than fifty meters, he would have seen him stumble into an aardvark hole and fracture his tibia. Through the worst pain he'd ever felt, Punpitak managed to pull his broken leg out the hole and began to crawl forward, sweating and whimpering. He managed to cover about ten meters before his resolve to escape the leopard gave in. He pulled himself into a sitting position with his back against a large mopani tree and tried to see the stars through the dense branches. He wondered what Vixay would say when he told him what had happened and why he and Loy had failed to bring in the man Vixay blamed for his son's death. He could still hear the leopard chomping on Loy in the distance, and he knew that, should he make it back to Laos, Loy's unpleasant death would seem merciful compared to what Vixay would do to him.

He looked down at his leg and watched the blood begin to pool where the broken bone protruded from his shin. He thought of ripping his shirt and tying a tourniquet around his thigh, but the shock and loss of blood had weakened him. Perhaps there was a merciful God out there who'd forgive him for all the evil things he'd done in his life. Then he thought of the animals he'd killed and the way they'd suffered, and he knew there'd be no mercy for him. He closed his eyes and tried to meditate to alleviate the pain. But whatever peace he sought would not come, and in between bouts of unconsciousness, the hapless Laotian shivered and waited for the leopard who, judging by the eerie silence, seemed to have finished with Loy and in Punpitak's rapidly diminishing sense of reasoning was no doubt contemplating him for desert. Fortunately for Punpitak, the leopard was still happily chomping on a juicy piece of Loy's liver and reveling in just how effortless tonight's meal had been. He tugged what was left of Loy up into the tree and went to sleep.

When the Mambas found Punpitak, he was alive but barely so. Loy, whose half-eaten body was found in a nearby tree a little later, was most definitely not. The question on everyone's mind was *where was Roger Storm?*

Roger, who'd witnessed the leopard drag the quivering body of Loy up the tree, was in fact very much alive and was at that moment on his way to a clearing where a helicopter waited to take him on the first leg of his journey to Zanzibar.

Chapter 9

In which the full range of primary negative emotions are experienced

Hunter's Folly, Limpopo, and a house on the
Mekong River, Laos

Gosego Modise was not his usual happy self when he greeted the four guests who were climbing out of the Land Cruiser that had picked them up at the airstrip thirty minutes before. He greeted the guests as if they were no more than a food delivery and wouldn't engage on any level.

"He's not the friendliest person," whispered Lizzie Florence to her husband, David.

"Maybe he's had a bad day," replied David as Gosego threw both their heavy duffels at the poor man who was supposed to show them to their tent. This was the Florence's first safari, and David had read several books on the intrepid explorers of the 19ᵗʰ century in preparation for the adventure. "I know this place is supposed to be a 'more authentic' bush experience, but Gosego does appear to be displaying the habits of Henry Morton Stanley, who was rather abusive to his porters."

"There's tea and coffee and welcoming drinks on the porch," Gosego snapped. "Abigail, our manager, will fill you in on the camp rules. You will have a good time. Welcome." With that he stormed off.

"I've gotten a friendlier welcome from our neighbor's pit bull," said Lizzie to one of the other guests, who was still cowering in the back of the Land Cruiser. "I hope the rest of the staff are a little nicer." Fortunately for David and Lizzie, they were.

No one who'd known Gosego at any point in his thirty-four years would have said he had a nasty streak. His parents had thought of him as obstinate at times. The troops he commanded as first lieutenant in the elite unit of the South African Defense Force known as 5 Special Forces Regiment thought he was extremely tough but fair. The poachers he caught—those that survived—found him sympathetic provided, of course, they were prepared to give up poaching. Even the many women—and there were many—whose hearts he'd invariably broken over the years couldn't bring themselves to say a bad word about him. And yet here he was stomping about like an ogre, terrifying both guests and staff. The truth was Gosego was angry at himself for leaving Roger alone, even if it was for no longer than the ten minutes it had taken him to go back to the main lodge to pick up a rifle and ask the kitchen to make Roger some dinner. And his anger was palpable to everyone within a two-meter radius.

He'd known something was wrong the minute he returned to Roger's tent. The lights were out, the door was open, and the umbrella stand at the door had been knocked over. By the time he'd raised the alarm with the policemen, his own rangers, and Sergeant Warona's Mambas, Roger and his captors were at least forty minutes ahead, deep into the dark bush. The moon was a waning sickle behind silver-blue clouds, and were it not for the heavy-duty flashlights and the expert tracking ability of the rangers and Mambas, they'd never have found the trail made by the kidnappers.

The rescue party—which consisted of Gosego and four armed rangers; Sergeant Warona and five of her Mambas; and Darmstaedter, Patel, and Bunter blundering along at the back—had made their way along the path. They found the pole that had been carried by the two bearers first. They saw the crumbled grass where Roger had been dumped and the body of a man with a bullet hole in his forehead. Then they heard the awful sound of a creature in pain. Gosego, throwing everything he'd learned about tracking and bush-craft out the window, made a mad dash toward the source of the moans. When he saw that it was Punpitak and not Roger, he grabbed the unfortunate Laotian by the arm and dragged him up, accidently snapping his leg in a different place. By the time the rest of the party rushed up, Punpitak was lights out and incapable of imparting any information about Roger's whereabouts.

Despite warnings to stay with the group, Bunter had wandered off, and it was his flashlight that illuminated the leopard in the tree with a long piece of Loy's intestine hanging from its mouth. "Shoot it, shoot it!" he screamed as the leopard who'd eaten its fill by then retreated to a higher branch leaving the major-organ-depleted body of Vixay's trusted female killer to fall with a resounding splat onto the ground below.

"Not a chance," said Patel. "The business end of a leopard's incisors is a perfectly fitting death for such an evil entity. I'm just sorry the leopard didn't finish its dinner."

"Good Lord," Bunter blanched. "That's pretty harsh, old chap."

"Really? You don't think what these bastards do to our wildlife every day isn't harsh? Get real, man."

On reflection, and as terrified as he was by the vision of the leopard's blood-stained jaws, Bunter couldn't disagree. He believed in the rule of law with all his heart. But decency cannot tolerate inhumanity under any circumstances, and Bunter, despite his flaws, was a decent man.

The search for Roger continued for another hour, but other than a few broken twigs and lightly trampled grass, there was absolutely no trace. It was if he'd simply vanished.

"I know you want to keep searching for your friend, Gosego," said Sergeant Warona, "but we're wasting our time. Let's take the prisoner back to the camp and see if we can revive him enough to question him. Then we'll come back and search."

Gosego reluctantly conceded. "You're right, Sergeant. If Roger was injured or taken by a lion, we'd see traces. I honestly don't understand it. He is a rather clumsy man, so he couldn't have walked off by himself either. No, I am at a loss." He picked up the limp Laotian and flung him over his huge shoulder as if he were lifting a heavy backpack. Then, together with his exhausted colleagues, he walked back to the camp. One of the rangers who'd been trained in first aid tried his best to set Punpitak's broken leg. He botched it horribly, and just before the ambulance from Allday's arrived on the scene, Punpitak gave a gurgling moan, spit up some strange looking bile, and his heart beat for final time.

At 7:30, just as Gosego and the sergeant were about to go back into the bush to resume their search, his phone beeped. It was a message from Roger, though not from Roger's number, that read, *I'm okay. With a friend. Will let you know when I can say more. But don't worry; just carry on. In case you're wondering if this is really me – Manx kippers and eggs.*

Gosego grinned for the first time in eight hours. "Ha, well we know it really is from him. It's his favorite breakfast."

"Kippers and eggs could be a lot of people's favorite breakfast." Patel was unconvinced.

"Not Manx kippers," Bunter said. "Those are an acquired taste."

"I have a feeling, a very distinct feeling," said Inspector Darmstaedter, looking at the text, "that I know who this friend is."

"Ishea Payamps?" asked Patel.

"Ja, the very same."

"Oh, Jesus," said Bunter. "This really complicates things. What the hell is wrong with this bastard? Why can't he just stay out of things? I don't even know where we go from here. As far as I can see, without the two assassins, Ishea Payamps, and now Roger Storm, this whole thing falls apart. I'm sorry Constantin; you may be back on traffic duty by tomorrow."

"Perhaps not, Matthew. Before we give up entirely, let's see if any small planes have flown from near here or across the river in Botswana in the last few hours. Nagesh, can you help us in this regard?"

"I'll see what I can do," replied Patel, who was still stroking the missing half of his mustache as if it were a ghost limb.

"Well, I have to make good with our guests," groaned Gosego. "It's the last thing I feel like doing, but I acted badly. This is a real mess and it's my fault."

"Nonsense," replied Bunter, who could see the big man was suffering. "None of it's your fault. As I said before, I'm afraid Roger brought it on himself when he took the money to buy this place. It proves once again, you can't have your cake and eat it too."

"I fail to understand that logic," said Darmstaedter. "If it's your cake, why can't you eat it?"

"Because," replied Bunter, "if you eat it you won't have it anymore."

"But if you don't eat it, it will get stale."

At that point, Patel decided to shave off the remaining half of his mustache. It was far preferable to hearing an Englishman trying to explain the illogical to a very logical German.

Twelve hours later in his compound on the Mekong River, Vixay Keosavang, the kingpin of wildlife crime, began to bang his balding head against a teak screen in the room that served as his office. It was not a large room, and the lack of windows made it feel stuffy. The only access to the outside world was the heavy steel bulletproof door and a secret tunnel that led from a trapdoor under the desk to a small dock on the river where a high-speed boat waited in case Vixay had to make a fast exit. It was the kind of room that may have excited an IT enthusiast and enraged a conservationist. High-tech surveillance and communication equipment covered every square inch of the large desk while the walls were filled with the heads of unfortunate animals and photos of Vixay and his lieutenants posing with their trophies. A single candle burned in a small shrine under a portrait of Vixay's recently murdered son, and an object that looked suspiciously like a nose encased in Lucite lay next to the candle.

"I'm really sorry, Mr. Vixay." The voice, with its heavy Afrikaans accent, came from one of the monitors on the desk.

"Oh, you are sorry, are you, Steyl?" replied Vixay, turning around to address Eldad Steyl, the game farmer who'd been involved in a number of his poaching expeditions. "Normally, I appreciate an apology. It shows good manners. But in this case, I give you a simple task to find out who runs the place where my son was killed—"

"Ja, well, I managed that. Wasn't hard, by the way. He's a well-known bastard. Responsible for my brother-in-law having to have his balls amputated after falling into a thorn bush."

"Shut up about your brother-in-law's balls. I also pay you to make sure that my people can bring that son-of-a-whore dog back here for torture. Now you tell me he has disappeared. Both you and my people have failed me miserably. They will be punished severely on their return. You will never get another cent from me ever again."

"Well, um, there's a slight problem about them returning, Mr. Vixay. You see, they're both dead."

"Liar!" screamed Vixay, smashing his hand down on the desk and causing the monitor to almost topple over. "You're telling me that gutless exploding penis killed my two best lieutenants?"

"No, not exactly. I believe the woman was actually eaten by a leopard from what my contact in the police told me. Crushed her skull like it was a coconut. The man died from a broken leg, which I've never heard of, to be honest." The connection was cut. Rather abruptly, thought Steyl as he fixed himself another neat brandy. He didn't understand Asians at all. They were certainly not the friendliest people to do business with.

Lao is a monosyllabic language with six distinct tones, and yet had a Professor of Linguistics from the National University of Laos been present at the time Vixay ended his Skype call with Steyl, he or she may have confidently prepared a paper on a number of new syllables and tones that had suddenly emanated from a large compound on the Mekong River.

Fifteen minutes later, Vixay Keosavang, sporting an open gash on his forehead from the continuous beating of his head on the heavy wooden screen, initiated a call with the heads of his global organization.

"I want this cancerous goat testicle, Roger Storm, found. I don't care where he is or who he is with. But find him you will, and then you will ensure he is brought to me. The person who finds him will be rewarded with a million US dollars. The person who lets him go will suffer a slow and painful death. Not dissimilar to the one I have planned for that stinking, sperm-swallowing bastard." He was about to further articulate his desires relating to the dispatching of Roger Storm, but the others had already hung up.

Chapter 10

IN WHICH ROGER STORM BEGINS TO BELIEVE IN
RESURRECTION. NOT THE RESURRECTION, JUST
PLAIN RESURRECTION.

Yet another secret and secure hideout,
this one on the coast of Zanzibar

Roger came to long before he and Ishea Payamps, who'd
carried him effortlessly for nearly five kilometers,
reached a clearing in the bush where a strange, silver-
colored helicopter stood like some mechanical, predatory
bird. Though his knowledge of military helicopters was
limited, and his brain wasn't functioning at a quarter of its
capacity, and his desire to show signs of consciousness was
low, Roger realized the helicopter was different to any he'd
ever seen before. Ishea lowered his shoulder, and Roger
flopped onto the ground. The pilot, who had been peeing
against a mopane tree, turned around, greeted Ishea, and
wiped his hands on his pants.

"Who's he?"

"Someone I should probably have left lying in the bush for the hyenas. He was in the process of being kidnapped by two nasty Laotian killers and in danger of being eaten by a leopard when I found him. Anyway, everyone seems to think he's worth saving, and who am I to argue? Now, I know you're awake, Roger. So unless you want me to sling you onto the floor of the helicopter, start acting like a live person. And you'd better hurry up because someone is going to be after us pretty soon."

Roger blinked his eyes a few times and struggled to his feet with an awful moan. He looked up at the man to whom he owed his life but in whose company he had hoped never to find himself again. His head hurt horribly, and once again he felt the familiar fear, confusion, and despair that, despite the relative peace and happiness he'd experienced over the past year, had been a huge and debilitating factor in his life over the years.

"My goddamn head hurts like a bastard and I think I'm going to be sick."

"I can give you something for your head, but you'd better resolve your nausea before we take off because I'm not traveling 800 kilometers in the same aircraft as your vomit."

"What's 800 kilometers from here?" asked Roger, gratefully accepting the two pills and water bottle from Ishea. He had a list of questions he'd been contemplating while Ishea carried him on his back through the bush, but he was so conflicted between hope and despair at who and what lay ahead that he didn't know where to begin.

"Quelimane in Mozambique. From there we're taking a Citation X to Zanzibar. Now climb up and strap yourself in. You can ask all the questions you like when we get there. I need to get some sleep."

"Okay, fine, but you have to answer one question: Who's the 'they' who thought I was worth saving? And if you tell me it's Freddy, then I'm probably not going to believe you. Because I know he and Conchita are dead."

"Well, if you're so sure, then I'd be an idiot to tell you that. So no, I'm not saying or telling you anything. Now shut up and let me sleep."

By the time Roger had oriented himself to his situation, and it was vague at best, they were skimming above the bush at an incredible speed. Ishea had fallen asleep the minute they took off, and the pilot, who'd ignored him up until then, turned around and grinned.

"This, in case you're wondering, is a Eurocopter X3. It's the fastest helicopter ever built, so nothing is going to catch us. And don't worry about how low we're flying—I'm doing it to stay under the radar, so to speak."

Roger wasn't wondering or worrying about any of those things, and so he just nodded.

"There's water in the back, and if you have to pee, use your empty water bottle. Otherwise you're on your own till we reach Quelimane." With that he turned back to his controls and left Roger to his jumbled thoughts of just who was waiting for him in Zanzibar. It was true he hadn't seen Freddy actually die—he'd only had Ishea's word for that—but he had very definitely seen Conchita Palomino tumble over the cliff and heard her scream. Weeks later, once he'd

111

recovered somewhat, he'd begun to mourn her. He'd felt a deep sorrow and a loss like nothing he'd ever experienced before. It was as if someone had put an ice cream cone in front of him and then whipped it away before he'd had a second lick. And yet, as one of the mercenaries he'd met in Addis Ababa had said to him, "In this profession people live and die many times." He closed his eyes and thought of Conchita, and he wondered if perhaps he were wrong and she might still be alive. And if she were alive, what would he say and do? Most of Roger's worries and musings soon gave way to even more anguish and apprehension as he thought about the fact that he had neither money nor passport. Then, when the agonizing had sucked every last ounce of energy from his already depleted brain, he too fell asleep. As for the passport, it wasn't an issue when they landed in Zanzibar. When you're dealing with ghosts, those sorts of things seldom are.

Ishea had slept all of the way to Quelimane and most of the way to Zanzibar. For the hour he was awake, he refused to answer any of Roger's questions and sat staring out the window or reading from the pile of Cigar Aficionado magazines in the rack at the back of the plane.

Once Roger realized that he wasn't going to get much more than an emphatic "shut up!" from Ishea, he picked up one of the magazines and tried to read an article about an obscure law in Zion, Illinois, that prohibits owners from giving a lit cigar to their dogs and cats. He may as well have been looking at a book on advanced calculus for all the sense it made. Finally, he decided he couldn't take the silence any longer and decided to make one final and concerted effort to elicit anything that could assuage the conflict that raged in his tired brain.

"Look, Ishea, I know you're not going to give me any information on who or what is waiting for us in Zanzibar, but your silence is totally screwing me up even more than any answer you could give me."

Ishea looked up from his magazine and regarded Roger as if he were a bowl of porridge that needed a spoon of honey to make it palatable. The beginning of a smile played at the corner of his mouth. He thought back to the time he'd met Roger in London the previous year and how at first he'd thought him a weak and whiny individual deserving of mistrust and derision. And yet, when the situation had seemed hopeless and he'd witnessed Roger beaten to a bloody pulp by Demetri Guria and about to have his head cut off by Zecheriah Corn, Roger had surprised Ishea with a gritty desire to survive and enough courage to warrant a review. That's when he'd come to realize that Roger was simply a poor though brave schmuck who'd got caught up in a world that was far beyond anything he was capable of dealing with. At that point, he'd developed an affection for Roger. In truth, not a great deal of affection but enough to make him palatable.

"Okay, I'll tell you a few things, but only because I don't want to talk at the moment. I need to detoxify after the last few weeks, and answering questions isn't part of the process."

"Fair enough. Anything, and then I promise to shut up."

"Good. Well, I came to South Africa to see how you were doing. Not my idea, I promise you. As it turns out it was quite fortuitous. Someone told me Vixay Keosavang's son and heir, whom I've been trying to find for a long time, was in the area. I didn't expect to find him on your game reserve, though."

"Not so fortunate for him."

"No, it wasn't, and while I take little pleasure in ending life of any sort, I must admit that his death gave me a certain amount of satisfaction."

"And I'm glad. What he did was absolutely despicable, and the world's better off without him." Roger let out a deep sigh. "I only wish his father didn't blame me. Those bastards were going to torture me to death."

"Oh, you have no idea what they'd have done to you. Trust me, Demetri Guria was an amateur compared to Vixay. Look, I'm sorry you got the blame. Couldn't be helped. But that's why you're on your way to Zanzibar. At least you'll be safe for a while. And that, pal, is it for the moment."

"Fine," said Roger, thinking that it could damn well have been helped if Ishea had actually owned up to the killing, but he realized anything he said would have been pointless, and in any case, he supposed Ishea had saved his life more than he'd put it in danger.

"Thanks for your advice on stopping a charging elephant. I'll be sure to remember it."

Ishea looked up from the magazine and, much to Roger's surprise, laughed. "You're welcome. And my advice is: If you're going to live in the bush, you may want to learn a few basics."

A Citation X needs a 1600-meter runway for takeoffs and a slightly shorter one for landing. The runway near Matenwe on Zanzibar's north-east coast was exactly 987 meters, but the pilot had flown Lockheed C5 transport planes, and short runways held no fear for him. It was a hard landing, and the plane came to a screeching halt a meter from a large mango tree.

"Sorry about that," said the pilot over the speaker system, "but that's the best I could do. Sit tight while I turn her around and park her."

The plane taxied up to a small hanger and stopped a few meters from the entrance, where a black SUV was waiting. The pilot came out of the cabin and whispered something to Ishea, who listened and turned to Roger.

"Wait here. I just need to make sure we're okay here without you having a passport. Those guys you see, the ones getting out of the truck, are the Idara ya Usalama wa Taifa, the Tanzanian secret service. They're a little unpredictable, and I don't think you want to spend any time in a Zanzibari prison. I'm told it's a brutal experience."

Roger slunk down into the seat, trying to make himself as invisible as possible. After a few seconds, he gingerly lifted his head so he could see out the window. The front doors of the SUV were open, and Ishea was talking to two men dressed in identical black suits and sunglasses. They seemed to be listening intently to Ishea with the sort of expressions that made Roger think they'd be happier pulling someone's fingernails out than eating ice cream for dessert. Ishea stopped talking, and both men looked puzzled for a second, then burst out laughing. When they'd calmed down, they looked over at the plane with big grins on their faces and waved at Roger, who, despite his efforts at invisibility, was quite conspicuous through the window. They fist bumped Ishea, climbed back into the SUV, and drove off just as another SUV, this time a white one, pulled up.

"Okay," Ishea said, sticking his head back in the plane, "this is us. This is our ride."

"I'm assuming that I'm not headed for a Zanzibari prison?"

"No, they were cool. I gave them a few anecdotes, and they decided someone like you wouldn't constitute a threat to the national security of Tanzania. I exaggerated a little, of course."

"What the hell is wrong with you? Why does everyone have to think I'm the world's biggest half-wit? First those idiot policemen in South Africa, now the cops here. Jesus."

While the put-down was annoying, Roger knew it was probably more true than not. He had no illusions as to his abilities, and clearly, neither did anyone else. There were times when he genuinely wondered how the hell he'd made it so far in life. At best, he was average at anything he did. Excelling was certainly not a word that teachers, coaches, bosses, or lovers for that matter would readily have included in any discussion involving Roger Storm. Then the apprehension at what lay at the end of his journey took over, and he began to tap his knee nervously. He stared out the window deep in thought as they drove through small towns and randomly spaced houses till they hit a road that ran parallel to the ocean. He so much wanted to believe that both Freddy and Conchita were alive and yet at the

116

same time hoped they weren't. It would be just too much to process at this moment.

"Ishea, I wish you'd tell me who I'm going to see when we get wherever it is we're going. I honestly don't know why you won't. I mean, what difference does it make? If I'm going to see Freddy or maybe Conchita, then why won't you just say?" Ishea was in the front of the SUV with the driver, who hadn't said a word to either of them.

"It doesn't make any difference to me, but then I'm not the one making those decisions. And in any case, here we are."

At that moment, the SUV pulled up to two huge metal gates set in a three-meter-high wall that obscured whatever it was and whoever it was that lay ahead. The gates opened automatically, and the SUV made its way along a sand road that led to a stone house partially obscured by tall palm trees. The size of the thatch-roofed mansion became clear as they pulled up to a paved path bordered by two pools. It was enormous. Perhaps one of the biggest houses that Roger had ever seen. It could quite easily have been a hotel or a palace of some exotic eastern potentate. But there was no signage or parking lot or liveried doorman standing at attention.

"Jesus, this is huge," said Roger as they walked up to the front door.

"Well, you know your friend."

"Ha, so Freddy is alive!"

"Well, alive may be pushing it...." said a voice that seemed to come from a pillar to the right of where Roger stood. To Roger's credit, he didn't jump away or scream.

But he did feel the blood begin to drain from his head, and he swayed on his feet and would have fallen if Ishea hadn't caught him as a blissful darkness enveloped him.

"What the hell's wrong with him, Ishea? Every time I come back from the dead, the bugger faints."

Chapter 11

IN WHICH A RELUCTANT ROGER LEARNS THINGS THAT SCARE THE PANTS OFF HIM

The Zanzibari headquarters of the recently deceased Freddy and friends

Freddy Blank was not dead.

That much was clear to Roger. And yet the person who stood/lay in the strange contraption on the porch overlooking a beautiful strip of white sand and clear blue sea was not the man he'd seen a year or so ago. His wavy blond hair, while still moppish, was now totally white, and his face, normally the color of a pomegranate, was pale and blotchy. To his credit, despite the tubes and restraints that connected and held him in the high-tech mobility device like a Michelin Man, it was obvious that Freddy was still large.

"Christ, Freddy. You look like Hannibal Lecter in *Silence of the Lambs*. Oh, Jesus, I'm sorry—I just blurted that out."

"Hmm, a fine way to greet an old friend, I must say."

Roger's face fell, and he tried his best to embrace Freddy.

"Whoa, you nearly pulled out my colostomy bag!"

"I'm sorry, Freddy!" Roger jumped back in sheer horror and embarrassment. Then Freddy began to laugh.

"I'm joking, I'm joking. I do look like Hannibal Lecter. Though I haven't yet developed a taste for human flesh. Food here's too good. Go on, give me a kiss on the cheek. That way you'll do the least damage. Hey, you're crying?"

"Of course I'm bloody well crying. I thought you were dead. Again."

"No, but there are times when I wish I was, trapped in this device. I'm almost totally paralyzed as you can see. I can talk, and I can eat and swallow, and I can use this finger on the control panel. But that's about it. What do you think about this thingy, though? It can do just about everything for me, except wipe my arse. Which, fortunately, with the bag, I don't have to do."

Roger looked at his friend and shook his head sadly. "Uhm, I don't know, Freddy. I have so many questions. God, I'm so emotional, I don't even know where to begin."

"It's based on the original iBot," said Freddy, ignoring Roger's visceral shock and confusion. "Developed by Dean Kamen, the guy who invented the Segway. But, of course, I had some brilliant young engineers modify it for me. I'd sell the plans, but I'm not sure there are many people who can afford a $2 million wheelchair. Now come on, follow me and we'll get something to eat. That'll settle you down. You must be starving." Freddy tapped the panel with his working digit, and the device transformed into more of a wheelchair, spun around, and began to move silently along the outdoor porch to where a long wooden table, set for one, stood. "Sit, I've already eaten because I know you're going to want me to talk, and I can't do both at the same time. Here, look. There's a great local-lobster salad and a goat biryani. You'll love it."

A waiter in a long white dishdasha set the dishes in front of Roger. "Can I offer you something to drink, sir?"

"Uh, well, um, what do you have?"

"We have fresh watermelon juice, avocado juice with lime, or maybe some mango juice. Whatever you prefer?"

"Oh, come on, Juma. Can't you see? He wants a damn martini." Freddy laughed. "Make him one with that Beluga Gold Line Vodka."

"Very well. Freddy, are you going to have one too?"

"Absolutely, my friend. And use those big martini glasses."

Juma nodded and walked over to a bar cart, where he discreetly began to shake up the drinks.

"I honestly don't think I've seen you drink a martini before," Roger said.

"Well, in all honesty I didn't used to," Freddy replied. Juma handed Roger his martini in a large frosted glass and clipped Freddy's, which was in a blue plastic bottle, to a cup holder on the side of his device. Juma attached a long plastic straw to the bottle and positioned the end a few inches from Freddy's mouth. Freddy moved his head and sucked on the straw. "However, after what happened in Ethiopia and losing Jamie...."

"Oh, Jesus, Freddy. I'm so sorry. He didn't make it?"

121

"No. I'm going to tell you the whole story, but bottom line is he didn't. Which has been devastating because he truly was the love of my life, and it's been damn hard to carry on without him." Freddy took a long suck on his straw. "Especially in this state. But that's how it goes. Now, I know you're wondering about Conchita. Well, I'll get to her in a minute. She's alive and she's okay."

As many times as Roger had been through the "Conchita-alive-or-dead" scenario on the trip from South Africa and projected how he'd react either way, nothing he'd imagined prepared him for "she's alive and she's okay." His lip began to tremble, and his appetite, normally immune to good or bad news, receded into his intestines. "She's alive? How can she be? I saw her tumble over the cliff."

"Here, take a sip of that martini, and I'll tell you what happened when we tried to storm the monastery of Kunda Damo to try to rescue you and Menelik. And eat, for Christ's sake. It's going to be okay."

Roger took a bite of the biryani, but his stomach felt as if someone had shoved a sandbag into it, and he pushed his plate away. "I honestly thought you'd all died."

"We probably should have. My fault entirely for trusting Zecheriah, that treacherous bastard. He convinced Jamie, Conchita, and me to take the main staircase up while he created a 'diversion.'"

"He told me that just before he tried to cut off my head."

"Yes, Ishea told me. I'm sorry."

"Don't be. Ishea saved me."

"Anyway, just as it looked like we'd made it to the top of the stairs, he turned around and tossed a grenade at us."

"Jesus!"

"Conchita was in the front, and I was at the back, and the grenade landed between Jamie and I, and...." Freddy's voice broke, and he began to cough and choke. Roger jumped up to help him, but Freddy moved his head and pushed a button on the control panel. There was a horrific sucking sound and his coughing stopped.

"Sorry, I literally get choked up, and this has to suck up whatever I can't swallow. It's quite disgusting. Don't worry, this contraption is designed to keep me alive for as long as I want it to. It can also put me out of my misery, by the way, if I decide I've had enough. All I need to do is push this button."

"Please don't. I don't think I can take you dying for a third time—well, not yet."

"No, I'm not quite ready to go to the great beyond. Too many things to do. So, where was I?"

"The grenade."

"Ah yes, the grenade. Jamie did the bravest thing you can imagine. He fell on the grenade seconds before it exploded. I survived with my spinal cord severed by a piece of shrapnel. Jamie didn't. There wasn't even enough left of him for us to bury. I'd cry if I could, but I can't really. Not anymore."

"Well, you went through all of that to rescue me. I'm not sure what to say."

"There's nothing to say. Yes, we desperately wanted to rescue you and Menelik, but at that point we also had to take out Geoffrey and his mercenaries. So, don't feel guilty. We got you into that horrible situation in the first place."

123

Roger knew Freddy was right. He and Conchita and Jamie had gotten him into the harebrained scheme to help Menelik, the supposed descendant of Solomon and Sheba and true heir to the throne of Ethiopia, to position himself as the African messiah. The plan was to then organize the overthrow of the neo-colonialists who were slowly buying up traditional tribal land, displacing millions of people, and systematically wiping out the great herds of animals, all to feed their own growing populations.

"Anyway, at that stage I was pretty much out of it. I had no idea what happened until the next day when Ishea and the two mercenaries, Khosan and Erku—you'll remember them I'm sure—flew back from Addis Ababa in one of our helicopters to see if anyone was alive. They found me, probably hours away from death, and then they found Conchita, clinging to a ledge about ten feet down from where she'd fallen. Her shoulder and left leg were broken, and she was still stunned from the grenade. But otherwise she was okay."

"But why didn't you contact me . . . or let me know you were alive?"

"I thought we did when we gave you the money."

"Well, that's true. Archibald Rossiter did say it was from you, but I assumed you'd arranged that before we left London. I couldn't even thank you for it."

"There was no need. You earned it, and what you did with it, buying up that game reserve, more than made up for any thank you. You've done a great job with Hunter's Folly, by the way. Especially taking Gosego on as a partner. What an enlightened man he is."

"You're not going to tell me you know him?"

"No, not personally. But there are certain people in conservation that we try to support—mostly without their knowledge—in different parts of Africa, and he is definitely someone we have our eye on. It's too bad about the rhino, but at least Ishea settled that."

"Except I got the blame."

"You did, and that's both unfortunate and fortunate. But Ishea will fill you in."

"I can hardly wait. Well, okay...." The martini was doing its job, and the shock and pure insanity of the situation was beginning to succumb to the calming effects of the alcohol. "But first you have to tell me about Conchita."

"You're still in love with her, aren't you?"

"I don't know. I mean I think I am—yes, of course I am. How could I not be?"

"I'm glad to hear that because I'm pretty sure—well, the last time I spoke to her anyway which was about an hour ago—that she has similar feelings for you. Although she wasn't too happy about that woman Maggie giving you a blowjob."

"What? How the hell do you know that? No, don't even tell me. Everyone in the world knows."

"Fortunately, not Maggie's husband, and I'm kidding about Conchita. She doesn't know a thing. She is, however, waiting for you."

It's a universally accepted axiom that unanticipated blows to the lower abdomen are not immediately followed by euphoria. Take the case of the late Harry Houdini: When, on the afternoon of October 22, 1926, he was unexpectedly punched in the gut by a McGill University student who believed the famed escape artist could withstand any blow to the abdomen, he grimaced in agony and died shortly afterwards. Roger's reaction to Freddy's mind-shattering blow followed the rule to the letter. It caught him like a haymaker to the spleen and he gasped, slumped forward, then retched horribly.

"Good God, man. What the hell is wrong with you? That's supposed to be good news. What are you going to do when I tell you the bad news? Juma, bring a wet towel for our friend here. He seems slightly incapacitated."

In addition to his skills as a mixologist, Juma was a registered nurse, and his duties included emptying Freddy's colostomy bag, and so he was unfazed by Roger's condition. He emptied the ice bucket into a towel, put it on the back of Roger's neck, and then remade the martini Roger had spilled on the table. When Roger had recovered his composure and sipped his martini, he turned to Freddy, who'd said nothing during the clean-up and recovery.

"Where is she?"

"She's in Hong Kong."

"Hong Kong. I thought you said she's waiting for me?"

"She is—in Hong Kong. No, don't look at me like that. You'll hear everything tonight. Now, you need to take a nap, have a shower—you stink to high heaven—and Ishea and I will meet you back here for dinner."

Roger slept for a good two hours, showered, searched for his clothes which had mysteriously vanished, and finally put on the long silk robe that he found hanging behind the door of the bathroom. He was feeling a lot better physically, but emotionally it was as if he'd walked into the back of a bus. His head was buzzing with possibilities, and his stomach felt like a bottle of Tabasco had been added to its contents. He was looking through the chest of drawers and closet for anything else to wear when there was a not-so-discreet bang on his door. He opened it and jumped back in total surprise.

"So sorry," said the man at the door. "I didn't mean to startle you. I just wanted to bring you these clothes. But you must to try them on. I couldn't really take accurate measurements while you were asleep. My name is Destructive Wang."

Destructive Wang was the biggest Asian—man, woman, or elephant for that matter—that Roger had ever seen. It wasn't as much height or breadth, or size of hands or head or limbs that conveyed Wang's substance. Rather, it was the sum of all body parts. Destructive Wang was simply immense. Even his voice, which seemed to emanate from deep within his massive belly, gave the impression of a volcano about to erupt.

"You like this color?" He held out what, in his ginormous hands, appeared to be a puppet-sized cream-colored suit. "Here, take it and try it on. If it doesn't fit, I fix it for you."

Roger's capacity for being flummoxed, already strained by the events of the past few days, was once again put to the test. He stood with his mouth wide open, as if in some catatonic state, staring at Destructive Wang.

"You no like the color? I knew it. I should have used navy cloth. You look like a navy person. Very dull." Destructive Wang shook his head sadly.

"No, no—I like the color," Roger stammered. "I just . . . I'm sorry, you said you made this?"

"Yes, I had only a few hours, so it's not my best work." Wang grinned, displaying a set of teeth that rivalled a small billboard in Times Square.

"Please," said Roger, regaining a certain amount of equilibrium, "come in."

"Here." Wang handed Roger a shirt and a pair of boxers that had been concealed under the suit. "You put these on as well."

Roger took the clothes and retreated into the bathroom. He thought of locking the door but realized Destructive Wang could have taken it off its hinges faster than the Big Bad Wolf. In any case, there was no lock. He took a deep breath and began to dress. To his amazement the shirt and suit fitted him almost perfectly. The pants were a little tight around the waist but nothing he couldn't handle. He looked at himself in the mirror and wondered if the image reflected of a middle-aged man with disheveled grey hair would please Conchita. A year in the bush had left him tanned and leaner than he'd been in years, and even the heavy bags under his eyes from his previous diet of booze and little sleep had all but vanished. He found a hairbrush and made the best of his untamed mane and wondered if a Panama hat would complete the image that in his mind resembled a spy from a le Carré novel.

A grunt from the bedroom brought him back to reality. He gingerly opened the door to the bedroom to find Wang waiting with an impatient expression on his face.

"Hmm, hmm, hmm." Wang held his hands up to his face and tapped his fingers on his nose as he contemplated Roger.

"You stand up straight. Yes, yes. Not bad. The pants are a little baggy round your bum, but you don't really have one, so no worries. I don't have proper shoes for you, and your bush boots will spoil the way the pants hang. You take these flip flops. We get the right shoes in Hong Kong."

"Thank you. Um, are you a tailor?"

The giant laughed. "No, not a tailor. I was with the Flying Tigers, the Hong Kong Special Forces. But I now work for your friend, Freddy."

"But you made this suit?"

"Yes, and the shirt and underwear. I see you are confused. No worries. My father was a tailor. Now he owns a big, successful clothing store in Central shopping area in Hong Kong. Very fashionable. Very expensive. I'll take you there once we arrive. You get special treatment. I worked there as a boy, but I wasn't very good. Now sometimes I make clothes for Freddy's guests. Keep my hand in. I know my father hopes I will one day take over the business. Who can tell. Now, we go to dinner."

Roger decided the scenario was just insane enough to sound like every scenario involving Freddy Blank, and so he simply smiled and followed Destructive Wang down a long white corridor back to the porch where a table was set for three. Freddy and Juma were standing at the railing looking toward a wall of black clouds billowing in the winds and churning up the waves as the storm moved rapidly across the sea toward the island.

"There's a huge storm coming," Freddy said. "We should move indoors."

There was a sudden crash of thunder, then a lightning show that lit up the beach like a fireworks display. Then it began to rain. "Ha," laughed Freddy. "The gods are pissing on our little party." He took a look at Roger and blinked his eyes rapidly. "My dear Wang, you've outdone yourself. The suit fits him perfectly. Now let's get inside before the storm ruins it."

"Where's Ishea?" Roger asked as they moved into a dining room off the porch. "I thought you said he'd join us for dinner."

"Unfortunately, he has a little something to take care of in the Seychelles. It's not that long of a flight, so he may be back before you and Destructive Wang head for Hong Kong the day after tomorrow. If not, he'll join you there."

At that moment a bolt of lightning hit the house, and the light went off for a few seconds before an auxiliary generator kicked in.

"Jesus," yelled Roger.

"Don't worry. This house can withstand hurricanes. You're perfectly safe."

Once again, Roger didn't believe a word of it.

The dinner was an elaborate affair of fresh seafood and spicy curries that Juma fed to Freddy in between his stories of how they'd finally sold PaloMar—the international arms business that was owned by Conchita, Jamie, and

Freddy—to a Qatari company for billions and were now firmly focused on environmental issues.

"Well, I'm really glad to hear that," Roger said when Freddy had finished. "I have to say, I never really understood why you got into guns and weapons in the first place. It's not something I'd have ever thought would appeal to you."

"Money," Freddy responded. "That's what drove the decision. Well, money and Conchita. Jamie and I probably never would have had anything to do with guns if we hadn't met Conchita. She's the one who made it possible."

"Could you tell me about that? About her . . . I realize just how little I know of Conchita's life."

"I'll tell you what I think she'd probably be okay with you knowing. Conchita is an enigma that few people have ever even begun to unravel. I probably know more about her than most, and what I can tell you is that she's a puzzle best left unsolved. But, if you like, I will tell you a bit.

"You'll remember back in London when we first began to talk about Ethiopia, she told you that her father was Columbian and a pretty powerful figure in FARC?"

"Yes, and her mother was an Israeli Mossad agent on assignment to the CIA who'd infiltrated FARC."

"Precisely. Well, after her dad died, she and her mom returned to Israel where Conchita grew up and served her time in the Israeli Defense Force. Soon after her service was over, she was recruited by Mossad, I guess because of her mom or her extraordinary skills, or both. Jamie and I met her in London shortly after she'd been fired for almost killing her case officer when he apparently made inappropriate overtures."

"Yes, I can imagine how she'd react to something like that."

"Oh, my dear boy, you have no idea what Conchita is capable of when riled up. I've seen her do things that would make your hair stand on end. Anyway, Jamie and I were looking to invest our money—and we obviously couldn't put it into anything that would be overly scrutinized for obvious reasons."

"I get that."

"Well, a mutual acquaintance told us about this woman who needed money for some sort of black ops, and we agreed to meet her at an Indian restaurant called Veeraswamy...."

Freddy and Jamie were already seated at their table dipping papadums into mint chutney when the restaurant went strangely silent. Conchita Palomino, who had caused the forks to pause in midair and the conversations to come to an abrupt halt, was making her way to the table. She was not beautiful in the classical sense. There was no softness to her face, no roundness to her body. Her silver blond hair was pulled back in a tight ponytail, and in the body-hugging jumpsuit she wore under a black leather jacket, she looked like a cobra about to strike. And yet for all that, Conchita was positively spellbinding. Certainly, like no other woman that either Jamie or Freddy or any of the gawking diners had seen before.

"My name is Conchita Palomino," she said in an accent that was as exotic as the lips that formed the words, "and I need four million dollars."

"Well," replied Freddy with a big grin on his face, "would you mind if we ate first? I'm much more prone to loosening the old purse strings after a lamb vindaloo."

Conchita took the opportunity to observe her dinner companions closely for a moment and then laughed. "I'm sorry. That was probably quite rude of me. I haven't had many occasions lately to engage in anything but short exchanges. Too many people after me, I'm afraid."

"That's okay," said Jamie, who was totally gobsmacked by Conchita. "We're keen to hear about your proposal." He beckoned a hovering waiter who handed out menus and took their drinks order.

"Would you mind if I ordered for all of us?" asked Freddy. "I know this place pretty well. Do you enjoy fiery food?"

"Yes," Conchita replied with a dismissive wave. "Go ahead. You look like you enjoy food."

"What's that supposed to mean?" Freddy sounded peeved.

"You're a fatty. But it's good. I appreciate people who are confident in what they are."

"That's a tad presumptuous. You're saying I'm fat and happy to be so...."

"Yes. I was trained to understand people quickly. I can also tell you and Jamie are very comfortable together and you don't really care what people think."

"That's true," Freddy said. "But how do you know?"

"I observed the way you were looking at each other while I was walking to the table. Only people in love look at each other like that." She smiled and took a sip of the gin and tonic that the waiter had put down in front of her. "But let's get the order in. I want to tell you my proposal, and I have very little time."

As soon as the food was served, Conchita began to talk. "I have the opportunity to purchase a thousand Uzi submachine guns with extra 32-round magazines and ten Matador rocket launchers from a reliable source, and I have the buyers. The problem is the deal needs to be concluded in four days."

Freddy took a piece of roti and dipped it into the remaining sauce of the now-depleted lamb vindaloo. "Conchita, I'm not going to insult you with a myriad of questions that follow a proposal of minimalist details. I assume that the fact you're even bringing it up means you know—and not just from your observations tonight—something about us."

"That is a safe assumption. I know a great deal about you. I know about your fake deaths and the assumed names that you use for the authorities. I also know you have a great deal of money you need to invest. If I didn't, I wouldn't be meeting with you."

"You certainly don't waste time," said Jamie. "And you're very impressive for someone so impetuous. We, however, don't have your access to sensitive information, so how do we know we can trust you?"

"You don't, yet. But that's what will make this relationship work. We're both going to have to prove we can trust each other." She looked over at the next table where four young men dressed in expensive suits were getting rowdier and rowdier with every bottle of wine they consumed. They were staring at her and making lewd comments to each other.

Conchita rolled her eyes and continued. "What I will tell you is that I was with Mossad up until two months ago when I was kicked out for defending myself against my superior, a pig of a man who thought he could take advantage of me without any consequences. He was wrong. Unfortunately, the Mossad is still a boys' club and so my bosses took his side. I'm not exactly on the run, but I think they'll kill me if the opportunity arises."

"Then," Freddy interjected, "we'd better make sure the opportunity doesn't arise."

"Thank you. I appreciate that. But you can see why time is of the essence. So let me explain the situation. During my service in Mossad I made many contacts, a lot of whom owe me favors. This is why I can get my hands on the guns and arrange for the sale. You don't need to know all the details."

"Except," said Freddy, "if Jamie and I are going to fork over four million, we'd like to know a few things. And I'd certainly like to know what the return is projected to be."

Freddy was interrupted by one of the men from the next table who'd walked over to them. The man, whose lips were stained a deep purple from the wine, leaned in to Conchita. "My friends and I would like to buy you a drink."

"That's very sweet of you," replied Jamie, flickering his eyes at the man. "But we're all good."

The man jerked back. "Fuck off, Nancy. I wasn't talking to you." He leaned back over Conchita and touched her cheek. "I'm talking to you, sweetheart. Come on over to our table and talk to some real men."

Conchita smiled up at him. "Of course, my dear." She stood up and took the young man's elbow. "Why don't you come outside with me for a moment so I can tell you something in private." Whether the man would have gone willingly or not made no difference. The grip that Conchita applied to the pressure points of his elbow gave him no choice. They disappeared out the door and down the stairs to the whooping and hollering cheers of his mates and much to the amazement of Freddy and Jamie. Less than a minute later there was a horrific shriek, and shortly after that Conchita reappeared. The young man did not.

"What in God's name did you do?" asked Freddy.

"Very little. I scraped the edge of my boot down his shin. There is a very high concentration of nerve endings in that area. I doubt if he'll be back. Now, you wanted a few details?"

Freddy looked over at the drunks at the next table. They had gone pleasantly silent and were focused on their food. "Yes," he said to Conchita. "A few details would be appreciated."

"The weapons are in the hands of a disgraced general of the Israeli Defense Force currently residing in Somalia. He wants $2 million. I estimate bribes and shipping will cost close to $750 thousand. I will need $250 thousand for my expenses and any unforeseen costs. The buyers will pay $5.5 million partially in dollars and the rest in uncut diamonds and rubies."

"That leaves $1 million of our money unaccounted for," said Jamie.

"Yes, and that money will be put into an account at The Cayman Islands Bank and Trust Company held by you but accessible by me once the transaction is concluded. Now, do we have a deal?"

"And you gave her the money just like that?" asked Roger.

"Just like that," replied Freddy, signaling to Juma for another martini. "I tell you this, Roger, because it demonstrates not simply the charisma of your lover but the sheer mastery she has over people. That alone would make Conchita one of the most remarkable people I've ever met. But there is so much more to her. Those are intricacies and secrets that no doubt she will tell you when she feels it's appropriate. All it took for Jamie and me to trust her was that one meal. And by the way, she came through in spades. Once we'd sold the diamonds and rubies to some Russian oligarch, we netted over $2 million in literally two weeks. That was the beginning of our relationship."

"Phew," said Roger, leaning back in his chair. "Well, as you say, she certainly is remarkable. But that makes me wonder even more what the hell she sees in someone as insignificant and inglorious as me?"

"She sees kindness and generosity and a genuineness that she doesn't get to see in the people she deals with every day. I suppose she also sees your vulnerability, and that probably appeals to a side of her she keeps hidden. Anyway, my friend, I can see you're ready for bed. Go, sleep. Dream of her."

Chapter 12

In which stages are set, revenge is exacted, and conclusions are drawn

Limpopo province, South Africa. The Seychelles. The departure lounge, Oliver Tambo International Airport, Johannesburg.

Gosego Modise stood on the porch of the Hunter's Folly main lodge and looked over toward the water hole where a family of warthogs were happily playing in the mud. The sounds of black-fronted bushshrikes in the surrounding trees competed good naturedly with the shrieks from four hadeda ibises dipping their long beaks into the water. All was well with the world—or would have been were it not for the fact that everything, in Gosego's opinion, sucked. For the first time in ages, he felt totally alone. The three policemen, whom he had begun to quite like, had concluded that the mystery of the dead poachers and disappearance of Roger Storm was better solved back in Johannesburg and left early that morning. Sergeant Bontle

Warona and her Mambas had vanished back into the bush, and all of the new guests were out with the rangers looking for animals to photograph.

Gosego's musing on the pain of loneliness was interrupted by a sudden silence that fell over the bush. It was a thick, ominous silence, the kind that in Gosego's experience usually pre-empted the death of some unfortunate creature. The birds had stopped singing, and the warthogs ceased their happy frolicking. Their tales stood straight up as they stared intensely into the trees that surrounded the water hole. Then they began to run. Gosego held his breath. For a second, he thought that Roger might emerge from the shadows with a big grin on his stupid face and everything would be okay. His brief elation quickly vanished as two young male lions, their bellies full from a baby impala they'd killed and eaten that morning, sauntered out of the shadows, not even glancing in the direction of the hastily departing warthogs. Gosego recognized them as the same two who'd recently left the northern pride to set up on their own. It was their first solo kill, and their swagger brought him some respite, however brief, from his rapidly deepening depression.

Where in God's name was Roger, and why had he left him all alone? Gosego sat down in one of the big armchairs and covered his face with his hands, hoping none of the staff would see his sadness. He looked down at the floor, and his mind drifted back to the restaurant in Lephalale where he'd first met Roger Storm, and his life—which was going nowhere as the head ranger on a small, private game reserve—changed beyond anything he could have imagined.

"I've just bought a small game reserve," said the strange man sitting opposite him with an American lilt to his South African accent. "I need someone to partner with me, and from everyone I've spoken to—and I've spoken to a lot of people around here and in Joburg—you're the guy."

"How small?" asked Gosego.

"It's about 23,000 hectares."

Gosego laughed. "That isn't what I'd call small, and I don't know who you've spoken to, but a partnership usually involves money, and I don't have any."

"I don't need money. I've got plenty. You'd be putting in your experience and your knowledge. That to me is worth more than money."

"Hmm," Gosego snorted. He narrowed his eyes and contemplated Roger as if he were some deranged lunatic. "You know, my father told me that the only rewards that are genuine are those you've worked for. So you can see why I'm a little distrustful of some stranger who asks me to lunch and then offers me something that is beyond belief."

"Oh, I totally do. But I can prove I'm absolutely serious about what I'm saying." Roger reached into the small backpack hanging behind his chair and removed a large envelope. He pulled out a legal document and handed it to Gosego. "This gives you 50 percent of the game reserve. All we need to do is agree that we both have the same ideas about conservation. Then at the end of this meal, if I like you and you like me, you can fill your name in at the top and we can sign it in front of my lawyer who's sitting at the next table."

141

Gosego looked over at the woman at the adjacent table about to take a bite of a hamburger. She gave him a big grin and a friendly wave. Gosego lifted his large hand and waved back.

"I realize this all sounds too good to be true, but when I tell you the story of how I got the money to buy this reserve, I promise you this lunch will seem perfectly normal." With that, Roger told Gosego about Freddy and Conchita and the whole ridiculous adventure. The only thing he left out was the death of Harry Bones. He didn't feel that part would add anything to the veracity of his offer.

It was clear to Gosego that Roger had done his homework. He knew everything about Gosego's background. His military career. His graduation from Phinda, the toughest game-ranger training course in the world. Roger knew about his hatred of poachers and disdain for trophy hunters, and perhaps it was that discussion that convinced Gosego that Roger was indeed genuine. As they both took their last bite of sticky-toffee pudding, they shook hands and walked back with the young lawyer to her offices where they signed the papers.

Two things were clear to Gosego from day one. The first was that Roger saw him not just as a partner, but a friend whom he trusted implicitly. The second was that Roger was extremely lazy when it came to actual work. He loved the food and the wine part of the safari experience, and he never seemed to get bored going into the bush—which he did as often as he could—but that was about it. And in truth Gosego was perfectly happy with the arrangement. There was more than enough money to hire the right people and

buy the best equipment, and Roger never questioned anything he felt he needed. It had been an ideal and happy year
up until a week ago.

Gosego didn't want to think about the worst-case
scenario, but he knew he had to. What would happen to
Hunter's Folly if Roger didn't return? Would Roger's half go
to his two sons? Gosego had met them a few months before
when they'd come out with their wives to see the place. He
liked them a lot and they liked him, and while they clearly
loved the bush, neither had expressed any interest in moving to South Africa. In his experience silent partners didn't
work. One thing he was certain of was that he couldn't
afford to run the reserve on his own. Which would mean
they'd have to sell it, and while that would probably give
him enough money to live really well for the rest of his life,
it wasn't what he wanted. He wanted his friend back and
things to revert to the way they'd been.

"Gos...."

Gosego looked up to see the young office manager holding out a piece of paper.

"What's that?"

"It's an email that I think you're going to want to read.
It's from Roger."

Gosego snatched it out of her hand and began to read.

*Gos, first of all get a phone that allows you to get
email, not just texts. This is too long to text. I'd call
you, but I need this to be a one-sided conversation
because you'd ask too many questions which I'm not
in a position to answer just yet.*

The good news is I'm fine. It was Ishea Payamps who found me. I'm sure that's what you and the three cops surmised. I heard those two Laotian bastards are dead and I'm pleased about that, but of course it's put me in more danger. The good news is that I'm with people who are going to help. I'll tell you who at some stage, I promise. I'm not sure when I'm going to be back with you and the others, but hopefully it won't be too long. Tell everyone I'm good, and please carry on as necessary. I've arranged for you to have access to any funds you need. My lawyer will contact you tomorrow. She'll also give you an agreement that hands over my 50 percent to you provided I don't return within sixty days. There'll be enough money to run the reserve for at least two years, at which stage it should be self-sustaining. You can sell it—but not to anyone who hunts (not that I believe you would). However, I plan to return. I want to live the rest of my life there, and I'd like to do it with you, mate. Although I think we could both do with some female company. Maybe you should consider asking Sergeant Warona out. She's more your age than mine as you pointed out, and in any case, I have someone else in mind. I guess that's all I can say at the moment. Sala gahle, my friend.

Gosego stood up and turned away from the office manager who'd been standing attentively waiting for Gosego to finish. He stared out towards the river.

"Hamba gahle, my friend," he said to no one but the wind, using the Zulu response of "go safely" to Roger's "stay safe."

"Are you okay, Gos? And is Roger okay? I think everyone here wants to know."

"Yes, Martha. I'm okay, and in case you didn't read the email first, Roger's fine. Though I don't know where the hell he is. Why don't you arrange for a staff meeting when everyone gets back from the drives, and I will fill you in as best I can. Sorry that I've been in such a bad mood. It's been tough. Oh, and ask David and Lizzie Florence if they'd have dinner with me. They seem like a great couple, and I'd hate them to leave here thinking I was a rude bastard."

"Hey, we all get it. Of course, I'll send out texts. And I just want to say that I'm so happy that you're both okay. I don't think any of us can imagine this place without you."

The Eden Island Marina, close to Victoria, capital of The Seychelles, is a deep-water marina capable of handling super yachts up to 100 meters in length. *The Mystery*, a 90-meter yacht owned by the soviet billionaire Gregor Sapiskiva, was anchored safely in the harbor together with a number of smaller yachts. It was early, and the sea, a metallic grey against the almost tangerine dawn sky, was eerily calm. That was about to change.

All in all, *The Mystery* was a yacht that lived up to her name. Her enigmatic notoriety, however, had very little to do with her sleek lines or avant-garde technology, nor to the fact that her guestlist read like the *who's who* of Russian organized crime. What made *The Mystery* truly mystifying was that she was rumored to be decorated with the hides of hundreds of exotic and endangered animals. Rugs made from the skins of tigers, jaguars, and lions were said to be strewn over the floor of the entertainment deck like someone had dropped a box of Animal Crackers made from real animals. Animal rights groups reported that even the barstools were covered in the skins of reticulated pythons and three of the lounge chairs made from the hides of critically imperiled saiga antelopes. Most of the information, as sketchy as it was, had come from a crew member whose body was found nailed to his parents' front door two days after talking to a news reporter—anonymously, or so he thought—about elephant tusks and rhino horns and an entire stuffed lion on display to the fawning guests who were enthralled—or at least pretended to be—with the hunting exploits of Gregor and his son.

The crew had been up until after midnight catering to every need of the Sapiskiva guests and had yet to surface to begin the final cleanup after the previous night's debauchery. That was good and bad news for the two people who were on deck, one of whom was at that very moment about to jump into the water. The other was a little less active and would remain so for a good deal longer. They were joined shortly by Oksana Sapiskiva, Gregor's second wife, who'd woken up to find her husband's side of the bed empty.

She'd long suspected Gregor was sleeping with the twenty-three-year-old Swedish stewardess, and so, armed with one of his hunting rifles that he kept in a display case in his study and a fierce determination born from her early life in a Georgian brothel, she set out to find and kill them both. Oksana knew Gregor wouldn't be stupid enough to perform his acts of matrimonial treachery in the stewardess's own cabin, and so she headed directly to the entertainment deck where the safe room was hidden behind the elaborate bar. The safe room was a prized feature of the yacht maker and was designed to withstand anything short of a nuclear blast. No one other than Gregor and Oskana knew the combination to the electronic lock that opened the door, and other than the captain, no one else on board even knew it existed.

As it turned out, Oksana didn't need the combination to get into the safe room or the hunting rifle to blow the head off her husband. As she tip-toed across the deck past the unfortunate stuffed lion, she felt something wet and cloggy under her bare feet. She looked down at the tiger-skin rug and saw a large pool of what looked suspiciously like blood close to its open jaw. Then she looked up and saw her husband. He was draped over a zebra-skin-covered Eames Chair with a horrific snarl on his face. It was, thought Oksana, just before she went insane, reminiscent of that of the tiger.

The crew members who heard her screams didn't have much time to examine the neatly skinned remains of Gregor Sapiskiva, who'd unwittingly (judging by the bullet hole through his left eye and look of sheer terror on his face) joined the ranks of his taxidermized kills. Just as the captain held up his hand to stop the advancing crew from contaminating the crime scene, there was a loud explosion that blew out a sizeable portion of the hull.

"Grab the others," yelled the captain to the stewardess, who had given up her attempt to comfort Oksana after she called her a whore and tried to claw her eyes out. "Get them into the life boats and head for shore."

"What about the guests?" the stewardess asked, narrowly avoiding a stuffed armadillo thrown by Oksana.

"Screw them. They're lousy tippers. Let them go down with the ship."

A day or so later, police divers found the bodies of the drowned guests, who'd all been locked in their cabins by person or persons unknown. All they recovered of Gregor Sapiskiva was his shriveled penis, which had somehow got wedged between the paws of the stuffed lion. Not even the sharks wanted to swallow that.

Inspector Constantin Darmstaedter contemplated the bland cheese and crackers that stared sadly up at him from the plate resting on the glass coffee table in the Lufthansa Business Class Lounge at Oliver Tambo International Airport, Johannesburg. He felt stumped, and stumped was not something he often felt or enjoyed feeling. He, Bunter, and Patel had spent the past two days going over every detail surrounding the deaths of the two Laotian killers and the disappearance of Roger Storm. Like Gosego, they believed that Roger had been rescued by the mysterious Ishea Payamps, but as to his whereabouts, they were clueless. No one in either South Africa or Botswana had reported any small planes in the area of Tuli and Limpopo at the time when Roger and Ishea would have made their escape, and no European agencies had any record of either arriving, legitimately or not, in Europe. It seemed that Matthew was right, after all. With no clues left to uncover, no leads to pursue, he would be back behind a desk the minute he stepped off the plane. His pondering, however depressing, was lightened by the arrival of a grinning Inspector Bunter, who'd left him in the lounge to find a gift for his girlfriend, Clare, at the Out of Africa store.

"What do you think?" Bunter asked, pulling a decorated ostrich egg out of the zebra-striped bag. "You think Clare will like this?"

Darmstaedter took the egg and examined it. It was kitchy and crass. Just the sort of thing that someone whose taste levels rivalled those of a Bulgarian brothel owner would enjoy. It was true that his knowledge of Clare and her ability to discriminate when it came to objet d'art was slim yet valid when one took into account her choice of Matthew Bunter as a lover. All he knew for sure was that she was brilliant and had exceptional breasts.

"Ja, I imagine it will be appreciated so long as she doesn't sit on it."

"What are you talking about? Why the hell would she sit on it?"

"You said she likes to sit on big round objects?"

"She uses a big rubber exercise ball as an office chair, not as some sexual aid. Give it back before you break the damn thing, and for God's sake get your mind out the gutter, especially when it comes to Clare."

"Of course, but now we need to go to the gate. Our plane is leaving shortly." Darmstaedter smiled to himself. Clearly Matthew had forgotten about telling him how he and Clare had first had sex while trying to balance on the exercise ball in her office in her London flat. He'd thought about it a lot.

As the two policemen got up and grabbed their luggage for the nearly eleven-hour flight to Frankfurt, their phones beeped. The identical messages were sent from Interpol headquarters in Hong Kong. A man fitting Roger Storm's description had just passed through customs and, much to Bunter and Darmstaedter's surprise, had presented a valid passport. They were surprised because they had taken what they thought was Roger's real passport from his bedside drawer in his tent at Hunter's Folly.

"It seems," said Bunter as he settled into his business class seat in front of Darmstaedter, "that the game is once again afoot. We'll have to do a quick turnaround and head to Hong Kong."

At around the same time that Bunter and Darmstaedter were enjoying their business class meal somewhere over the African continent, Vixay Keosavang got a phone call from his associate in Hong Kong.

"I have just received a message from a friend at Hong Kong customs. Roger Storm arrived here three hours ago."

"Are you positive?"

"Yes, Khun Vixay, he fits the description we received from you perfectly."

Vixay took a deep breath and stuck out his tongue like a toad contemplating a fly. "Excellent. I will be in Hong Kong tomorrow. Make sure you know where he is and have The Bach Brothers alerted. We'll need their soldiers."

He put the phone down and walked over to the shrine where his son's nose lay ensconced in the Lucite box. He'd thought of trying to save the hands, but by the time they arrived they'd looked more like those of a small monkey than a human. The nose, on the other hand, had been remarkably resilient. Vixay held up the box and examined it carefully. It had been beautifully preserved in formaldehyde by Prakeet Phibunsongkhram, Vixsay's most trusted Thai taxidermist. He could still see the blackheads on the sides where the nose would have attached itself to his son's face and traces of nasal hair in the wide nostrils. Vixay shook his head sadly. "My son, I swear that we will have revenge on that baboon-breathed pudenda of a syphilis-ridden whore's offspring." Then he picked up a book on particularly nasty methods of torture and went to his bedroom to read.

Chapter 13

IN WHICH ROGER STORM FINDS THAT WHERE
THE FLAME OF LOVE BURNS, THERE'S ALWAYS
SOME BASTARD WITH HIS FINGER ON THE FIRE
EXTINGUISHER

On the way to Hong Kong and the House on
Gough Hill Road

A Citation X has a maximum range of 3,700 miles. Not
enough for a direct flight from Zanzibar to Hong Kong,
and so Roger and Destructive Wang were forced to refuel
in Colombo, Sri Lanka, where they were joined by an exhausted but elated Ishea Payamps.

Ishea nodded a greeting to both Roger and Destructive
Wang and then slumped into his chair, not even bothering to
fasten his seatbelt on takeoff. Roger knew better than to try
to ask questions, but Destructive Wang was not intimidated
by the extremely grim look on Ishea's normally grim face.

"Ishea, you need a beer. No, you need more than a beer. Here, I make you a Bikini Girl. It's a Hong Kong special. Guaranteed to make you happy."

It wasn't easy for someone of Destructive Wang's girth to move through the cabin, but he managed to make his way to the liquor cabinet and within a few minutes was mixing together white rum, lychee puree, cucumber, rosewater, and lychee syrup. He poured the cocktail into a tall glass and handed it to Ishea.

Roger, slightly miffed at not being offered a drink, watched in amazement as Ishea emptied the drink down his throat in one quick gulp.

"Jesus fucking Christ! What the hell is this?"

"You don't like it? You crazy bastard. It's the latest drink in Hong Kong."

"It tastes like the Sugar Plum Fairy pissed in a glass. Now I need to sleep for an hour. Then we need to discuss what happens when we arrive." And with that, he closed his eyes and fell into a deep sleep.

Destructive Wang looked more hurt than annoyed. He took the three-quarters-full bottle of Fiji White Rum and returned to his seat, where he sucked on it like a giant baby and looked out the window. When the bottle was empty, he dropped it on the carpet and began to snore loudly.

Roger felt his eyes closing too, but every time he began to nod off, visions of Conchita Palomino raced through his mind, and he knew he wouldn't sleep till he saw her. Freddy had been purposefully evasive in his explanation as to precisely why Roger had to meet her in Hong Kong but assured Roger that it was necessary and that Ishea would explain everything once they were together. It wasn't a satisfying send off, but Roger had resigned himself to the fact than anything involving Freddy seldom was, and so he settled back, took a long sip of water, and waited for Ishea to wake up. As he was paging through his "new" passport for the tenth time wondering just how Freddy had managed to obtain it from his contact in the American Embassy in Dar es Salaam in under twenty-four hours, Ishea opened his eyes. He grunted at Roger and walked back to the bathroom. When he emerged a few minutes later, he looked quite refreshed for someone who hours earlier had turned a Russian trophy hunter into a chair cover.

"Come and sit here opposite me, Roger, and let's talk."

"What about him?" Roger pointed to Destructive Wang, who was slumped in his chair, drooling copiously.

"Don't worry about Destructive Wang. He's a soldier. He doesn't care about all the details. Now, here's what's going to happen."

"You're implying that this isn't going to be a back-and-forth conversation."

"Good, you're learning. No, I'm going to tell you how things are going to go down, and if you have questions, save them for when we meet up with Conchita. And don't worry—you're going to have plenty of time to catch up with her."

"I'm not sure I like the sound of 'how things are going to go down.'" Roger felt the familiar horror make its way from his head to his bowels. He tried to think of just how many times he'd been overcome with abject horror since that fateful night in Paris when he found himself in the same

155

restaurant face-to-face with his supposedly dead friend, Freddy. He decided it was just too much to contemplate or comprehend, so he slumped back into his seat, gave a long sigh, and waited for Ishea to speak.

"What part of 'no questions' do you not understand?"

"That was more of a statement than a question, but since you ask: quite frankly, all of it. Why do you think you can control my life? It's quite annoying."

Ishea dismissed Roger's response with a shake of his head. "Once we land at Chek Lap Kok Airport and go through customs, we'll be met by one of our associates who'll take us to the house on The Peak where we'll meet Conchita. I'm not sure whether Vixay's men will try to intercept us on the way, but I doubt they'll be that obvious."

"Whoa, hang on a second." Shock multiplied by shock is never a good thing, and Roger's nerves, now shot beyond any obvious means of repair, gave one final spark. "What's this about Vixay's men? Are you telling me they're in Hong Kong?"

"Oh, Jesus. Okay, so obviously Freddy didn't tell you? I thought you seemed remarkably calm for someone with a bunch of blood-thirsty poachers after him." Ishea sniggered in a very uncharacteristic fashion.

"What in God's name is wrong with you guys? I wasn't calm; I was just apprehensive about seeing Conchita. No one said anything about Vixay or his killers. I had no idea those guys would be here."

"Typical of your pal Freddy to let me be the bad guy."

"You are a bad guy, Ishea. You kill people."

If Roger expected Ishea to be pissed off—and he did—he was mistaken. Ishea's chortling commuted down the track towards full-blown laughter, which unnerved Roger even more if that was possible.

"That's actually quite amusing. Know what? I'm kind of beginning to understand you, Roger. Not fully, but a little bit. You're a funny guy. Anyway, to answer your question, which I honestly didn't want to be the one to have to answer, yes. We knew, through our own network, that Vixay had sent out a directive to his organization to be on the lookout for you. I suggested to Freddy that Destructive Wang, with his connections, and I could control the Hong Kong theater better than some other random place."

"So, it wasn't as if Conchita was just here? You pre-arranged the whole thing?"

"I'm not going to lie to you. That's partly true, but it isn't that simple."

"Nothing with you or Freddy ever seems to be."

"That's also true, but in this case there's a good reason for the partial deception. First, Conchita is here and has been for the past six months putting together a new operation involving Vixay Keosavang and two other animal traffickers, The Bach Brothers from Vietnam."

"Never heard of them."

"Ah, but you will."

"Oh, now I get it. You're using me as bait. You know Vixay's looking for me. How very bloody convenient."

"I'm impressed, Roger. I wouldn't have said that deductive reasoning was one of your immediate strengths."

Roger clenched his fists in frustration. He knew Ishea wasn't trying to be an asshole. His assessment of Ishea was that he was mostly incapable of empathy. He was under no illusion that Ishea regarded him as an abject weakling, incapable of looking after himself. And yet there were times, like now, when he felt that Ishea quite liked him. Or "tolerated" may have been more appropriate. He doubted Ishea liked anyone.

At that moment, the pilot came back to tell them to strap in for the landing, and everything but trivial conversation ended until they'd made it through passport control and customs and were in a Mercedes S600 Maybach. They set off toward Gough Hill Road on The Peak, Hong Kong's most exclusive neighborhood, where whatever company Freddy and Conchita now owned had rented a house.

Despite the size of the Maybach, the sheer bulk of Destructive Wang and Ishea made it feel like a clown car to Roger, who remarked, "Hopefully no one attacks us in this car; I'd never be able to squeeze past you to get out."

"Hah," sniggered Destructive Wang. "This car totally bulletproof and bomb-proof too. Just relax. No worries."

"I told you I didn't think they'd attack us on the way from the airport. So now, shut the hell up and enjoy the scenery. You're perfectly safe until I tell you otherwise." Ishea tapped the driver, a much smaller though just-as-tough-looking individual, on the shoulder. "Wang Wei, can you make sure they've got food for us when we get there. I'm starving."

Wang Wei nodded and pushed a button on the steering wheel, which connected him with someone at the apartment. "They want food when we get there," he said into the hidden microphone.

It was a woman who answered, and Roger's heart skipped a beat. He hadn't heard Conchita's voice in over a year, and for a second he wasn't sure. "Tell them not to worry. I have Ishea's favorite dim sum and something extra special for our extra special guest."

"Conchita?" But Roger's question went unanswered as Wang Wei cut the connection before Conchita, if it truly was her, could reply. He turned to Ishea for confirmation. Much to his surprise, Ishea squeezed his shoulder and smiled. He didn't need to say anything.

The house on Gough Hill Road was one of a seven-unit development in what had once been the German consulate. The Maybach made its way up the hill along the narrow street that was lined with exotic vegetation. It seemed like the perfect location to pull off an attack, thought Roger, but both Ishea and Destructive Wang looked remarkably calm as they arrived at a set of heavy wrought-iron gates in front of a very modern house.

The front door was opened by a beautiful Chinese woman whose blue silk dress clung to her body like Saran wrap. "Good morning," she said, giving Ishea a kiss and bowing to Destructive Wang. "I'm Pansy Pong, Conchita's assistant, and you must be Roger Storm." Roger stammered a hello and a gave a lopsided smile. "Ishea and Destructive Wang, the guest rooms are ready, but Roger," she said, taking his hand, "you are to come with me."

Roger didn't hear Ishea's snigger. In fact, he couldn't hear a thing. His veins had begun to throb, and images and

159

sounds boomed in his head as if someone had fired a rocket at a dinner gong. "I should probably wash my face first," he said, thinking how disheveled he must look after the long flight. "And maybe brush my teeth too." He was beginning to panic and was stalling for time. But Pansy just laughed and led him along a corridor to an enclosed patio. Roger closed his eyes in an involuntary reflex, and then he opened them.

Conchita's silver-blonde hair was pulled into a tight updo, and she had a mysterious smile on her face. Roger froze because he couldn't comprehend what it was he was seeing. The woman he'd loved and made love to and tried desperately to save as she toppled to her death from a clifftop in Ethiopia was standing in front of him. She was wrapped in a black silk robe that did little to hide anything. She was, he decided in his brief moment of contemplation before she glided towards him, more beautiful than he had ever imagined in the thousand dreams he'd dreamed over the past year.

He tried to say something, but Conchita's lips stopped his from opening as she pulled his head down, drawing whatever breath he had left from his body. Then they were kissing and holding and groping like lovers who've been separated by more than time and distance, but by death itself.

In many fictitious accounts of frenetic fucking, impetuous lovers embroiled in the act of passion "tear off their clothes." Bodices rip with abandon, and buttons and underwear fly off in all directions. In reality, this is seldom the case. Clothes, at least well-made clothes like those sewn by tailors as competent as Destructive Wang, do not tear easily, and so after a few seconds of struggling, Conchita pushed Roger down on the divan and began to slowly remove his crumpled suit. Roger's tumescent penis, trapped inside his boxers, began to writhe like a cobra woken from a long hibernation, making it difficult for Conchita to divest him of his pants. But where Roger was precipitant, Conchita was deliberate, and within what felt to Roger like hours but was no more than seconds, she'd let her silk robe slip to the floor and climbed on top of him. She was slow and rhythmic, more skilled than any lover Roger had ever known. At first, her body was like an electric blanket, spreading warmth and comfort. Then, as she sensed his impatience, she ground her hips down and brushed his nipples with hers, causing him to buck like a rodeo bull controlled by an expert rider. Whatever performance anxiety he'd felt when he saw her vanished as she reached down between their bodies to take his penis and slowly and deliberately insert him into her wet sex. They started off slowly, but Roger was undisciplined and desperate, and his thrusts became wild and uncontrollable. Eventually, Conchita gave up any semblance of control and began to move at his pace until what began as a slow ripple turned into a convulsive orgasm. She pulled herself forward, allowing his flaccid member to slip out, and rolled over onto her side, staring into Roger's face. She saw his brows crease and his eyes begin to fill with tears. His mouth moved but no words came out. She took his face in her hands and squeezed gently.

"Say nothing, my love. It's better that way. There is too much to say but nothing that matters more than being here with you in this moment. Just know that I never stopped thinking of you." She paused. "Or loving you."

Roger pulled her towards him, marveling at the firmness of her flesh. "I thought you were dead, Conchita."

"I know, and you have no idea how much I wanted to tell you I wasn't."

"But why? I don't understand. Why didn't you? You say you love me—"

"Yes, and for that very reason I couldn't. Freddy and me, we nearly killed you, *mi amor.* I didn't want to put you in danger again."

"And yet, here I am, and you know what? I don't care. I'd rather die with you than live apart from you."

"Oh, my love...." Conchita rolled back on top of him and bit his lower lip. He winced. "Still the baby." She laughed and mashed her pubic patch onto his groin, causing his penis to stir once again.

Roger moved his hands up her thighs to her buttocks, which he squeezed. He'd missed them desperately. They were as round and warm and smooth as butter. The second bout was slower and sloppier, mainly because Roger was exhausted and Conchita was content. It ended before it was really over, but neither of them seemed to care.

"Excuse me, Conchita." Pansy Ho peered in as if two people rutting like aardvarks was a scene she encountered on a daily basis. "But lunch is ready."

Roger squeaked and grabbed the sheet to cover his nakedness, but Conchita laughed, stood up, and walked toward the marble sink at one end of the patio. "Thank you, Pansy. We'll be there in a few minutes." She wet a washcloth with warm water and tossed it to Roger. "Here, do the best you can. We'll shower later."

Ishea and Destructive Wang were already sitting down at the round table on the patio. Both had changed and showered and were looking a lot more refreshed than Roger, who felt decidedly sweaty and disorderly in his crumpled suit. He had a stupid grin on his face, and as hard as he tried not to, he couldn't help smiling as he looked at Conchita. She, despite their half hour of vigorous sex, looked as fresh as a croissant that had just come out the oven. She still wore her black silk robe, slightly more creased than it had been, as she bent down to kiss Ishea and Destructive Wang on their respective cheeks. Both stood up and gave her a hug.

"Sorry to have kept you, my dears, but Roger and I had some catching up to do. Now, I know you must be starving. Pansy," she signaled to her ever-present assistant, "why don't you tell Chef Ho to begin the service. Let us eat, and then we can discuss our plans." She turned to Roger, who was gazing out at the incredible view from The Peak. "Isn't it magnificent?"

Roger, who'd thought he would never see anything that could compete in the "magnificent view" category with the one of the Limpopo and riverine forest from his tent on Hunter's Folly, had to admit that it was. "It's fantastic. I've never seen Hong Kong from this height. Look at the ships!"

"Forget the ships," said Destructive Wang, who'd walked up beside him. "What you need to be looking for is my father's clothing store. You have nearly ruined this suit. I am humiliated."

"I'm sorry," replied Roger, who genuinely felt bad at the state of his clothes. "I'd take it off, but I don't have anything else to wear."

Destructive Wang grunted. "It's okay. I call the store and give them your measurements. You have two new suits and shirts by tonight. Then I'm taking this one and sending it for cleaning."

"That's fantastic, thank you. But I don't have any money on me. I didn't have time to grab my wallet before I was kidnapped."

Destructive Wang slapped him on the back. "You pay me later. After the job. No worries."

Roger turned to Ishea and Conchita, who were arranging what was enough food to feed a small country onto the table from trays held by two waiters. "What job are you all implying I'm going to be doing? I think I should know."

"Of course, my sweet. But come and sit down and eat, and we can tell you what we're doing and where you will help."

From where Ishea and Conchita sat, it looked like Roger was in some kind of food-induced trance as he stared at the myriad bamboo steamers of dim sum and dumplings and dishes of vegetables that covered the round table. Roger was certainly in a trance, but it had very little to do with food. His emotions, which at this stage should have been accustomed to the death-defying rollercoaster that plagued every encounter with Freddy and Conchita and their odd group of colleagues, were spinning around his head, causing partial paralysis of vital parts of his body. Love, rekindled and requited by Conchita, was in a savage fight with Fear, and it was a toss-up which would win. Seconds passed until suddenly the fog lifted and a sense of clarity overcame the confusion. He was not in control of his life, and he hadn't been for a long time—that much was obvious. And yet, as distressing as that should have been, it was strangely comforting. Whatever force in the universe had its fickle finger firmly planted in his ass had got him through the worst horror he'd ever imagined, and for some unknown reason he had the feeling it would do so again if called upon. He smiled, picked up one of the dumplings from an open steamer, and took a bite, scalding his mouth and sending the contents cascading over his shirt.

"That is a soup dumpling, you ignorant *gweilo*," said Destructive Wang. "You don't eat it like that. No more suits for you if you continue to eat your food like some savage."

Ishea didn't even look up, but Conchita laughed and wiped Roger's mouth and shirt with a napkin.

"Here, you look closely," said Destructive Wang, picking up a soup dumpling with his chopsticks and moving it smoothly onto a spoon on which he'd put a few drops of black vinegar sauce. "Then you bite the top so you don't burn your mouth and pop it in. Ha, brilliant." After a few more failures, Roger moved onto dumplings packed with fat shrimp and mushrooms, and barbecued pork buns that melted in his mouth. Dumpling followed dumpling, each more delicious than the last. Crab competed with chicken and black truffle. Potstickers with crispy beef were replaced with lobster and ginger dipped in a fiery chili vinegar. No one said a word until Destructive Wang belched loudly, contemplated the empty steamers, and pushed his chair back. "Okay, we're done. Let's talk." Then his head fell forward and he began to snore.

Chapter 14

IN WHICH ROGER LEARNS ABOUT HIS
POTENTIAL AND/OR IMPENDING DEATH

The House on Gough Hill Road

When the plates and bamboo steamers had been cleared and coffee had been served and they'd woken Destructive Wang and asked him to go and finish his nap somewhere else, Conchita began to tell Roger what she'd been doing for the past few months.

"Do you know how lucrative animal trafficking is today, Roger?"

"No, but I imagine it's ridiculously profitable judging by the number of rhino and elephants being slaughtered on a daily basis."

"It's worth an estimated $23 billion. Not far behind drug, people, and arms smuggling. And it's not just rhinos and elephants. It's lions, tigers, bears, pythons, and pangolins, and different birds too. Thousands and thousands of animals dying to satisfy the illogical needs of some Chinese, Vietnamese, and Laotian morons who believe that a few grains of ground rhino horn mixed with tea can cure a hangover, or help them get an erection, or cure cancer. And the chief architects of this evil empire—the two people I'm determined to destroy—are Vietnamese brothers: Boonchai Bach and Bach Van Limh, who are based in Nakhon Phanom on the Thai side of the Mekong River. Just Google their names if you want to see the extent of their operations."

"I don't know about The Bach Brothers. I thought everyone was talking about Vixay Keosavang," said Roger, putting his coffee cup down and wishing it were a cocktail instead.

"You're right," Ishea said. "But it was a total surprise to come across his son on your game reserve. To be honest, we all thought he'd given up after the US government put up $1 million to end his operation. But he's obviously back in business."

"Yes," said Conchita. "I didn't know either until you killed his son. I didn't even have him on the radar, I was so focused on The Bachs. But everything I've managed to uncover since then suggests they're working with Vixay."

"It's a really complex situation," said Ishea, "and the landscape changes on a daily basis. A few years ago, Vixay and some of the others including a really horrible bastard named Fatty Tiewcharoen owned farms where they slaughtered the animals supplied by The Bach Brothers and shipped the carcasses and parts to Vietnam and China. Now, from what Conchita says and the fact that Vixay's son was in South Africa, it means they're doing the same thing again. And I take it Fatty's involved?"

"Yes, he's definitely been working with The Bach Brothers."

"How do they get away with it? Why don't their governments stop them? It's almost incomprehensible," Roger said.

Conchita shrugged. "A lot of people are trying to stop them. But there's just too much money changing hands, and Laos and Vietnam aren't exactly on the United Nations list of least-corrupt countries. What I've told you, as Ishea pointed out, is just one element of a global criminal enterprise. These men, The Bach Brothers and Fatty, work very closely with white South African farmers who breed lions for hunting. These farmers charge rich Americans $35,000 to hunt the lions and then double-dip by sending the body parts and bones to Thailand to be used in medicine as a cheap alternative to tiger bones. Then the American hunters go back and tell everyone they're encouraging conservation because the meat from the lions supposedly fed an entire village."

"It's hard to know who to hate more. The Bach Brothers of the world, the farmers, or the trophy hunters."

"That's the problem," said Conchita, brushing Roger's arm and causing a jolt of electricity to shoot through his body. "But we can't think in terms of hate, my love. To hate, as Freddy says, is the quickest way to unfocus the mind. What we are doing—me, Freddy, and Ishea, with the help of Destructive Wang and some of the others that survived Ethiopia—is trying to come up with a way to destroy these

169

networks. If we can kill the kingpins—Fatty, The Bachs, and now Vixay—then maybe we can slow things down. We've managed to expose a few of their shipments and even arrange for some of their people to meet untimely ends, so they know we're on to them. I am reasonably sure they want to kill us in return."

"What I don't get, and Freddy said you'd fill me in, is why you're here in Hong Kong?"

"It's a lot easier to set up an operation in Hong Kong than it is in Laos and Thailand. Of course, there's corruption here but a lot less. It's not China yet, but they've imposed some of their anti-corruption programs, so for the most part we have faith in who we're dealing with. Not everyone, but a lot of the people."

"We've set up a trust here called WildWorld Fund," said Ishea. "We sponsor all sorts of ecological programs, mainly in Hong Kong but in other Asian countries too. So we have access to top people and information. Freddy, Conchita, and Destructive Wang are the principals."

Roger wanted desperately to ask just how much money they were talking about but decided it would be inappropriate. At least they weren't back in the arms business. That much he knew from Freddy. "What about trophy hunters? Please tell me they're still on the hit list."

"Yes, but that's a side job for Ishea at the moment while I put the plan together. Look, we may never be able to stop trophy hunting, but we can damage the lion-breeding farmers by drying up one of the sources of income. And then maybe, if we manage to do that, we can start taking them out too."

Silence followed, and Roger could sense that Ishea was waiting for him to start whining about the danger he was about to be put in. But he didn't because whatever epiphany had hit him during the meal still filled him with an un-flustered serenity that he only ever experienced when he smoked a joint while sitting on the porch of his tent looking over at the Limpopo. The idea that he could be involved in something as vital to the survival of all the things he loved and lived for was both intriguing and thrilling. It was a feeling as surprising to him as it would have been to anyone who'd ever known him in his past life.

"Okay, so now tell me how I fit in. What's my role? And I understand this is going to be hard for you to comprehend, Ishea, but I really do want to help."

"Hmm, not the reaction I was expecting," said Ishea, raising a quizzical eyebrow. "What did you do to him before lunch, Conchita? No, I'm not sure I really want to know, but I believe you finally fucked the fear out of him."

Conchita's reaction caught Roger by surprise. She began to laugh. It began as a quiet little laugh and then intensified into a full-on guffaw. Roger had seen her smile and he'd heard her giggle, but he'd never really experienced her laugh. It was high and cheerful and seemed to emanate deep within her breasts. It came out her mouth and her nose until fat tears ran down her cheeks. "Oh, Ishea, I knew you'd come around. I think for the first time you're seeing the real Roger."

At that moment, Roger's heart melted into his rib cage, and then he too began to laugh because he knew that Ishea had finally accepted him.

"I think," said Conchita, "this momentous occasion calls for a drink."

As if on cue, Destructive Wang sauntered up. "Aha, you want drinks?"

"Yes," replied Ishea, "but not that shit you gave me on the plane."

"Don't worry, you uncultured slug. I will make you the best martini you've ever had."

"Make that two," Roger said.

"Three," said Conchita. "Then come back, Destructive. We have work to do.

"So, Roger, you asked what your role will be. I don't know because Ishea and I haven't even discussed the details yet. All I can say is that you being here is probably the most important and opportune factor in making this whole thing work. But I have to tell you: It will be dangerous if we don't plan everything perfectly. And I don't want you to be in danger because I don't intend to lose you."

"Bottom line," said Ishea before Roger could kiss Conchita, which he desperately wanted to do, "is that we need you to flush out Vixay and hopefully The Bach Brothers, who we think will help him because their Hong Kong network is a lot stronger than his. If we can get them all together in one place, then maybe we have a chance."

"They don't seem like the kind of people who'd help if there's no money in it for them."

"Perhaps," said Conchita, "but as I said, they know that I'm after them, and by now they also know that we—you, me, and Ishea—are connected. And if they know that, then maybe they will work together to try to destroy us."

172

"How would they know that we're together?"

"Oh, trust me, they know you, Destructive Wang, and I arrived together early today. They'll have one or two customs officials on their payrolls, and we were followed from the airport. A silver-grey Toyota Corolla with two men. No more than a scouting party."

"It seems I am just in time to enlighten you," said Destructive Wang, who had four martini glasses and a cocktail shaker the size of a small fire hydrant precariously balanced on a large tray. "While I was mixing up the best martinis you've ever tasted—even for the uncultured Ishea—I received phone call. A very enlightening phone call. But first...." He set the glasses down, shook the cocktail shaker a few times, and filled the four glasses. "Here, try this. I make it with Strane Ultra Cut Gin. 165 proof. Strongest gin in the world. You sip slowly or your head explode."

Destructive Wang wasn't kidding. Roger took a small sip and his eyes began to water. He could taste hints of mint and lime, but the alcohol was overpowering. He looked over at Ishea and Conchita. Neither appeared to be in any distress, and Roger decided they were made of sterner stuff when it came to liquor. Destructive Wang on the other hand had already knocked his back and was pouring himself another.

"So, what was this mysterious phone call about?" asked Ishea.

"From an old colleague in the Flying Tigers. He tell me Vixay Keosavang landed in Hong Kong this morning and was met by a young man named Devil Lam. I don't know him. This means whatever he has planned for my timid friend Roger is imminent."

"Shit," gulped Roger, feeling his balls ascend into his pelvis.

"I won't let him get to you. No worries."

Roger gulped a few more times. He looked at the huge man and decided that while Destructive Wang could probably hold off a small army, he was not reassured in the least. He took a deep breath, determined not to show fear in front of Conchita. "Thank you, I appreciate that, but obviously I have to put myself out there." His attempt at sounding calm didn't fool anyone.

Chapter 15

In which nasty people consider nasty things to do to Roger Storm and others

Vixay Keosavang's headquarters near Wong Chuk Hang

There are not many places in Hong Kong that still qualify as *seedy*. Wong Chuk Hang may indeed have been one a few years ago, but the trendy restaurants and fashionable businesses and galleries were quickly replacing all of the things that had made the gritty South Side industrial area appealing to Vixay Keosavang and his associates ten years before. Their headquarters, hidden inside a large, ugly concrete block that had once been a commercial printing company, had ample space for both the unfortunate caged animals and the parts that had already been separated from their slaughtered relatives. Tight security and lots of money had ensured it was off the radar for both the Hong Kong Police and the Customs Anti-Smuggling Bureau.

Vixay sat at a round table in his glass office overlooking the warehouse floor eating a bowl of noodles that Devil

175

Lam had picked up at The Green Curry House. He put his spoon down, spat a mouthful of noodles onto the floor, and pushed the bowl aside. "This food isn't fit for a pig. Why couldn't you get me some proper food?"

"I'm sorry, Boss," replied Devil Lam, who was enjoying his curry, "but it's hard to find anything authentic around here anymore. All these new fancy restaurants, gyms, art galleries . . . they've pushed all the old places out. You wouldn't believe it."

"It's sickening at what's happening to the world. Nothing's good enough anymore. Everyone has to be pure and clean and environmentally conscious. You know, it's almost impossible to bribe an official under the age of thirty-five? I'm not sure how long we'll be able to even operate here."

Devil Lam did not know either. His position as a lowly chauffeur and general factotum did not expose him to information relating to bribes or other important facts. He was quite surprised that Vixay was even talking to him. The man had an awful reputation when it came to his employees, and Devil Lam was terrified by some of the stories. And yet here he was, sitting with one of the greatest animal trafficking kingpins, having a reasonable discussion about the state of the world. Perhaps the stories were simple fabrications. But his illusion was about to be shattered.

"Where are The Bach Brothers? They should have been here by now."

Devil Lam looked at his phone. "It's just five minutes to one, Boss. They promised they'd be here by 1:30. I wouldn't worry if I were you."

"Oh, you wouldn't, wouldn't you?"

"No, Boss. I'm sure they'll be here on time."

"Oh, excuse me, are you perhaps a therapist?"

"No, Boss—"

"So, you are simply contradicting me?"

"Not at all, Boss. I'm just—" Devil Lam froze in horror as Vixay picked up a heavy electric cattle prod from the desk and walked towards him. At that moment, Devil Lam knew he was screwed. Everything he'd heard about Vixay Keosavang was true. He was unhinged under normal circumstances and present circumstances were most definitely not normal. The death of his son and two top lieutenants had moved him along the "insane to off-his-fucking-rocker" continuum. Devil Lam noticed little bits of spittle beginning to form at Vixay's mouth, and his eyes began to blink at an alarming rate.

Please let him be having a stroke, thought Devil Lam, trying desperately to disappear into his chair. Vixay flicked a switch on the cattle prod, which was normally used to ensure cooperation from uncooperative animals, and held it inches away from his unfortunate employee's eye.

"You sperm-spewing sea slug. How dare you contradict me?"

"Please, Boss, I'm so sorry—"

"So, now you're sorry?"

"Yes, Boss. Please forgive me."

"Okay," said Vixay, putting the prod back down on the desk. "That's all you had to say. Just a simple sorry. Was that so hard? You know, I respect polite people. Your uncle was very polite. That's why I gave you this job when he was bitten by that black mamba. 'Please Khun Vixay,' he said, just before his jaw seized and his lungs collapsed. 'Please will you look after my nephew?' When I nodded, he said, 'Thank you.' Then he died. When your final words are 'thank you,' then you qualify as polite in my book. Now, where are The Bachs?"

Devil Lam took a deep breath. He had no illusions as to just how close he'd come to never needing glasses again. "Thank you, Boss. I will call to find out."

"Very good," said Vixay with a smile. "That's what I call polite and enterprising. I would say you have a future in my organization, but my gut feel is I'd be wrong. We'll see."

Devil Lam was still quivering from fear and having a hard time hitting "call." Fortunately for him, at that very moment the front door bell rang. Both he and Vixay looked at the screen that monitored the various cameras around the warehouse and saw both Bach Brothers with four of their body guards waiting at the front door.

"Well don't just sit there. Let them in, you brainless idiot."

Devil Lam jumped out of his chair and ran down the stairs to the heavy metal doors. He punched a keypad and then unlocked the door. He bowed deeply to both Boonchai Bach and Bach Van Limh, who walked past him without even acknowledging his presence. The bodyguards sneered at him and followed their bosses up the stairs to the office. For the umpteenth time since he started working for Vixay, Devil Lam cursed his dead uncle. He hated this job. He loathed Vixay and everyone he was associated with, and he couldn't sleep at night when he thought of the poor animals suffering in the cages. Like him, they were trapped in a world they couldn't escape.

Devil Lam locked the door, making sure to re-arm the explosive device that would be triggered if the correct security code wasn't entered on the hidden keyboard. Then he slowly and reluctantly walked upstairs. He didn't know exactly why Vixay was meeting with The Bachs. All he'd been told by his immediate superior, Feng Mian, who had returned to the mainland the previous night to attend to his dying father, was to pick Vixay up from the airport and get him to the warehouse for a meeting with The Bach Brothers at 1:30. Devil Lam did not expect to be included in the meeting, but no one seemed to notice him at the back of the room. Vixay had produced a bottle of Johnny Walker Blue Label, and the three kingpins were drinking but not laughing. There was no small talk.

"So," said Boonchai, "we have a mutual interest in destroying these filthy foreigners. My brother and I understand your pain and need for revenge on the man responsible for your son's death."

"But," said his older brother, "that cannot interfere with our plan to kill Conchita Palomino. She has caused our business irreparable harm."

Vixay didn't respond for a moment. Then he reached into his bulky leather briefcase and removed the Lucite box containing the preserved nose of his son. He placed it on the table between The Bach Brothers and himself.

"This…." he said. "This is all that remains of my son."

Bach Van Limh picked up the box and examined it closely. Then he looked at Vixay. "Hmm, your son had your nose, that's for sure."

"And now," said his brother, "you have his."

"That's true," replied Vixay. "It's better than nothing, I suppose. But I'm sure you can understand my need for revenge."

"Of course, of course, my friend." Boonchai's tone was conciliatory though devoid of sympathy. "What father would not want revenge? And no one can ignore the removal of a nose. That's too big an insult. We just want to make sure that you can be equally focused on the destruction of this woman, Conchita Palomino, and her compatriots for the sake of all our businesses. If you can assure us of that, then we can work together. After all, you are one of our oldest partners, and we envisage continuing our relationship."

"Excellent," said Vixay, refilling everyone's glass. "I am content to work with you on the destruction of this woman and her team so long as at the end I have that despicable pig testicle Roger Storm in my hands either in this warehouse or back in Laos for extreme torture."

"I believe we can guarantee that, and perhaps if you're willing, we can arrange a joint torture session for he and Conchita Palomino. I find those so much more enjoyable. People screaming in unison."

"You know," said Bach Van Limh, looking very pleased with himself, "maybe we can turn this whole thing into a torture party by killing some animals at the same time. Have you heard a sun bear cry when you remove its gall bladder? Pure music."

"I love it," Vixay said, pouring the last of the Scotch into their glasses. "And I will make contact with the one person who can set up the ambush."

"And who might that be?"

"Ah, not just yet. Let's just say he is a very high ranking official whose credentials are beyond reproach. We'll give him a call tomorrow morning when we're ready." He turned to Devil Lam, who'd heard every word. "Devil Lam, make yourself useful. Don't just stand there like a lazy fool—go to the liquor store and get more whisky. This is a time to celebrate."

Devil Lam didn't even ask for money. He bowed deeply and rushed once again down the stairs. The talk of torture, especially that of the animals, had almost caused him to throw up. He knew then he couldn't do this job anymore and decided then and there that he would have to do something about it. He wondered if there was a way to get to Conchita Palomino and warn her.

Chapter 16

IN WHICH INSPECTORS BUNTER AND DARMSTAEDTER FORM THE FIRST ALLIANCE

A Dim Sum restaurant in Hong Kong

The iclub Sheung Wan Hotel on Bonham Strand, Hong Kong, is a modern hotel near Victoria Peak. Bunter's Interpol connections had enabled him and Darmstaedter to get excellent rates on business class rooms. They were both exhausted after the eleven-hour flight from Munich that had arrived in Hong Kong at 16:30 but had decided to accept a dinner invitation from Inspector Norman Fok of the Hong Kong Police Force Organized Crime and Triad Bureau.

"Norman Fok," Bunter informed Darmstaedter as they walked from the hotel to the IFC Mall, "worked with me in Lyon when he was seconded there a few years ago. He's a jolly nice chap, and he's already working on finding Roger Storm and Ishea Payamps. And he won't get away this time. Of that I have no doubt."

"Perhaps, but my head tells me it isn't going to be any easier than it's been so far. We must focus on the animal traffickers. Payamps and Palomino will be the dessert."

"Ah, look. Here we are. I believe this is the restaurant."

"Tim Ho Wan? This looks like a fast food restaurant." Darmstaedter was not a huge fan of Chinese food.

"Yes, it does, but it's supposed to be the world's cheapest Michelin Star restaurant, so I'm sure it's excellent."

"Ja, well, just so you are clear, Matthew, I am not eating anything from above the neck, below the knee, or from somewhere deep inside whatever beast they are serving."

"You can't be rude to Norman, Constantin. We need him."

"I understand, but I promise you: He will consider me less rude if I don't eat certain things than if I projectile vomit all over him."

"That's pretty disgusting," snorted Bunter. "Well, it's famous for its dumplings and buns, so I'm sure you'll find something. And speak of the devil, there's Norman now."

Norman Fok—dressed in a black suit, white shirt, and black tie—looked exactly like the classic detective, one who could blend into a crowd in seconds. He rushed up to Matthew and much to Constantin's surprise gave him a big hug. "Matthew, my dear friend, how good it is to see you after all these years. And this must be Inspector Constantin Darmstaedter? It is excellent to make your acquaintance." He shook Darmstaedter's hand enthusiastically. "Welcome to Hong Kong. I hope you are hungry and prepared for some of the best Dim Sum you have ever eaten. Come, let us go in. It is not too crowded because Dim Sum is more a lunchtime food."

While Fok and Bunter caught up, Darmstaedter looked at the yellow paper menu. His eye immediately went to the "Steamed Pork Balls topping with pig's liver and pork belles." He knew what balls were and he knew what liver was (though *belles* stumped him), and he realized he was going to go to bed hungry.

"Allow me to order," said Fok. "I'll make sure you get to taste the most delicious things on the menu."

"Please do not think of me as being rude, Herr Inspector Fok, but my stomach is very sensitive after the flight, and I think I will just eat some rice."

"No problem," said Fok. "I understand perfectly. Perhaps you will feel better tomorrow. I know a place that serves some of the best chicken feet and snake soup on the planet."

"I doubt it," Darmstaedter whispered to Bunter, who pretended not to hear.

Small talk ensued until Bunter and Fok were well into their fifth plate of dumplings and Darmstaedter was still picking away at his rice, wishing to hell he could at least get a beer to go with it.

"So, down to business, gentlemen." Fok put down his chopsticks and took off his thick black-rimmed glasses, which he began to polish with a big white handkerchief. "You'll be pleased to hear that I know exactly where Roger Storm is at this very moment. And it's not that far from here. My suggestion, if you are up to it, is that we finish our meal and pay them an unannounced fact-finding visit."

"Who exactly is *them*, Norman?"

"Ah, yes. *Them* includes Conchita Palomino. Ah, I see that name rings a bell?"

"Yes," replied Bunter. "A rather large bell. But do tell us who else before we return to Ms. Palomino."

"Also at the house is a highly decorated and well-respected ex-Flying Tiger named Destructive Wang, and one of Ms. Palomino's colleagues, a man whose name you will also recognize immediately: Ishea Payamps. Wang, Payamps, and Storm flew to Hong Kong early yesterday morning."

"So," said Bunter, "It seems that we're finally going to get to lay hands on Ishea Payamps."

"Not hands," replied Fok. "Eyes only. You cannot touch him."

"We'll see about that."

"Yes," replied Fok, misinterpreting Bunter. "Only eyes."

Bunter ignored him. "But even more surprising, Conchita Palomino *is* alive. Well, I suppose we suspected as much all along, Constantin."

"Indeed," replied his colleague. "And, of course, that brings up the possibility of Freddy Blank being alive too?"

"I know that name," replied Fok. "I believe, if my memory serves me, that he is part of the Trust."

"Trust? You mean PaloMar?"

"I don't know PaloMar. No, I mean WildWorld Trust. They rent the house we'll be visiting and are the biggest supporters of our ecological education programs. Conchita Palomino and Freddy Blank are listed as the founding partners, but we have no record of Freddy Blank ever entering Hong Kong."

"Very little computes here." Darmstaedter scratched his head with his chopstick, depositing a few grains of rice just above his eyebrow. "This WildWorld—is it legitimate?"

"As far as we can tell. They support numerous programs in Hong Kong. They also offer grants to organizations involved in animal welfare, ecology, and the prevention of deforestation in many parts of Asia. Obviously, they have vast sums of money to be able to do what they do. The house is one of the most expensive pieces of real estate in Hong Kong. Which actually makes it one of the priciest pieces of real estate in the world. I cannot even begin to imagine what the rent for such magnificence is."

Bunter whistled. "I wonder if they're back in the arms business?"

"That I don't know, Matthew. What I do know is that they spend a lot and give generously and therefore, as you can imagine, they are most welcome here. So—and I want to emphasize *so*—there can be no arrests, or even talk of arrests. Your visit can be nothing more than to check up on Roger Storm. If we need to be more assertive, you will have to leave that to me."

"Ja, ja," said Darmstaedter. "This we know. To be honest, Norman—if I may call you that—Matthew and I realize we have no case against either Conchita Palomino or Ishea Payamps. We never have had. As much as we'd like to bring them to trial on charges ranging from murder to illegal arms dealing in any number of countries, they have proved to be far too clever. The evidence against them is almost impossible to verify and circumstantial at best. No, at this stage, we see this as a possible breakthrough into the prosecution of The Bach Brothers and Vixay Keosavang only. Which ultimately, if I may speak frankly, will be a most satisfactory outcome."

Bunter looked at Darmstaedter as if he were insane. They had every intention of nabbing Ishea and Conchita if the opportunity presented itself. Then Darmstaedter winked at him. Bunter didn't understand why, but he appreciated how smart his colleague was and decided to play along.

"Well, that's good to hear, and you have the backing of my entire team on this so long as you follow protocol."

"Of course," Bunter said. "There are so many different angles and aspects to this case that it's almost impossible to put everything together. Ishea Payamps, Conchita Palomino, Freddy Blank—aside from the fact that they've killed or been involved in the assassination of a bag load of highly undesirable people—have evaded us and numerous police forces in Africa for years and no doubt will continue to do so. Roger Storm is just a silly bugger who seems to end up in the middle of everything through no fault of his own. Getting as much as we can on The Bach Brothers and Vixay, as Constantin says, is probably the best we can hope for."

"Well, we too are most interested in these individuals along with their partner, Fatty Tiewcharoen. There is no doubt in my mind that they use Hong Kong as the entry to China. Unfortunately, and despite our best efforts, we've never been able to penetrate any of their organizations. But if all of this provides an opportunity to finally get enough evidence to make arrests, then it will be, as the Americans say, a win-win."

"I am uncertain as to why you have been unsuccessful, Norman," Constantin said. "With all of the power at your fingertips, it seems inconceivable. After all, these people are no more than gangsters." Something about Fok made him uneasy. He couldn't put his finger on it. Perhaps it was no more than exhaustion.

"These gangsters, as you rightly call them, have more tentacles into government than you can imagine. The organization that's had the most success in exposing them is the Freeland Foundation in Bangkok. They have been able to unmask a number of The Bachs' deplorable acts. Not just animal trafficking but human trafficking too. The only problem with the Freeland Foundation, unlike everything you have told me about Ishea Payamps and Conchita Palomino, is that they are legitimate. Unfortunately, legitimate organizations have a hard time in Laos and Thailand, where corruption and bribery run rampant and ensure protection for these traffickers. I am ashamed to say that to a much smaller degree the same happens both here and on the mainland, and this causes enormous difficulties every step of the way. Perhaps, and do not quote me on this, the methodology of WildWorld may be the most effective. Now, let me get the bill, and I will call my driver to take us to the house on Gough Hill Road."

On the ride from the mall to the top of The Peak, Bunter and Darmstaedter explained to Fok their endless frustration in trying to collect enough evidence against Ishea

Payamps for the murders of the various trophy hunters and other animal abusers around the world.

"Sometimes it seems impossible to distinguish good from bad," said Matthew. "We know Ishea Payamps is motivated by what he and the others see as essential to saving the world's wild animals, but his methods are wrong."

"I understand. Playing God is a dangerous game. Even if you are God."

"Or believe you are," said Darmstaedter. Fok made him decidedly uncomfortable. It was as if he knew precisely how things would pan out before they'd even discussed a plan. He decided to apply his extraordinary methods of observation just as Sherlock Holmes would have done. He almost slapped himself for even thinking of that name.

Chapter 17

IN WHICH INSPECTORS BUNTER AND DARMSTAEDTER PROPOSE THEIR SECOND ALLIANCE

The House on Gough Hill Road

The arrival of the three police inspectors coincided with the pouring of the first pre-dinner cocktails. It was Pansy Pong who interrupted Destructive Wang, whose skills as a mixologist, Roger decided, were only exceeded by his skills as a tailor.

"I am so sorry to interrupt, Conchita, but there are three police officers here who would like to talk to all of you. Only one is from Hong Kong, an Inspector Norman Fok—"

"I know Norman," said Destructive Wang. "Tell him to come in. He, unlike Ishea, appreciates my martinis."

"Whoa!" Ishea held up a giant hand. "Before we start inviting people in for drinks, who are the other two?"

Pansy looked at the business cards in her hand. "Inspector Matthew Bunter of Interpol and Inspector Constantin Darmstaedter of the Bundeskriminalamt in Wiesbaden."

"How the hell did they know I'd be here?" asked Roger, who was wearing one of the new suits that had been delivered from Destructive Wang's father's store. He was still wearing flip flops and was beginning to like the insouciant appearance they gave to the rest of his outfit. Even Conchita had remarked how interesting he looked that afternoon before she divested him of it and fucked what was left of his brains out.

"Well, let's find out, shall we?" Conchita said. "We have nothing to hide, and I promise you, Roger, nothing to worry about either. We are more than welcome here in Hong Kong. I swear to you that no one is going to harm you."

"Maybe," Roger said, rubbing his temple. His lovemaking with Conchita the previous night and that day had left him feeling quite chipper up until this latest bombshell. The self-doubt was receding, and his desire to spend the rest of his life with Conchita was stronger than ever.

"But what about you, Ishea? They were pretty adamant in South Africa that they had evidence against you."

"As they and various others have thought they've had for a long time. I'm not in the least concerned. Whatever they suspect I've done, they have absolutely no proof. I'm very careful, and that's how I've survived for so long. Conchita's right. Just relax."

"So, what do I tell them? The last thing they know is that I was kidnapped by Vixay Keosavang's thugs. I did send

Gosego a message to say I was safe and with friends. But I never mentioned who."

"They aren't stupid. They'll know I was involved in your rescue. We just have to be careful not to lie about it. If we need to construct a scenario, I will do so. You shouldn't attempt to explain anything you don't have to. In fact, say nothing. Let's see how they handle this."

As it turned out, Roger didn't have to fabricate much at all. Inspectors Darmstaedter and Bunter did it for him.

Pansy showed the policemen in, and after the initial introductions, Darmstaedter turned to Roger. "I'm very glad to see you alive, Roger. How lucky you were to have friends like Herr Payamps, to rescue you."

"I'm lucky to have friends to take care of me—lots of friends. You wouldn't believe how many. Tons of friends all over in the most unlikely places." Ishea glared at him, and he realized he should shut up.

"Relax, Roger." Bunter shook his hand. "We know what happened, and we aren't here to question or accuse anyone of anything. We aren't going to grill you either. Our biggest concern in coming here was to make sure you were alive. That was a particularly nasty situation you were put in."

"Yes, it was. And as I recall, you, Constantin, and Nagesh were the guys who put me in it in the first place."

"Yes, we did. Or at least we were going to. But someone else did it for us." Matthew looked at Ishea, who brushed him off with a bored expression on his normally impassive face.

"And you, Ms. Palomino," Matthew said, turning to Conchita, "are to be congratulated as to the current state of your mortality. Last we'd heard, you'd fallen off a cliff in Ethiopia."

"Ah, yes. That was unfortunate. But as you can see, I survived and am quite fine."

"I do not suppose," Darmstaedter said, "that you know what has happened to Freddy Blank?"

"The good news, Inspector Darmstaedter, is that he too survived. Unfortunately, he is completely paralyzed, or I'm sure he'd be here to greet you. Together, as you may already have discovered, we have set up a charitable trust here in Hong Kong."

"I'm sorry to hear about Freddy. But yes, The WildWorld Trust. Inspector Fok has explained it. Most commendable."

Roger thought the whole situation was weird and uncomfortable. Everyone knew everything, but no one was saying it. Suddenly, the all-too-familiar nervousness that had taken over his vital organs so many times in the past few years welled up. His fingers began to tingle, and he experienced a shortness of breath. Just when he was sure the policemen would notice, Destructive Wang, who'd said nothing until then other than a quick hello to Inspector Fok, jumped to the rescue.

"Inspectors! None of you are on duty. That is clear. So, now I make you all a pre-dinner cocktail, and I will not take no for an answer. Especially from you, Norman Fok."

"Well, technically, my dear Wang," replied Fok, "we are always on duty. But seeing as this is more of a social visit than an official one, I will indeed have one of your cocktails." He turned to Darmstaedter and Bunter. "Destructive Wang was not only one of the most highly decorated members of the Flying Tigers, but he is renowned for his ability to mix cocktails."

"Okay," said Matthew. "Just a quick one because we don't want to interrupt your dinner. But we do have a few things that you can help us with."

When everyone had a drink—martinis made with an odd-tasting grape vodka distilled at a small winery on the shore of Lake Michigan for everyone other than Darmstaedter and Ishea, who were drinking beer—Inspector Fok revealed the purpose of the visit.

"None of us have need to cover old ground, especially what happened in South Africa other than as it relates to issues that I and my two colleagues will outline. What we would like very much to do is get your cooperation on our investigations into the operations of The Bach Brothers, Vixay Keosavang, and Fatty Tiewcharoen. What I can tell you is that they are all—other than Fatty—here in Hong Kong, and we suspect that their aim is to kidnap and kill you, Mr. Storm."

"Yeah, well that's been the case from the minute Ish—" He nearly said Ishea but managed to save himself. "The minute whomever it was shoved a rhino horn through the back of Vixay's son's head. I have to say, for someone who'd had absolutely nothing to do with anything, I seem to be the prime patsy of everyone's desire for revenge or blood."

"Your situation is indeed unfortunate," Darmstaedter said, taking a swig of his beer. "And yet as Freud said, 'Nothing comes out of the blue.' The situations you constantly find yourself in are as a direct result of your inability or

195

perhaps lack of desire to extract yourself from company that is so, how shall I say, provocative."

"I'm not exactly sure what you mean?"

"Pardon my use of English. It is not always perfect. I mean only that the company you seem to find yourself in is extremely stimulating."

While Roger was confused as to Darmstaedter's meaning, Bunter was not. He'd seen the way Constantin had eyed Conchita the minute they'd walked in. Jesus, he thought, the bastard's at it again. The man's libido is insatiable. "Just ignore Constantin. He's so abominably jet-lagged even a man with a brain like his gets muddled. This is a damn fine drink, Destructive, if I may call you that."

Destructive Wang nodded.

"So," said Ishea, "now that we've got the bullshit out the way and you've established that Roger is alive—for the moment at least—how do you think we can help you?"

"I think," Inspector Fok said, taking off his glasses and cleaning them for the umpteenth time, "that we need to understand what each of us knows about these criminals. I realize we have imposed on you and that may not be possible to achieve tonight, but what I would like to do is establish some ground rules."

Conchita put down her martini. It was not an abrupt put down, but every man in the room turned to her. "Inspectors Bunter, Fok, and Darmstaedter: We are very flattered that you would consider coming to us. But I hope you don't believe that we have any intention of committing any acts, legal or illegal, towards the *criminals*, as you call them, Inspector Fok. As you know, WildWorld is involved in many ecologically oriented undertakings, including the exposure of animal trafficking. And naturally, any information we have or get will be passed on to the authorities. So, I am not sure what it is that you're asking us."

"We do appreciate that, Ms. Palomino," said Bunter, "and yes, as Mr. Payamps says, we should dispense with the bullshit. Constantin and I are here as guests of Inspector Fok and the Hong Kong Police Department, and as such have no jurisdiction. As you all know, we have long suspected you, Mr. Payamps, of a number of killings over the past few years. Whether we will ever find proof is pretty much up in the air. Quite frankly, at this point neither of us really care. No, that's not entirely true. We do care as sworn officers of the law. But at this moment in time more than anything else, we'd like to get enough evidence to be able to help put away The Bachs and Keosavang and his cohorts, and effect the shut-down of their organizations. We feel that would serve the greater good. We know you have information and resources at your disposal that we may not have."

"What sort of resources?" Ishea asked.

"Him," replied Bunter, pointing at Roger. "He is the resource we'd like to use to help capture them. We need to use him as bait."

"Why not?" Roger stood up and walked over to the window. "By all means, use me as bait. That's become my primary purpose in life, to be the worm at the end of everyone's line and hook."

"Excellent," said Darmstaedter, failing to hear the irony in Roger's voice. "I must congratulate you, Roger, for your bravery and sense of civic duty."

"Absolutely not!" Conchita joined Roger. She took his hand and kissed him on the cheek. "No one is using him as bait. He's been through more than enough."

"My dear Ms. Palomino." Inspector Fok put down his martini and walked up to Conchita. He was not a tall man, and he came up to just below her nose. But all the pretense of friendship and goodwill vanished as he looked her in the eye. "This is neither a suggestion nor a friendly request. I can with one phone call make sure that you are forced to leave Hong Kong within twenty-four hours. I can tie up your assets here, including this magnificent property. I can arrest Mr. Payamps on suspicion of murder and have him extradited to certain African countries that still employ the death penalty."

Inspector Fok was not used to foreigners challenging his authority. He looked around the room with his dark eyes as if daring any of them to confront him. Roger swallowed as he saw Ishea clench his massive fists, but Ishea's face didn't change at all, and much to Roger's amazement he simply smiled back at Fok. Bunter had turned away as if embarrassed by their colleague's threat, but Darmstaedter narrowed his eyes and examined Fok carefully. Conchita clicked her tongue and held Roger's hand even tighter. It was Destructive Wang who surprised everyone. But then, he was not a *gweilo*.

He stood up slowly, his enormous frame exiting the leather armchair like a blackhead from a particularly deep pore, and lumbered over to Fok. The blow from his open hand was so unexpected and so loud that Roger jumped. Fok did not. He crumpled to the floor where he lay, his glasses broken and his left cheek resembling a split pomegranate. "Mein Gott in Himmel," yelled Darmstaedter, who was the first to react. "What have you done?"

Destructive Wang ignored him, bent down, grabbed Inspector Fok's tie and pulled him upright, almost strangling him in the process. Then he steadied Fok, who looked as if he'd keel over at any moment, straightened his tie, and lowered his face until his eyes were level with Fok's. "Your impudence is unacceptable. You dare to come into this house and act like some peasant farmer who has not learned manners? Now you will apologize to Ms. Palomino immediately, or I will see you are sent to Xingtai, where you will work as a traffic inspector and die from pollution within a year. Do you understand?"

Roger almost wet his pants. This wasn't going well at all. Even Ishea pursed his lips in a surprised whistle. Then much to everyone's surprise, Fok took a step back, bowed to Destructive Wang, and turned to Conchita. "My humble apologies, Ms. Palomino. I hope you can forgive me. My impertinence was driven by my eagerness to rid the world of Vixay Keosavang and The Bach Brothers. My delivery was ill-thought-out." He tried desperately to balance his broken glasses on the end of his nose but failed.

Conchita shook her head in disbelief. Then she let go of Roger's hand and walked back to the couch and sat down. It was clear from the ensuing silence that no one knew what to say. Bunter, to his credit, walked over to Inspector Fok and patted him on the back. Then Conchita spoke.

"Inspector Fok. I appreciate your apology and I accept it. I hope in the future that we can maintain a level of decorum that will be beneficial to both our objectives. My aim and that of my colleagues is the same as yours. We do wish to rid the world of these criminals, as you call them. Now it is time for our dinner. My colleagues and I will discuss how we can work together and contact you tomorrow. Is that acceptable, Inspectors Bunter and Darmstaedter?"

"Ja, of course," replied Darmstaedter, standing up quickly and joining Bunter, who was helping a still-dazed Fok towards the door. "We look forward to hearing from you. Let me give you my card."

"That's unnecessary," said Destructive Wang, who used his body to herd the confused Inspectors out the room. "We already have a card. We will contact you should we decide to go further."

Twenty minutes later, after Fok, who'd said nothing on the ride, had dropped them off at their hotel, Darmstaedter and Bunter were sitting in the bar trying desperately to make sense of the evening.

"Most unusual behavior if you ask me, Constantin. Wouldn't be tolerated back home."

"Ja, in my experience it's usually the police who slap the suspects. I must tell you, Matthew, that there are things going on that are beyond 'unusual' as you say. I must think on it tonight, and I will enlighten you in the morning."

A similar though more enlightening conversation was about to take place at the house on Gough Hill Road, where Roger, Ishea, and Conchita were eating Peking Duck expertly carved by Destructive Wang, who was pouring the last of the Bockenauer Felseneck Spatlese Riseling into his own glass. "This is such a good wine with the duck. High acidity. Dissolves the fat. Really excellent."

"Look," Roger said putting down his chopsticks. "I realize none of you may want to discuss what just happened, but I honestly need to know."

"It's not a big deal, my confused friend," replied Destructive Wang, shoveling what looked like half a duck into his mouth. "My uncle calls Norman 'Upstart Fok.' He is in constant need of reminding of his position. That's all I did. I am sure he is used to it."

"Good God. Who's your uncle?"

"He is the Secretary of Security for Hong Kong. You'll like him. I introduce the two of you soon."

Roger gave a polite smile and decided not to pursue the subject. He was used to being surrounded by lunatics, and on reflection this was no different to any number of dinners with Conchita, Freddy, and the mysterious friends that attended them.

"What we do need to talk about," said Ishea, "is how we use you to lure The Bachs and Vixay into a place where we can take them out."

"Hang on." Roger put down his wine glass. "Conchita said I'd been through enough. And I couldn't agree with her more."

"No, my darling. I said that to the policemen. Unfortunately, we do need you to do this. But I promise you," she reached over and kissed him again, "I won't let anyone hurt you."

But once again, like all the other people who'd promised Roger he'd be safe, she was wrong.

Chapter 18

IN WHICH DEVIL LAM PUTS HIS ESCAPE PLAN INTO ACTION AND A TRAITOR IS EXPOSED

The headquarters of Vixay Keosavang
The next morning

Vixay Keosavang was having a hard time keeping down the preserved egg and salt pork congee that Devil Lam had secured for him, The Bach Brothers, and their bodyguards earlier that morning. All three of the kingpins had awful hangovers after washing down mountains of yellow crab curry with four bottles of Johnny Walker Blue Label at Mango Tree, Boonchai Bach's favorite Thai restaurant.

"What's wrong, Vixay?" asked Bach Van Limh. "You can't handle your liquor?"

"Of course I can," responded the queasy Laotian. "My stomach is a little sensitive, that's all. It's been that way since I was a child. Devil Lam!"

"Yes, Boss?" Devil Lam had been hanging out in the back of the office with a bucket and mop just in case. "What can I do for you?"

"You can bring me my tiger semen, you impudent ape. That's the perfect remedy for a bad stomach."

"Certainly, boss. Please forgive me, but where is it kept?"

"Where do you think, you imbecile?" said Boonchai with a huge grin on his face. "In the tiger's balls. You go and masturbate the tiger."

"Uhm." Devil Lam began to shake. "I'm not sure...."

"You are a fool." Bach Van Limh had decided to join his brother in his attempt to prank Devil Lam. "You go to the tiger's cage, reach in, and grab his penis. Then you wank him till he cums. Don't worry—he'll enjoy it more than anything else he will soon experience. Don't forget to take a big cup."

Much to the amusement of The Bachs and their bodyguards, who were sniggering like school boys, Devil Lam picked up an empty tea cup and, with his knees knocking together like a pair of maracas, backed out the room. Vixay shook his head and walked over to the desk where he kept the Tiger semen in a small vial. He took a swig and turned to The Bachs. "Well, a handless assistant isn't much use to me, so we'll use him as meat after he attempts to choke the tiger's chicken. In fact, if you don't mind, maybe your bodyguards can just go and throw him straight into the cage. I've had more than enough of that impudent fellow."

"Certainly," replied Boonchai, signaling to the three goons. "Go after him, boys, and have some fun. We'll watch from up here."

As stupid as his bosses may have thought him, Devil Lam had no intention of touching the tiger's penis. He ran down the stairs from the office onto the warehouse floor, past the suffering animals, between the rows of preserved parts, and headed straight for the door. He opened it, reset the explosive device, closed the door, and walked out, determined to find Conchita and hopefully some safety.

The bodyguards had seen him slip out and began to sprint. They reached the door, flung it open, and promptly blew themselves into hundreds of little pieces. The explosion was designed to be contained by the thick doorframe, and so neither The Bachs, Vixay, or the animals were hurt.

"Well," said Vixay, who'd observed the entire scenario from the large glass window in his office, "we're going to need some replacement items around here. First, a new door. Second, more bodyguards, and third, a driver, because I'm certainly not going to start taking Uber." He turned back to The Bachs, who were gaping in disbelief at the scene below. "And we will add Devil Lam to the list of people to die most painfully when we locate him. Now, I need to make a phone call to that one person I said was going to help."

Devil Lam's plans, however, did not include being caught by Vixay any time soon. He walked quickly from the smoking building, hailed a passing taxi, and gave the driver an address in Sheung Wan, one of Hong Kong's oldest districts. The apartment building on Queen's Road Central, between a paper store and a clothing outlet, looked run down from the outside, yet Devil Lam knew that the small apartment on the fifth floor would be filled with high-tech equipment.

The young man who answered the door was known as Scorpion, and he was, at twenty-two, one of the most accomplished hackers in all of China. He'd been arrested when he was sixteen for hacking into the teleprompter at the 14th National Congress of the Communist Party of China and replacing the trade speech of one of the top government ministers with a recipe for moon cakes. A judge had offered him the choice of a bullet to the back of his head or the opportunity to join the ranks of the thousands of independent hackers employed by the Chinese government to disrupt as many organizations in the West as they could without getting caught. Scorpion had chosen wisely. He allowed few people into his apartment, which would have resembled an operations room at the headquarters of a cyber security firm if that cyber security company was run by a complete slob. Dirty laundry was draped over monitors, and empty food cartons covered every available space on the large desk that wasn't already occupied by high-tech equipment. Scorpion dressed only in a pair of boxer shorts and resembled a large slug that had spent too much time buried in a heap of manure.

"You smell worse than our grandfather's underpants," said Devil Lam, holding his nose.

"Nice to see you too, cousin," replied Scorpion with a huge grin. He was extremely fond of Devil Lam, who'd been his closest companion growing up. "Come in quickly and tell me what brings you here into my humble abode?"

"More like your humble commode. It really stinks in here."

"Yes, yes. I know. My mother is coming along later to clean up."

"Look, Scorpion. I am sorry, but this is not a social visit. I'm afraid I need your help if I am to live to see my next birthday." It took Devil Lam thirty minutes to explain his situation to his cousin and Scorpion less than five minutes to come up with an address for the house on Gough Hill Road.

"You know," said Scorpion after he'd reprogramed Devil Lam's phone to make it untraceable by his previous employer, "if you need me to, I can totally make you disappear. Consider it, please. You need to get as far away as possible from those horrible people."

"Thank you, cousin. I have considered it, and I realize that I cannot go away until I have tried everything I can to help destroy Vixay Keosavang and The Bach Brothers. Those poor wretched animals in the warehouse. You cannot believe their suffering."

"Well, blowing up some bodyguards is a pretty good start, if you ask me."

"Maybe, but those guys have countless people who work for them all over the place. No, I have to do more. I am convinced that this woman Conchita Palomino can help. I only hope she will see me."

"Leave that part to me," said Scorpion. "I'll send her a text message from the head of the World Wildlife Fund to say she should see you."

"How will you do that?"

"Easy," replied Scorpion. "Look." He pointed to one of the monitors. "I have both their mobile numbers. And I hope you know, cousin, if you need my help, I will do what I can."

An hour later just as Devil Lam arrived at the house on Gough Hill Road for his appointment with Conchita Palomino, kindly set up by the President of the WWF, a man pulled up in a taxi at the headquarters of Vixay Keosavang in Wong Chuk Hang. Workmen were covering a large hole that had been the doorway to the warehouse with plastic and plywood. They pulled aside a sheet of plastic to let the man in. He walked passed the cages, barely giving the suffering animals a second glance, and waved up at Vixay, who was looking down from his office. Then he climbed the stairs and sat down at the round conference table where the animal traffickers were sitting drinking tea.

"What happened to your door?" asked Inspector Norman Fok.

"Probably a similar thing that happened to your face," replied Vixay, pointing at the large purple bruise on Fok's face where Destructive Wang had slapped him. "Now, Inspector Fok, prove that you're worth the hundreds of thousands I pay you every year. How are we to get Conchita Palomino and Roger Storm?"

"Perhaps easier than you imagined, Khun Keosavang. I am babysitting two European policemen, both more stupid than your driver, Devil Lam, if you can believe that. They are here as representatives of Interpol and the German police to—like everyone else—collect evidence against all of you. I believe that Roger Storm knows them and therefore will trust them more than he will me."

"This complicates things." Bach Van Limh lit up a cigarette that smelt to Inspector Fok almost as foul as the horrific stench from the floor below. "Too many people."

"In my experience," replied Fok, "the more people involved, the less chance of suspicion falling on any one individual. The only complication is getting rid of two more bodies."

"That will be the least of our worries. We will just feed them to the animals. Save us on meat."

"Then," said Fok, ignoring Vixay's suggestion, "all we have to do is work out a location where they think they will find you. This is something I can easily accomplish using my two colleagues. We lure them there and then you take them. It's that simple." Inspector Fok glanced around the room. "But, if you don't mind me saying so, you seem rather low on personnel to take care of so many people."

"Yes, yes," replied Boonchai Bach, waving dismissively. "That traitorous lizard Devil Lam just blew up all our bodyguards before vanishing. But have no fear: We have many, many more men who will be here soon."

"In fact," said Vixay, "while you're at it, you can help us find Devil Lam. I have something special in mind for him." He closed his eyes and realized his list of people to torture was getting increasingly longer and he was running out of ideas on just how to kill them all. He'd have to consult his manual.

Chapter 19

IN WHICH ALL THE PLAYERS HATCH THEIR PLANS FOR THE SHOWDOWN

Various locations around Hong Kong
That same day

Inspectors Bunter and Darmstaedter were sitting in the lobby of their hotel drinking coffee, trying to make sense of the events of the night before and wondering what had happened to Inspector Fok, who hadn't returned their calls.

"Nothing makes sense to me, Constantin. I have a horrible feeling the two of us will be on a plane this evening headed back to our respective headquarters to report our failure and suffer further humiliation. Let's face it: We haven't got anywhere on this, and we're definitely not, of this I am certain, going to get a call from Conchita Palomino or Roger to say they want to work with us."

Darmstaedter, who'd been contemplating the ceiling as if it were one of the Upanishads, lowered his head and looked at his colleague. His headache was gone, but he hadn't been able to sleep more than a few hours, and his brain, normally whirling like an out-of-control carousel, had slowed down considerably. "I am uncertain as to the accuracy of that belief, Matthew. Though I must warn you that my brain is only working at approximately 47 percent of its capacity."

"Well, that's a damn sight better than mine. "

"Yes, of course. I know that."

Bunter ignored the put-down. "If you have even an inkling of an idea of what the hell we should do, then spit it out, man."

"Very well, but 'spitting' would imply speed, and speed is inadvisable when one is jet- lagged. So, let me explain the situation in as precise a manner as I am capable of at this moment. First, Ishea Payamps and Conchita Palomino have every intention of using Roger Storm as bait."

"Hmm, not sure on that point, old boy. She seemed rather adamant that he'd been through enough already."

"Ja, but too adamant. You did not observe her body language or that of Ishea Payamps when she said it. She squeezed Roger's arm, and Ishea Payamps rolled his eyes. These, if you have studied Dr. Patricia Nasshauer's book, *A Comprehensive Study of Twitches, Tremors and Convulsions*, are obvious indications of lying." He didn't give Bunter, who'd most definitely not read it, a chance to comment. "Second, you have ignored the fact that they brought Roger Storm here to Hong Kong. Why Hong Kong? If they were trying to find a location safe from Vixay Keosavang, why bring him close to the asshole of the devil?"

"That's a good point—"

"It's an excellent point, not merely a good one. You must learn to understand the difference. Third, and while this has nothing to do with the motivation of Conchita Palomino or Ishea Payamps, it is something you will have missed entirely." Darmstaedter sat back and sipped his coffee, waiting for Bunter to respond.

"How can I answer if I have no idea what you're talking about?"

"Exactly, you cannot because, my dear Matthew, there is something vital that you failed to observe about your friend and colleague, Inspector Norman Fok."

"Enlighten me, please."

"Inspector Fok talked of using Roger Storm as bait as if we had discussed it in detail first."

"Yes, but I brought it up."

"Indeed you did. However, and however is the operative word here, you brought it up as a suggestion. Fok turned that into a threat, and there was no need to threaten Conchita Palomino in the manner that he did. Our need was for cooperation. We were not at that point where threats were called for. No, Matthew—and I will quote Dr. Nasshauer once again: *When a subject goes from nice to nasty, from polite to repugnant, he or she has something to hide.* Fok is sloppy and undisciplined. This means he is not being entirely honest. As yet, I do not know precisely what it is that he is hiding."

"Good Lord, Constantin. That's a bit of a stretch. Really, even for you. Norman Fok is an outstanding police officer—"

"Outstanding he may be, but upstanding he is not. Trust me on this, Matthew, and let us observe his actions with great vigilance going forward, if and when he shows up."

"You know I respect your intuition, Constantin. But I must say I think perhaps your jet- lag is clouding your judgement a little. Look, here's Norman now."

At the house on Gough Hill Road, Roger had finished his shower and was examining his penis. It looked awfully red, but he put it down to the excessive lovemaking with Conchita. Happily, certainly in the case of his sexual activity, past performance was not an indication of future let alone present outcome. His ex-wife had told him he was a pathetic lover, and yet here he was shagging the most beautiful woman he'd ever known like a horny badger. He looked in the mirror as he applied shaving cream to his face and marveled at himself. He felt great. Other than his cock, nothing on or in the rest of his body ached. He thought he detected the hint of a six-pack just above the towel he'd carefully wrapped around his waist but decided it was most likely just a shadow. Still, for someone his age he was in pretty good shape. Then he began, for the hundredth time, to wonder whether Conchita felt the same way. Every feeling he'd had for her from the moment he'd first laid eyes on her at the restaurant in Paris the year before had resurfaced with a vengeance. Love and lust, but most of all uncertainty and paranoia. How could anyone so utterly beautiful and mysterious have feelings for him? And yet every moan and fondle appeared to indicate that his love was requited. He pushed his emotions to the back of his mind and began to shave. He'd just whistled the first few bars of Leonard Cohen's *Hallelujah*, his favorite shower song, when Pansy Pong stuck her head round the door.

"Sorry to interrupt you, Roger," she said, wondering just what it was that Conchita saw in this flabby *gweilo*. "Conchita has asked that you meet her, Ishea, and Destructive Wang in the drawing room. A visitor has just shown up, and they want you to hear what he says."

The mood in the drawing room when Roger walked in was anything but amiable. Conchita and Ishea were sitting on the couch watching Destructive Wang, who had the arm of a young Chinese man pinned behind his back. From the expression on the young man's face, he was not enjoying the interaction.

"Ow, ow, ow," cried the young man as Destructive Wang pushed his arm further up his back till Roger feared it might snap. "I promise you I'm telling you the truth . . . I just want to help."

"Then why did you send us that fake message?"

"My cousin—aargh. My cousin thought it was the only way that you would see me . . . please stop."

Destructive Wang relaxed his hold, and the young man snatched his arm back and began to rub it furiously. "I promise I will tell you everything. I just want to help."

"Okay," said Ishea. "You have one chance. Tell us everything, and if I or Destructive Wang think you're lying about anything, anything at all, I will snap your neck. Is that clear?"

"Yes, it is clear. But I am very nervous, and I don't know where to start."

215

"Right at the beginning, my dear. And here, have some tea. It will help you calm down." Conchita poured Devil Lam a cup of green tea and beckoned for him to sit beside her on the couch. The ploy worked, and Devil Lam began to talk.

A lot of what he told them they already knew. What they didn't know was the location of the warehouse, the extent of Vixay's bond with The Bach Brothers, and the fact that Vixay had someone who was acting as a double agent.

"So, you have no ideas who this person is? You have never seen him?"

"No, Ms. Palomino. I have never seen him. All I heard was Vixay telling The Bach Brothers that he was an important official and that he was the one who could set up the ambush of you and Mr. Storm. I also know that once they capture you, they intend to torture you and some poor animals to death. Either here in Hong Kong or back in Laos."

"Thank you, Devil Lam. You are very brave, and you have been very helpful."

"Yes," said Destructive Wang. "Only problem is you are of no further use to us. You can't go back to Vixay or The Bachs, and we have no need for your skills as a driver. So, sorry, Devil Lam, but now you must disappear."

Roger couldn't believe what Destructive Wang had just said. "Hang on just a second. I'm not going to sit here and allow you to kill this man. He risked his life to help us."

"I never said I was going to kill him. I said he had to disappear. I will get him into my father's store. He will be quite safe there."

"I'm surprised at you, Roger." Ishea was laughing. "Do you honestly believe that we kill indiscriminately?"

216

"I'm not sure what I believe. But I'm glad to hear it. There's just one thing—what about Devil Lam's cousin, Scorpion? He sounds like he might be very useful."

"Roger's right," said Conchita. "We don't have anyone like him. If he's capable of hacking my phone, then he can hack into any of those criminals' mobiles. Do you think you could persuade him to help us, Devil Lam?"

"I don't know, Ms. Conchita. I think the government keeps a very tight reign on him."

"No worries," Destructive Wang said, taking out his cell phone. "My uncle will fix it."

"Good," replied Conchita. "Let's get him here and make our plans. In the meantime, call our friends from the police department and invite them to join us tomorrow. Tell them we've decided to work with them after all. If Vixay's informant is indeed an important official, I'm sure he will know exactly what the police are up to, and if Scorpion is half as good as you say he is, Devil Lam, we can set our trap."

An hour later, Vixay Keosavang received a phone call from Inspector Fok informing him that he, Bunter, and Darmstaedter had been invited to the house on Gough Hill Road the following day to discuss working together. He clapped his hands together in glee and pulled out his manual on torture.

"Oh, yes," he said to The Bach Brothers, who'd just finished interviewing twenty new bodyguards. "Get ready for the Butcher's Picnic, my friends. Everything is coming together."

Things indeed were coming together. They came together for Conchita, Roger, Ishea, Destructive Wang, and

Devil Lam at around 16:25 that afternoon after a two-hour session with Devil Lam's cousin, Scorpion. They came together for Inspectors Bunter and Darmstaedter an hour later when Destructive Wang pulled up in front of their hotel in a black Mercedes Maybach as they were about to take a pre-dinner stroll and asked them in a polite yet firm manner to please get in and not use their mobile phones. When Bunter told Destructive Wang that he wasn't going anywhere without informing Inspector Norman Fok, Destructive Wang reached back and put him in a sleeper hold that kept him unconscious until they reached the house on Gough Hill Road Darmstaedter hadn't made the slightest objection. Things were going more or less as he expected.

Chapter 20

IN WHICH KNIVES ARE SHARPENED, SIDES ARE
CHOSEN, AND TRAPS ARE SET

The House on Gough Hill Road
That evening

"Just what the hell do you think you're playing at?"
Bunter stood up from the armchair into which he'd
been unceremoniously slung. He took two staggering steps,
wobbling dangerously until Destructive Wang steadied
him. He was pissed. "First, you assault a senior member of
the Hong Kong Police Force. And now me. These are serious crimes, and I must warn you that I shall call Inspector
Fok—"

"No," Ishea said, "what you should do is shut the fuck up
and listen to what we have to say. You won't call Inspector
Fok, and we will tell you why that's a bad idea. You wanted
to work with us, and here's your chance. Your only chance."

"Ja, Matthew," Darmstaedter said, giving his colleague's
shoulder a reassuring squeeze. "For once in your life listen.

I have a feeling we are going to hear something that I have suspected since this morning. May we sit down?"

"Please do, gentlemen, and have some tea. It's very rare and very refreshing." Conchita poured each of them a small cup from an elaborate porcelain tea pot.

Constantin took a small sip and nearly gagged. "I apologize, but this is not to my liking. It tastes a little like *scheissedreck*."

"How observant of you, Inspector Darmstaedter. It's called Poo Poo Pu-Erh Tea, and it's actually made from the feces of insects in Yunnan that have been fed tea leaves. Take another sip."

"Jesus." Bunter put his cup down without taking a sip. "Now you're trying to poison us too."

Conchita laughed. "Not in the least. My intention in serving you this tea was to show you just how much we value your potential partnership. It costs about $1000 a pound."

"We appreciate that," Darmstaedter said, "but I'd rather have a beer."

Roger felt the same way. He'd never understood why anyone who worked with Freddy and Conchita never served anything that didn't have a back story. There was no normal, no comparative in their world. Everything was either the most exotic or most expensive. If he hadn't been enjoying the dark liquid that had a distinctly mellow and smooth finish, he would have spat it out.

Once Pansy Pong had poured beers for both Bunter and Darmstaedter, Conchita introduced Devil Lam. Scorpion had chosen to stay in another room. He had no desire to meet foreign policemen.

"Earlier this morning, this brave young man, Devil Lam, took a very courageous decision to meet with us after leaving, under explosive circumstances from what he has told us, the employ of Vixay Keosavang. He has supplied intelligence that we didn't have and together with his cousin, a government-employed hacker who has chosen to remain anonymous, given us information that we believe is critical to your operation."

Bunter, who'd mellowed slightly after gulping half the beer, raised his eyebrows, but Darmstaedter just smiled. "That is excellent, but I must inform you that I suspect I know what this information is. Or perhaps I should say who this information refers to."

"How could you possibly know?" asked Ishea.

Now it was Bunter's turn to smile. Any opportunity to promulgate what he considered the greatest detective mind since Sherlock Holmes was a triumph for policemen everywhere.

"We could possibly know, because my friend here has an intellectual capacity that far exceeds anyone I have ever come across. His ability to reason deductively, to see clues where others see only fly specks, in my opinion has not been experienced since the death of the world's previously greatest detective. That's how we could know."

"And who was that?" asked Ishea.

"Why, Sherlock Holmes, of course," replied Bunter.

"Okay, ignoring the fact that Sherlock Holmes was a fictional character, what do you know, Inspector Darmstaedter?"

"It is not what I know, Herr Payamps. The fact is I know nothing. Rather it is what I suspect, and I suspect everything. What I suspect at this precise moment, or more accurately have suspected since last night, is that Inspector Norman Fok is not what he or his credentials would suggest."

"I'm impressed," said Ishea, who genuinely was. "It took our hacker thirty minutes to establish that. And he was using technology supplied by the Chinese government. How the hell did you figure it out?"

"Do not feel bad, Herr Payamps. Bunter and I had had the benefit of speaking to Inspector Fok at dinner before we met you. I observe the behavior of people I first meet very carefully. Within minutes I detected an irregularity in his breathing and eye movement. Having studied Dr. Nasshauer's manual on suspicious habits of extraordinary criminals, something I have encouraged my colleague Matthew Bunter to do, I was convinced that Inspector Fok was hiding something. His aggressive behavior last night in this very room served to increase my suspicions by a factor of three."

"He's brilliant," chirped Bunter. "I'm telling you, what goes on in that large noggin of his defies belief. He didn't let on to me how he felt about Fok until this morning. And even then, I had my doubts."

"Well, Inspector Darmstaedter, you're correct. Our hacker was able to get into Vixay Keosavang's phone from the number Devil Lam had used. Four of his calls were traced to a burner that had been bought on the street. We couldn't establish the owner until our hacker was able to unlock the GPS. It showed various locations including your hotel, this house, and a location in Wong Chuk Hang that we now know, thanks to Devil Lam, is Vixay's headquarters.

"You do understand that this complicates things considerably for us," Bunter said, rubbing his nose. "I told you last night that Inspector Darmstaedter and I have no jurisdiction in Hong Kong, and if Fok is working against us—"

"Then you," Destructive Wang said, speaking up for the first time, "must work with us. How does that feel?"

"Herr Wang," said Darmstaedter, "feelings cannot enter into this. It is clear that you and we have similar goals. Our motivations, however, are contradistinct—a good word, ja? And our methods as different as breast reduction is from buttock enhancing. If we are to work with you, and I am confident that you have a plan and that I know what that plan is, then our relationship must be devoid of feeling and focus on reason alone. So now, tell us your plan, or would you prefer that I do it for you?"

Destructive Wang looked at Darmstaedter as if he were insane and decided he'd never really understand some Westerners. He got Ishea, and he sympathized with Roger, but the German was off his radar.

Roger knew exactly what the plan was: Roger equals bait. Only this time Conchita would join him on the proverbial hook. He wasn't sure if that made him feel any better. He decided it didn't.

"Gentlemen," Conchita said, standing up and giving Darmstaedter an eyeful of her breasts, which looked as if they'd burst out of her low-cut silk robe at any moment, "why don't you join us for an early dinner and we can talk plans over the best hairy crab you've ever tasted."

Much to Darmstaedter's and Roger's relief, hairy crab, that odd delicacy from Yangchenk Lake, was a minor part of a spectacular meal that included more than enough dishes from body parts they felt comfortable eating. The conversation for the most part was amicable, and the wine, chosen by Destructive Wang, varied with each dish. Barbera with its high acidity and red-toned fruit with the Peking Duck. Off-dry Gewurtztramminars from Alsace, Chenin Blancs from South Africa, and a Vouvray from the Loire Valley with its fig and pear notes went perfectly with the other dishes. Destructive Wang explained each choice carefully, and by the end of the meal as they began to discuss the plan, both Bunter and Darmstaedter were feeling a lot better about their new partners. Darmstaedter, who'd drunk far less than Bunter, still regarded Ishea with the same degree of distrust, but he was enamored of Conchita. As Bunter had discovered in their various discussions on the subject, Darmstaedter, who lived for the most part in a binary world, saw women as art. A neck, a nose, a thumb would grab his attention, and he'd become infatuated to the point where everything else would blur. Conchita was different, however, to any woman Darmstaedter had ever encountered. She was almost unworldly in both her looks and her ability to understand human nature. He regarded her carefully when he thought she wasn't looking, trying to understand her first from a holistic perspective, and when he failed at that, he focused on her breasts, which were making him extremely uncomfortable. The one thing that confused him totally was why she had any interest in Roger

Storm. Storm was a weakling. Well, perhaps an opportunity would emerge down the road.

"And so," Ishea said, finally putting down his chopsticks, "let's talk strategy."

"Why don't you start," Bunter replied. "You've clearly given it more thought than us."

"What we know is that while Vixay wants Roger, The Bachs want Conchita. Vixay has the facilities, but The Bachs have—despite Devil Lam blowing up their bodyguards— access to some of the most dangerous thugs in Hong Kong. Inspector Fok, we must assume, will be the one to try to construct the scenario in which they can take Roger and Conchita—"

"And he will use Matthew and I to arrange that," interjected Darmstaedter, "after our little get together tomorrow morning. This much is obvious. Setting up the location, I must assume, is something that you with your knowledge of Hong Kong will be able to do with ease. The question I have is how will we, with our limited manpower, foil their plan?"

"What makes you think we lack manpower?" asked Destructive Wang, downing the last of the wine. "I assure you we don't."

"Are you saying you still have access to the mercenaries you used when PaloMar was in operation?" Bunter asked.

"No," replied Conchita. "That's not what we are saying at all. As both you and Inspector Darmstaedter know, Freddy Blank and I are no longer involved in the international arms trade. Other than Ishea, who is our head of Security for WildWorld, and Destructive Wang, who is head of operations in Hong Kong and mainland China, we have no association with mercenaries at all. Destructive Wang, because of his service in the Flying Tigers, has access to a number of people who help us out when necessary."

"What she said," mumbled Destructive Wang, who seemed upset that Conchita hadn't allowed him to answer.

"Very good." Bunter looked relieved. "Well, I'm going to assume that your fellows will be a lot more experienced than anyone The Bachs or Vixay can come up with. And so what are our next steps?"

"Those are what's going to make this plan so interesting. Destructive Wang is going to arrange for The Bach Brothers to recruit *his* men...."

The plan as laid out by the two police inspectors and Ishea with input from Destructive Wang was absurdly simple, Roger thought. But as Conchita explained to him later that night as they lay in bed after another bout of lovemaking, the best plans usually are. "Most operations fail not because the plan isn't good, but because the details haven't been well thought out. Success lies in the minutest detail, and that's where Ishea is so brilliant and why he has never been caught no matter what he does or where he goes. He leaves nothing to chance. I believe Inspector Darmstaedter, as strange a man as he is, thinks the same way, and so, my love, you and I will be as safe as houses."

Comforted by that thought and Conchita's naked bottom tucked into his groin, Roger fell into a deep, almost-nightmare-free sleep.

Outside earlier on that evening, things had been slightly less cozy. Detective Norman Fok, hidden in the exotic shrubbery at the bottom of the drive, tried desperately to repress a sneeze. He'd failed to see the sprinkler head when he'd chosen his spot and was now drenched from head to toe. The sniffles had begun an hour before, and he felt a full-blown cold coming on. His legs had begun to twitch and his stomach rumbled. His new glasses had fogged up, and the big white handkerchief with which he normally polished them was sopping wet. In short, he was miserable and in the process of deciding to call it quits when, much to his relief, the front door opened and Destructive Wang, Bunter, and Darmstaedter emerged. He watched as they climbed into the Maybach and drove out the gates of the house on Gough Hill Road. Both inspectors appeared to be inebriated and, from the convivial way they'd waved goodnight to Ishea Payamps, in cahoots with the enemy. Not only perfidious, he thought, but imbecilic to believe they could out-think and out-maneuver a mind as brilliant as his. Did they seriously consider that he and his men had not been watching their every move? Well, this time tomorrow they'd be well and truly chopped up and a feast for some starving beast in Vixay's warehouse. He felt for his phone and punched in a number that would alert his driver to pick him up.

"Did he follow you back to the hotel?" Ishea asked Destructive Wang, who'd just returned from dropping off Bunter and Darmstaedter.

"No, I think he must have gone straight home. I saw one of his men outside the hotel, but no Fok."

"What an idiot. Did he honestly believe that we don't monitor the outside of the house? Seriously, Destructive Wang, the Hong Kong police force must have lost half its brain power when you left."

Chapter 21

IN WHICH THE SIMPLE BECOMES COMPLICATED
AND THE COMPLICATED BECOMES
UNFATHOMABLE

Vixay's headquarters and the house on Gough Hill Road
Late the next morning

At 7:30, Inspector Norman Fok began to sneeze in earnest.

"You'd better not be getting sick at this crucial time," said Fatty Tiewcharoen, who'd arrived that morning on the Cotaijet ferry from Macau, where he'd spent the last two nights gambling at a casino owned by the Golden Dragon Group. "And if I catch your cold, I'll rip your balls off."

"It's just an allergy." Fok pulled out his large white handkerchief and wiped his nose. He was beginning to sweat, and his stomach felt wonky. He hoped he hadn't caught a cold last night.

"Here, drink this." Vixay tossed him a small phial of yellow liquid. "It's pangolin urine mixed with echinacea. Very effective for all allergies."

"So," Boonchai Bach said as Fok tried desperately to swallow the foul-smelling liquid, "you are sure they don't suspect you? It seems odd to me that they'd go to the house without letting you know."

"I am convinced of it. I told you yesterday that foreigners trust the foreigners more than us. This is typical Western behavior. Extremely rude and inconsiderate in my opinion, but normal."

"Well, you'd better be right, or everything is going to blow up. And talking of blowing up, any news on the location of Devil Lam?"

"None. Are you sure he didn't die in the explosion with your bodyguards? I say that because we have found no trace of him anywhere in Hong Kong. And if he was still here or had attempted to leave, I would know."

"Of course, that's a possibility. I doubt those lazy workers counted every finger or toe after the clean-up. They just swept them up and fed them to the animals. The only good thing is that I've saved a small fortune on animal feed this week." Vixay gave a hyena-like cackle.

"And more to come after tonight, Vixay." Bach Van Limh rubbed his hands in glee. "Now that Fatty's here and we have our men, what can possibly go wrong?"

"Hopefully nothing. Yugh." Fok coughed up something that resembled a dead sparrow.

"That doesn't sound like an allergy to me," said Fatty, moving away.

"It's nothing." Fok was feeling decidedly unwell. "So, the plan is this: I will meet Bunter and Darmstaedter at the hotel in 30 minutes, and we will drive to the house on Gough Hill Road. I will tell them that my sources have let me know you will all be at the Jumbo Golden Boy Floating Restaurant for dinner tonight at 8 o'clock. I will inform them that I have a table reserved for them and that my men will be among the guests waiting for my signal. Which of course they won't be. Just your men. You need to make sure that they are dressed appropriately so it looks like the restaurant is full of guests, not gangsters." Fok's eyes were watering, but it still seemed to him as if the thugs who were sitting together at the back of the room looked like the bad guys in a Jackie Chan movie. He wiped his face with his handkerchief, leaving a small deposit of yellow phlegm just below his hairline. Fatty opened his mouth to say something, but Boonchai waved him to ignore it.

"One table in the middle will be for the four of you. Make sure that there is a table next to yours that is open for seven people."

"Why seven?" asked Vixay. "There are eight of you."

"Yes, but I will suggest Destructive Wang remains at the entrance in case 'you make a run for it.' I have special plans for that arrogant swine. We will then order, and I will insist they try the famous Jumbo Martinis—these dolts seem to be obsessed with martinis—which you can arrange to be doctored with knock-out drops. As soon as I'm satisfied they've had enough I will give the signal." Fok felt his stomach contract and a loud fart escaped.

"That better not be your signal," said Fatty, trying desperately to wave away the foul smell of sulphur. "You'll make the entire restaurant vomit."

"My apologies. That pangolin urine is playing hell with my guts. No, my signal to you will be when I say, 'You must try the snake soup. It's delicious.' I will be sure to say it loudly enough for you to hear. That's when you move in." Fok blew his nose into his handkerchief, stood up, and made a hasty retreat to the door. "I will see you tonight, gentlemen."

Fok was not a believer in traditional Chinese medicine. He made his driver stop at a Manning's Pharmacy and bought some Panadol Cold and Flu, which he took with a bottle of water he always kept in the car. When he got to Bunter and Darmstaedter's hotel, he rushed past them to the toilets, where he emptied both his bowels and the room of other guests. By the time they arrived at the house on Gough Hill Road, he was feeling decidedly worse.

Despite his growing malaise and the fuzziness in his brain, Fok was impressed at the acting skills of the other participants in the charade. There was not a hint nor mention of a meeting the night before. There were no slipups at all. That alone raised his suspicions somewhat, but both Bunter and Darmstaedter were cold and aloof towards Conchita, while Ishea Payamps' aggression toward the inspectors was palpable. The group was keenly interested in the intelligence Fok had received from his undercover cops concerning the dinner on the Jumbo Golden Boy Floating Restaurant. There was some initial anger when he told them that they would not be permitted to participate in the actual apprehension, but their objections were assuaged when he said they would have a front row seat at the arrest of the world's most-wanted animal traffickers. He waited for further questions, and when none came, he began to suspect that something might be wrong.

"Inspector Fok," said Conchita, "are you feeling ill? You look terrible."

"No," replied Fok, feeling a new spasm in his gut. "It's just allergies."

"Okay, good. Well, then I must inform you that an incident took place last night of which you were deliberately left out. During the afternoon I decided to invite Inspectors Darmstaedter and Bunter here for dinner—"

"You invited them here without me? But that is highly irregular, let alone rude." He began to shiver and had to clench his buttocks together to prevent more gas from escaping.

"I know, and I apologize. You see, we had to make sure that we could trust them the way we know we can trust you as a highly respected member of the Hong Kong police department. There has been a lot of history between us and them . . . a lot of bad blood, you could say. We didn't want that to get in the way of what we have to do. Having you present would have changed the dynamics. You do understand?"

Fok nodded.

"Our apologies too, old chap." Bunter gave Fok a sheepish grin. "It was most helpful. And now we can work together seamlessly."

"Yes, yes, of course. Very thoughtful and clever. Excuse me, do you think I could use your water closet? I'm not feeling very well." As Fok sprinted for the toilet, he let out a tremendous sigh of relief at hearing the truth and a fart that was almost as loud as the Noonday Gun.

"Mein Gott," said Darmstaedter. "That sounds not good."

"Oh, it is really bad," replied Ishea. "Last night, Pansy Pong saw Fok skulking in the bushes observing the house, no doubt spying on the two of you. It was the perfect opportunity for me to try out something I've been working on for a while. I'm actually very pleased with it. It's a modified norovirus that incorporates flu virus symptoms. I injected a small amount into the sprinkler system, and as you can see—and smell—the results are pretty good."

"Please don't tell us that you're now into germ warfare," Bunter said.

"Of course not. It's just a hobby. I haven't really tested it out on anyone else, so I wasn't sure what to expect. But I think in the future it's probably going to take a lot of physical pressure off me in some of my activities."

"It's not going to kill him, is it?"

"I doubt it, but it should take him out of commission, probably put him in a coma for a few days. Now, let's discuss our plans."

Roger sat with the group for a minute or two listening to Darmstaedter arguing with Ishea on logistics. He hadn't contributed much of anything so far. First, he really didn't have anything substantive to add to the plan and second he really didn't want to think about what was going to happen. He knew he should have been scared, but listening to the elaborate strategizing made him feel slightly more comfortable. He walked over to the window and looked down at the harbor. His mind drifted to Hunter's Folly, and he wondered how Gosego was coping and whether he should give him a call to tell him that in all likelihood he'd be back in a few days. Then he looked over at Conchita, and his heart sank. What would happen with her? He didn't imagine she'd want to come and live with him on the game reserve. Yet every indication was that she wanted to be together. How would it work? Would she ask him to stay in Hong Kong with her, or would she be moving on when this job was over? Maybe that's just how things were meant to be. Then he felt her by his side and the calmness returned. He looked at her and smiled, and she took his hand.

"Don't think too much, my love. I know what it is that's going on in your mind, and I promise you everything will be good. Don't think of tomorrow just yet."

He squeezed her hand and kissed her on the cheek, and somewhere deep in his heart a little alarm bell went off. Was that last statement a warning that tomorrow wasn't going to be how he'd projected it to be as he lay in bed with Conchita? He sighed deeply and walked back to the table where Destructive Wang was explaining how even more of his men would be waiting on the pier and in boats alongside the restaurant to board on his signal. He assured Bunter and Darmstaedter that while they had no authority to make the arrests, his uncle, the Secretary of Security for Hong Kong, would have the appropriate people on the scene to take care of everything.

235

"The only thing that is of concern to me," said Darmstaedter, "is how will they react if Fok isn't there. Surely they will be suspicious, no?"

"No worries." Destructive Wang gave him a thud on the back. "Devil Lam's cousin texted Vixay a message to say everything is in place but Fok is unwell. He even suggested they delay the dinner, but Vixay said that they are relieved. Fok was passing gas there too."

When Bunter and Darmstaedter had returned to the hotel to rest before the evening's activities and Fok had been cleaned, put on an IV, and left in the care of one of Destructive Wang's men who'd be dropping him off at Queen Mary Hospital later that night, Roger asked the real question.

"So Ishea, what's really going to happen tonight?"

"You don't need to know the details, Roger. Let's just say as soon as we're done tonight, you, Conchita, Destructive Wang, and I will be making a hasty exit from Hong Kong. So why don't you pack up your suits and get some rest? We have a lot of things we need to do to wind down this operation." Roger shrugged. He knew he'd get no more out of anyone, and so he went back to Conchita's room and lay on the bed.

He stared at the ceiling for a bit trying to project into the next day's events. But a gentle numbness had taken over his body, and he fell into a deep sleep. Later that afternoon, he felt Conchita slide onto the bed next to him. She was naked and warm and soft. For some reason he didn't want to open his eyes. He wasn't sure he could bear to see her this way for perhaps the last time. But Conchita was not as sentimental as Roger, and with a frenzy she began to undress him till he lay there as naked as she but with his eyes still tightly closed. He felt her get on top of him and begin to lick the tears that were forming at the corners of his eyes. She bit his lips till he tasted blood, and then she began to move down his body, stopping briefly to nibble his left nipple, until she arrived at his penis which she swallowed greedily till he grew hard in her mouth. Their lovemaking was not gentle or slow. They were like two sails in a strong wind, billowing incessantly and slapping together with every rise and fall of the ocean. They were two cats on the African plain mating violently for just one night and then moving on, never to see each other again. Through it all Roger kept his eyes closed, and when he came, seconds before her, he thought he knew what would happen that evening. He was so wrong.

Chapter 22

IN WHICH SOME THINGS GO AS PLANNED, AND OTHERS NOT SO MUCH

On the floating restaurant

The Jumbo Golden Boy Floating Restaurant was not in the same league as the more famous Jumbo Floating Restaurant, a multi-storied structure decorated in the traditional imperial style, which attracted hundreds of hungry diners every day. For a start The Jumbo Golden Boy had only two stories and was more like a traditional Chinese slop-house than a fancy eating establishment. Even from the outside Roger was convinced that the very visible grime would have provided any number of active bacteria for Ishea's new hobby. He made his mind up not to eat a thing.

The pier was crowded with locals, and Roger noticed that anyone attempting to enter the restaurant was stopped by two tough-looking individuals in ill-fitting tuxedos who were almost as big as Destructive Wang. He looked around, nervously trying to spot their reinforcements, but no one in the crowds jumped out. "Are your colleagues here, Destructive Wang?"

"Yes, they are. No need for concern."

"What happened to 'no worries'?"

Destructive Wang looked puzzled and then brushed it off. "Everything under control. I come with you to restaurant and make sure you get in, then I will wait at the entrance. Now follow me."

Conchita took Roger's arm and strolled with him as if they were a normal couple out on a date albeit to some perfectly horrendous restaurant. They followed Bunter, Darmstaedter, and Ishea up to the entrance where two goons were clearly expecting them. Destructive Wang said something in Cantonese, and the party made their way across the gangplank to the first floor, where a narrow staircase led up to the dining room. A thin man with slicked-down hair in an even more ill-fitting tuxedo bowed to them and escorted them up the stairs. Roger hesitated as he peered through the filthy glass doors. He could make out a crowded room filled with large tables around which sat men who could not, in anyone's wildest imagination, be there to enjoy a plate of General Tso's chicken or whatever toxic substance was on the menu. Waiters were bustling about with big carts of steaming food, and though he couldn't make out what they contained, he knew he was even more convinced he wasn't going to eat anything. "Relax, my love," said Conchita, pulling him forward. "Everything has been worked out to the last detail."

"Well, okay, but I'm not touching that food. It looks like it's as lethal as anything Ishea could concoct or Vixay has in mind for me."

Conchita laughed. "I doubt we will get to the food. You just sit next to me, and whatever you do, don't drink the martinis that will come to the table first. Things will begin to happen right after that, but as long as you stay seated and keep your head down, you will be fine. Do not stand up or try to run. Trust me on this."

Roger grunted in acknowledgment and looked over at Bunter and Darmstaedter, who looked equally uneasy. He wasn't sure what they knew or what they were expecting to happen or do when whatever was going to go down went down. Destructive Wang, on the other hand, was all smiles as he talked to the maître d'. After swatting him on the back and nearly sending him tumbling back down the stairs, he came over to them.

"Okay, all is very good. There is a table very close to Vixay, Fatty, and The Bach Brothers that is reserved for you. You will take your seats, and a waiter will bring over the restaurant's special martinis. Ishea will propose a toast. You must all sip your martinis and then put them down on the table. That will be the signal. Our men and my uncle's representatives will then stand up, surround their table, and make the arrests. Very simple."

"A little too simple," said Darmstaedter. "Do you not think they are equally prepared? After all, this has been arranged by the missing Fok."

"Look, Matthew and Constantin." Ishea sounded un-characteristically disarming. "This is not going to be easy

241

for either you or us. You'd like to make some arrests, and quite frankly Conchita and I would like to kill these bastards. But we have to trust Destructive Wang's uncle on this. He's been apprised of all the plans, and he's assured Destructive Wang that we will all be safe so long as we remain observers. Is that clear?"

Darmstaedter gave a harrumph, but Bunter seemed mollified. "Well, okay. We have to trust you on this, though it does feel a little strange. But then again, I wasn't expecting you to be as open and accommodating as you were last night and today, so maybe all will be fine." Bunter was more trusting than Darmstaedter, but he was no fool. He decided to be as vigilant as possible.

The table they were shown to by the maître d' was two away from the one occupied by Vixay, Fatty, and The Bach Brothers. Devil Lam had shown them a few shots of the animal traffickers on his phone, but even if he hadn't, they would have been easy to spot. They stood out from the crowd in every way imaginable. All, with the exception of Vixay, who wore a tight black turtleneck, were wearing Hawaiian shirts and sunglasses. They were laughing loudly and drinking heavily. The men and women at the other table were dressed in black suits and engaged in muted conversation while eating chicken feet and awful-smelling soup. No one looked up, but it felt to Roger that he, Conchita, Ishea, and the inspectors were being observed very carefully. Nothing felt right, but then nothing he'd ever been involved in with Conchita or Ishea ever had. His instincts told him to get the hell out of there, but before he could do anything, even if his legs would have allowed him, they were at the table sitting down, and Conchita and Ishea were making small talk and laughing. Within seconds, a waiter arrived at the table with glasses of what looked like decent-sized martinis. As he set them down, Conchita squeezed his hand and whispered, "Remember, whatever you do, don't drink it. Just pretend to take a sip."

Ishea looked around at the group and stood up. "This is a monumental occasion, so I'd like to propose a toast." He lifted his glass, and Darmstaedter, Conchita, and Bunter followed suit. Roger hesitated. Even he, with severe jitters, could tell just how insincere Ishea sounded. He managed to raise his glass, though his hand was shaking so much that he spilled half the drink down the sleeve of his suit jacket. "To a new alliance and what will be in a few minutes the beginning of the end of animal trafficking."

Bunter and Darmstaedter raised their glasses and both took large gulps. It was precisely what Roger wanted to do but didn't. Neither did Conchita or Ishea, who both slammed their glasses down. Bunter looked at Darmstaedter with an alarmed expression, and then his head crashed down on the table. Darmstaedter gave a muffled grunt and followed suit.

Then all hell broke loose.

Ishea pulled a machine pistol from under his coat and turned to the animal traffickers' table. At the same instant, Conchita drew a similar weapon from her large handbag and began to fire at the men at table next to theirs. Roger went into a catatonic state and watched the scene unfold in slow motion. It was as if he wasn't actually present in the room but observing from some place above the madness. He saw The Bach Brothers and Fatty reach for their weapons. They were a hair too late as Ishea emptied his clip with incredible precision. Fatty was hit in the face, Boonchai Bach in the groin as he jumped up, and Limh in the chest. All three flew backwards, crashing into the tables behind them. He saw Vixay dive under the table as half the restaurant stood up and began to fire at each other. Then the doors burst open, and Destructive Wang, wielding a long sword, rushed in followed by more men. Roger could hear the whizz of bullets and screams of injured and dying men, and still he sat, unable to move, as the macabre dance swirled around him. He lost sight of Ishea and Conchita, and then he felt a tremendous blow to the back of his head, and a darkness pulled him out of one nightmare and into another. He fell forward, and the martini glass shattered as his forehead hit it and he slumped onto the floor.

With more than half the bodyguards hired by The Bach Brothers on Destructive Wang's payroll, the firefight was over as quickly as it had begun. It wasn't more than five minutes later that Ishea and Destructive Wang carried the two sleeping inspectors to the pier and placed them on a bench as if they were two drunks sleeping off an afternoon of debauchery. Conchita, who'd been searching for Roger, turned to them in panic. "What the hell happened to Roger? Ishea, you were going to grab him?"

"Yes, but one of Destructive Wang's men had him over his shoulder headed for the exit."

"Let me find out," said Destructive Wang, turning to a nearby heavily armed man. They spoke in rapid Chinese, and Destructive Wang's voice rose a few decibels.

244

"What? What is it?" The distress in Conchita's voice was unmistakable.

"He say Roger was carried out by two men, one of which must be Vixay Keosavang. We failed to kill him. My man he tried to stop them, but they had other soldiers on the pier who shot three of his men. They escaped in a black van. I'm so sorry."

Ishea grabbed Conchita. "Come, we have to move. There's nothing we can do until we're safely away from here." He dragged her to the Maybach that had pulled up on the pier. The driver was Devil Lam.

"Quick, get in," said Devil Lam. "I hear police sirens. They will be here in minutes. The helicopter is ready, but we have to go fast."

Ishea lifted Conchita as if she were a rag doll and placed her gently in the back seat and then got in beside her. Destructive Wang hit a button on his cell phone, and the Jumbo Golden Jolly Boy erupted like a giant Roman candle, sending bits of wood, metal, and dead thugs into the water. Thirty minutes later they were in the helicopter heading towards a large yacht anchored in international waters off the coast of Macau, where Freddy Blank in his two-million-dollar wheelchair and Juma with a tray of drinks were waiting for them.

"Oh, Freddy," said Conchita, "we've lost Roger. I think Vixay has him."

"Well, old girl," Freddy said, sounding a lot more confident than he felt, "we're jolly well going to have to get him back."

If they'd looked out to their starboard side, they would have seen a smaller boat, not quite in the league of the

PaloMar Princess, as Freddy and Conchita's yacht was named, but sleek and fast and capable of reaching Vinh city in Vietnam without refueling. Somewhere below deck in a dark room lay a very unhappy, confused, and bloody-faced Roger Storm. When the room had stopped spinning, he managed to sit up and immediately vomited down the front of his suit. Then a door opened, and a light went on, and the ugliest face Roger had ever seen in his life made him fall back into unconsciousness.

Chapter 23

IN WHICH ROGER COMES TO UNDERSTAND THE
TRUE EXTENT OF EVIL

The compound on the Mekong River, Laos

R oger, his hands and ankles secured by nylon ties and
a filthy rag stuffed in his mouth, was sandwiched between a small, wiry imp-like creature with a large knife and
a smaller woman dressed in a black tracksuit who sat quietly with her hands between her knees. Vixay Keosavang
was in the front of the blue Toyota Land Cruiser chatting
to the driver in Laotian as they made their way down a dirt
road toward some iron gates set in a barbed-wire-topped
cinderblock wall. No one had said a word to Roger for over
an hour since Vixay had yelled something to him in what
he assumed was Laotian and which the small woman had
translated in extremely broken English as "Welcome to
hell, you cancerous pig testicle."

The gates to Vixay's compound were opened by a guard
with an old AK-47 slung over his shoulder, and the Toyota

made its way along the bumpy drive past moribund vegetation and a large corrugated barn to a sprawling white house
with peeling paint and decaying green shutters. A number
of armed guards were waiting for them as they pulled up.
The imp, who was a good deal smaller than Roger but looked
like he was made of coiled springs, got out first, then leaned
in, grabbed Roger by his hair, and yanked him till he fell out
the van face down onto the dirt. Then he cut the ties around
Roger's ankles, kicked him painfully on the thigh, and signaled him to get up. It was the last thing Roger wanted to
do, and so he pretended to black out again. The problem
was he was in the company of people who understood pain
well enough to know that he wasn't experiencing enough of
it to pass out, and so the imp kept up the kicking till Roger
opened his eyes and tried his best to stand. Vixay, who'd
walked up to the front door, turned around and yelled
something at him. The small woman, who'd walked around
to where Roger now stood, nodded and began to translate.
"Mr. Vixay, he say you can piss or shit now there behind
that tree. After that you will be given some water and rice,
and he will tell you what he plans to do to you. He wants to
know if you have any questions?" She pulled the rag from
Roger's mouth.

"Why—" was all he could manage.

Vixay yelled back something before the young woman
could translate. She turned to Roger and slapped him as
hard as she could across the face. "He said to hit you and tell
you next time you ask such a stupid question, he will cut out
your tongue first."

Roger's eyes filled with tears. It wasn't that the slap hurt—compared to the vicious beating he'd suffered from a professional torturer in Ethiopia a year before, it was nothing. Yet there was something about the total senselessness of the young woman slapping him that made him realize that whatever spark of hope he guarded somewhere in his scrambled psyche was well and truly out. There would be no reasoning, no forgiveness, no rescue. He was going to die, and he was going to die horribly. He needed to pee badly, but he had no idea how he'd do it with his hands tied. Roger's bladder began to loosen involuntarily, and he was about to pee in his pants when the imp grabbed him by the hair again, dragged him behind the tree, and pulled his pants down. After Roger was done, the imp pulled his pants up and prodded him with the tip of his knife him towards the barn that even from a distance smelled and sounded like a Turkish prison. As they got closer the stench intensified and the sound became heartbreaking. It was as though a thousand distressed birds and animals were all crying out in unison for a freedom they would never again know.

The imp pulled open a rusty iron door and pushed Roger forward. As dark and gloomy as it was inside, he could still make out hundreds of cages piled one on top of the other filled with monkeys and birds chattering and squawking in fear. They seemed to stop for a second as they noticed him, and then the sounds started up again, filling him with a sadness that drained whatever feeling was left in his tortured soul. The imp pushed Roger toward the back of the barn where a bunch of workers were stacking elephant tusks and rhino horns. None of them even looked up. There were two freshly slaughtered tiger carcasses hanging from hooks, and lion and leopard skins, stripped of their insides, were drying near an open fire.

But it was not the sheer horror of what was going on around him that nearly drove Roger beyond that point of insanity from which a return-ticket is seldom issued. It was the old dentist chair near the fire, its black leather seat torn, its white metal arms scratched horribly as if it had been witness to countless terrors and torments. His legs buckled, and his throat began to constrict. He tried to stop moving, but the imp had been expecting resistance. He jabbed the point of the dagger into Roger's buttocks and once again grabbed him by the hair and pulled him into the chair. The imp fastened his wrists with thin leather straps to the arms of the chair and then, pulling his head against the headrest, secured it with two sharp clamps that dug into his forehead like pin cushions.

Roger tried to move his head, but the sharp clamps dug in even more, tearing his skin and drawing fresh blood, which mixed with the dried from where his head had shattered the martini glass on the Jumbo Jolly Boy Floating Restaurant. He looked up, but all he could see were some monkeys looking down from the wall of cages. In his delirium it seemed as if there were sympathy in their frightened eyes. The imp poured water into Roger's mouth, which he swallowed as best he could, but he almost choked on the rice ball that followed. The imp took one last look and moved off. Roger heard some large animal scream in pain, and then he was left for what felt like an hour to his unspeakable thoughts. He wondered if Conchita had died again. He hoped not.

Just as Roger was beginning to wonder if he'd been forgotten, he felt rather than heard someone approaching. It was like a wall of unimaginable horror moving towards him, and he knew, in that part of his brain still capable of rational thought, that it was Vixay.

The hideous face of his tormentor reeking of whisky and garlic filled his vision and began to talk at him in a remarkably calm voice. When Vixay stopped talking, the young woman, whom Roger couldn't see, began to translate.

"Mr. Vixay say congratulations. This will be the first night of your suffering, which he expects will last two days and nights. He says tomorrow morning after he has initiated the preparation he will remove one eye, after which he will begin with the real torture."

Vixay's hand reappeared, and from it dangled three fishing lines, each with a grape-sized, glistening white ball at the end. Vixay began to talk in an almost happy, sing-song voice. His eyes sparkled, and he ended his description of whatever fiendish torment he had in mind with a loud guffaw. "Mr. Vixay say that these are what he calls pain and pleasure balls. They are fish hooks with ten barbs each that have been dipped in sugar and will be coated in butter. Tomorrow morning you will swallow them, and by the afternoon the sugar will dissolve, and Mr. Vixay will begin to pull them out of your throat together with your stomach and intestines and perhaps, but he is not sure, your lungs."

Then Vixay began to systematically slap Roger's face until he passed in and out of consciousness from the pain.

A long time afterwards, when he was finally home and lying on a chaise on the porch of his tent overlooking the Limpopo, someone had asked Roger to describe how he felt or what he thought at the time. He said that he couldn't. All he knew was that whatever chemical is released into the nervous system as the body's final act of kindness—gushing from the brain, imparting a warm, wet numbness that blocks the fear of what is to come—had flipped his on switch to off. In one of his few conscious moments, he stared up at the monkeys and realized he'd become just like them.

The storming of Vixay's compound just before dawn by Ishea, Destructive Wang, Conchita, and four others had gone relatively smoothly. They'd landed the helicopter in front of the house and taken out twenty of the bodyguards within minutes with rounds from Tavor TAR-21 assault rifles fitted with sound suppressors. They kept one of the guards alive for information, and after Destructive Wang had broken three of his fingers, he told them that Vixay had gone to the large barn to prepare for the day of torture.

Roger had survived the night and was once again conscious and, despite the terrible state of his face, doing his best to keep his mouth shut. He was determined not to make it easy for Vixay to feed him the sugar balls. Vixay signaled to the imp, who stuck the point of his knife between Rogers lips to force open his mouth.

Ishea's bullets took out the imp and the interpreter and two other men who were standing by watching. To Vixay's credit, he didn't try to run. He just stood there until Destructive Wang's massive fist broke his nose and the top half of his jaw. Then he fell to the ground and began to moan. He sounded like one of the monkeys.

Ishea rushed over to the dentist chair and unbuckled the straps and clamps that held Roger. He helped him up and almost carried him over to Conchita, who'd almost broken down at the sight of her lover. She put her arms round him and drew him to her and tried to wipe away the blood, and at that moment Roger knew he was finally safe, just as she'd promised.

"What should we do with him?" asked Destructive Wang, pointing at Vixay, who was still rolling on the ground like an imbecile. He'd somehow managed to pull the Lucite box out his pocket and was jabbering at it.

"What the hell is that?"

"It looks like a nose. Pretty sure it belonged to his son. Yes, it's the one I sent him from Africa. Glad it held up."

"Give me your gun," said Roger, stumbling up to Ishea.

"What?"

"Give me your gun, Ishea."

"No, Roger. Don't do it." Conchita put her hand on his arm. "This isn't you."

"You're right," Roger croaked. "It's not me. This isn't me at all. I'm not here. I'm in Chicago in my little apartment on Michigan Avenue drinking a vodka and wishing I could die. That is where I am. So this isn't me. But it has to be at this moment. For the sake of every animal this man has hurt. Now give me your gun, Ishea." He took the proffered assault rifle from Ishea and walked over to where Vixay lay. Then he pointed the barrel at Vixay's head and squeezed the trigger. He almost laughed as Vixay's head exploded in a fireball of brain and bones, and suddenly a great sense of relief came over him. It was as if right then he had killed both Vixay and Harry Bones.

When it came to killing Harry Bones, Brian had been right on two counts: Roger had motive and opportunity. What he didn't have back then was the burning rage brought on by the pain and suffering of the animals. Someone else had poisoned the bastard.

Destructive Wang and his men together with the workers, who simply carried on as if a change in management was a daily occurrence, began to open the cages and herd the monkeys and birds out into the surrounding jungle. They found some starving bears in an enclosure and fed them from the stockpile of animal feed in the storeroom. Then Ishea put in a call to his contact at the Freeland Organization, who promised they would send people to take care of the bears and a starving lion, who was now happily chewing on Vixay's body.

During the helicopter ride back to the PaloMar Princess, Roger slept with his head on Conchita's shoulder. When it got too uncomfortable for her, she tried to move him, but he whimpered like a child, and she cradled his head and whispered things in his ear which he never heard.

"Roger, my God but you're a bloody mess," said Freddy as the party exited the helicopter. "Here, Juma, old man, why don't you put those nursing skills to the test and clean him." But it was Conchita who took Roger to their stateroom, where she stripped him and washed him and then injected him with a sedative that knocked him out for eighteen hours. When Roger finally awoke, Conchita was next to him. She kissed him gently and stood up. "Let me go and tell the others that you are awake. They are all waiting for you."

"Please, Conchita. Please don't leave me. I don't know if I could stand it."

She kissed him again. "No, my darling. I won't leave you ever. Not anymore. But I must get you something to wear, and you must eat. So, use the bathroom and I will be back in five minutes."

"Does your face hurt?" asked Freddy, sitting in his chair sipping his second martini through the plastic straw from the bottle Juma had fitted to his device. "If it does, Juma has some marvelous drugs."

Roger smiled. "Surprisingly enough, it doesn't hurt much. It feels like someone used my head as a football, but the pain, whatever there is, is dull. I don't know how exactly to describe it."

"And how do you feel in other ways?"

"You can say it . . . You mean how do I feel about killing Vixay?"

"Yes."

"I don't really feel anything. I've been thinking about it a lot, but like everything that happened to me after Hong Kong and the suffering of those poor animals in that awful barn, it occupies a part of my brain that I have yet to come to terms with."

"Don't," said Ishea.

"Don't what?"

"Don't try to come to terms with it. You're a good person, Roger. The fact that you're also an enigma when it comes to some of the things you've done in the time you've been with us shouldn't change you. Be the good guy. The kind guy. The soft guy. Be all the things that we aren't."

"Ishea's right." Conchita said. She'd been sitting at the dining table next to him, her thigh touching his, giving him the comfort he so desperately needed at that moment. "Try to push all of that into some vault in your head, and don't open it ever. Now come, you must go back to bed." She squeezed his hand, and Roger knew that she'd join him. While he wasn't sure he'd be able to put on a star performance, he was determined to give it a damn good try.

That night he called Gosego from the SAT phone on the bridge. "I'm coming home, Gos. I'm finally coming home."

"About time," laughed his friend. "The wine cellar isn't going to restock itself, and to be honest, even though that's about all you do around here, it's not the same without you." Then he gulped, and Roger could swear he was crying.

Chapter 24

In which a very special wedding takes place

Hunter's Folly, Limpopo Province, South Africa
About three weeks later

"Are you ready for this?" asked Conchita, walking onto the porch of Roger's tent where he sat drinking a cup of coffee watching the sunrise turn the bush from grey to a soft green. The hippos were making their way back towards the river after their long and noisy night of grazing, and in the distance a lion roared.

He looked up at her and smiled. She was, he decided, even more beautiful at that moment than the day he first saw her at the restaurant in Paris just a year before. The light ricocheted off her hair, and he couldn't tell whether it was gold or silver, only that it framed the face he'd seen every time he'd tried to sleep since.

"When will you leave?" he asked, trying to keep his voice from sounding hollow.

"I think tomorrow," she replied, sitting down on his lap. The long shirt she wore rode up round her waist, and he touched her thigh with a hand warmed by the hot coffee. "I wish I could stay longer. It's so beautiful here. So peaceful and quiet."

"Ah, but that's the problem, isn't it? You just can't handle peace and quiet."

She said nothing but kissed him on the cheek. Then she picked up his coffee cup and took a long sip. "You'll be with me in Zanzibar next month. I do love it here, but there is so much to do."

"I know, and I'm looking forward to helping you do it. Especially since Brian is going to be there too."

"The three of you together finally . . . I hope you'll still have time for me." Conchita gave a provocative wriggle.

Roger laughed. "Somehow I don't think you need to worry about that. I wish Freddy could have been here for the wedding, though. I think he would enjoy finally meeting Constantin and Matthew."

"I'm surprised they even came after Hong Kong."

"I suppose, but then again they got all the credit for what happened and none of the blame. And they don't really know that it was Destructive Wang who Mickey Finned their drinks. They think it was the traffickers. In any case Gosego wanted them and Colonel Patel to be here. God knows why. No taste in friends if you ask me. But he's sentimental that way. Do you think Ishea will make it?"

"I don't believe so. Freddy told me that he's off on one of his solo missions taking care of some South African farmers who've been breeding lions for canned shoots. I don't even think it's that far from here, but I imagine he'd want to get away as quickly as possible. Anyway, my love, let's get dressed. They start weddings early here in Africa."

Roger slipped his hand between her thighs. "I think we have time for a quickie."

Conchita just laughed and stood up. "No, you'll have to wait till tonight. When you get to Zanzibar, you'll have a whole month with me on the beach. If you last a week without collapsing from exhaustion, I will be surprised."

The wedding of Gosego Modise and Lieutenant (as she now was) Bontle Warona of the Black Mambas was quite an elaborate affair. Roger had arranged for both their immediate families and close friends to be brought in. Stuart and Susan Stobbs had taken the day off from their animal-rescue hospital to be there, and Darmstaedter, Bunter, and Patel were already drinking heavily and watching the elephants at the waterhole before the actual ceremony took place.

Roger, still wearing flip flops and dressed in one of his new suits from the five he'd been sent by Destructive Wang's father, was best man.

He'd thought a great deal about what to give Gosego and Bontle as a gift but in the end surprised even himself by deciding to give them his remaining 50 percent of Hunter's Folly. "It was never really mine, Gos," he said to his friend later on that day. "I just borrowed it for a while. I needed it to heal myself, and I think I have. This is yours, as it's always been. I've written in a few stipulations, though—not that I believe you'd ever do anything with it that goes against the things we both believe in. You can never sell it off as a hunting preserve, and I must always have a place to stay because I intend to come back often to see the two of you.

Also, I insist that you become famous for not just the food but for the martinis. I don't know why, but I have a feeling that could be a big draw."

At first Gosego had refused. "I love this place, Roger, and I know Bontle is going to love it as much as me. But I can't imagine doing it without you, and if I have to insist that you keep your half just to guarantee you'll be back, then I must do that."

After Roger refused to even consider Gosego's offer, they shook hands and agreed. Roger looked down at his empty coffee mug. "I have to move on, Gos. Things happened to me in Laos. I'm not the same person I was when we first met."

"You say that, but as far as I'm concerned, you're still the same guy. The same lazy, good-for-nothing dreamer that bought me that terrible hamburger and gave me half of one of the most amazing places in the world. Now come here." He put his arms around Roger and hugged him so tight it squeezed the air from his lungs.

When Roger had recovered, the two of them walked over to the veranda to watch some zebras drink from the water hole. They said nothing for a moment, and then Roger turned to Gosego. "Finding Conchita again and knowing that in her own way she loves me—though perhaps not in quite the same way I love her—I really have to try to make it work. She wants me to go to Zanzibar and spend a few months together to see how things work out. We'll never marry, I know that much, but I have a feeling we can be together, for a while at least. And I have to give that a try."

It was a little over a year before Roger and Conchita returned to Hunter's Folly. Gosego was as thrilled to know

they were still together as Roger was to hear how successful the game reserve had become. The waiting list for ac-
commodation was over a year, and The Storm in a Martini
Glass bar was developing a reputation to rival that of the
famous Dukes Hotel in London. Or at least that's what one
of their guests told Gosego after his third martini

After dinner when Bontle was in her office finalizing the
next day's game drives and Conchita was on her computer
catching up on emails, Gosego made Roger a very special
martini.

"I've been saving this for you," he said, producing a
bottle of Caorunn gin from a locked cabinet behind the bar.
"This stuff is really hard to get here. Though I must tell you
I nearly drank it myself last week before you called to say
you were coming. What the hell happened? You said you'd
be here often."

"I know, and I apologize. As it turned out, a lot of things
happened. There are times, and I don't blame you by the
way, when you've thought I exaggerated half of the things
I've told you...."

Gosego snorted. "I certainly do consider you someone
who'd put my grandfather to shame when it comes to making up stories. But every time I doubt you, you produce odd
friends, dangerous enemies, and mysterious women. So at
this stage I will have to believe anything you tell me."

Roger laughed. "It's too long and complicated to tell you
tonight, but maybe tomorrow if you have a few hours."

"I have a feeling I should make them."

The next morning Roger skipped the game drive with
Bontle and Conchita, and over what began as coffee and

ended up in the bar, he told his friend one of the most bizarre stories that Gosego, no stranger to the devastation of poaching and trophy hunting, had ever heard.

"And it's not over yet," Roger said. "We have to fly back to Zanzibar in a few days to meet up with Freddy, Destructive Wang, and Ishea—if he gets back from Zimbabwe or wherever he is. I expect the next time you see me, I'll be able to tell you the ending."

"Roger, just do me one favor. Make sure you stay alive to get back here and tell me the ending. Jesus, after hearing what you've been through, getting charged by a wounded buffalo sounds a lot safer."

"What's he been telling you?" Conchita asked when they were all sitting down to dinner later that evening.

"More than I wanted to hear about things I'd like to believe don't happen," Gosego replied. "Do you people honestly not worry about being killed?"

Conchita squeezed Roger's thigh under the table. "Oh please, you know Roger. He exaggerates everything."

A week after Conchita and Roger had left, and much to the surprise of Gosego and Bontle, Ishea Payamps appeared. He emerged from the bush one evening like a ghost. He took a shower, had a drink with Gosego and Bontle, ate a huge plate of Peri Peri Chicken, and then vanished back across the Limpopo into Botswana. His fight to save the slowly dwindling herds of Africa wasn't over.

The End (for now)